Dreaming In Moonlight

Tricia Linden

Kingsburg Press
San Francisco, California

Kingsburg Press
P.O. Box 475146
San Francisco, California 94147
www.KingsburgPress.com

Editor: Deborah Fallon
Cover Design: Ravenborn@SelfPubBookCovers.com

Other Works by Tricia Linden

The MacNicol Clan Through Time
A Time To Begin – Book 1
A Time To Return – Book 2
A Time To Belong – Book 3
A Time To Forgive – Book 4

.

.

.

.

Jules Vanderzeit novels:
Set in the Gilded Age of New York
Until We Meet Again
Until Their Hearts Desire

.

Coming Soon: Until You Love Me

Dedicated to anyone who has a dream and follows their heart.

Special acknowledgements to Sherry Ewing, fellow author and partner at Kingsburg Press. To all my fellow authors at SFA.RWA, the best support group a romance writer could ask for. My sincere thanks to Deborah Fallon for her expert editing services. It takes a village of love and support to create anything of value.

Prologue

A small duchy in Central Europe 1692

There wasn't time to think about the pain burning through his shoulder from the heft of a sword he'd held for too long, or the weight of the armor chaffing against his flesh. There wasn't time to worry about the loss of his helmet, or to brush away the hanks of bloodied hair hanging over his forehead. There wasn't even time to consider the horror of the lives being lost. There was only time to fight against the foe advancing upon his kingdom.

The warrior prince had barely a moment to survey the devastation surrounding him before the next wave of barbarians descended upon his army like a black plague of angry rodents. The invaders, dark, dirty, hairy men, appeared as faceless beasts to his eyes, no longer human. And much like swarming vermin, they carried the stench of death and destruction with them into battle. Even the rain, pouring from grey, overcast skies, could not wash away the filth they inflicted upon his land.

With scarcely a moment to breathe, Lord Gavin Richard Montague, heir-apparent to the Maninberg throne, shouted to the heavens, "This madness must stop! These are my people, this is

1

my land. I must maintain control. By the gods and all the powers that rule, my kingdom must not fall to these undeserving beasts."

His father had already fallen under the enemy's sword. It was incumbent upon Lord Gavin to save his kingdom, or what was left of it. The sharp clank of metal against metal rang out, followed by the sickening sounds of crushed bones and tearing flesh. The smell of blood, death, and fear assailed his senses. He cut and slashed at the invading horde, only to be met with wave upon wave of attackers. Driving rain and rivers of mud turned the battlefield into a horrid bloodbath.

"My kingdom must be preserved!" Lord Gavin shouted skyward as his broadsword once again connected with deadly force against his foe. He ducked and dodged sideways to avoid the blade of his opponent as he swung his sword to strike the man. His blade sliced through leather and flesh, drawing blood as Gavin delivered a disabling blow. The barbarian fell to the earth, only to be replaced by another.

With fierce determination he fought against his attackers, spearing another faceless man with the blade of his sword. He needed a miracle to save his kingdom. All appeared hopeless, but he would not yield. With his last dying breath he would fight for is kingdom, he would not yield.

"By the gods above, I demand my kingdom be preserved," Lord Gavin cried out again, his voice thundering above the din of the fighting. "I demand my birthright."

The battle raging around him suddenly stilled. Every drop of rain, every breath of man, was held in place, unmoving, except for Lord Gavin. In awe, the warrior prince lowered his sword, stunned by the power holding the ferocious battle at bay.

A voice as powerful as the wind pierced the stillness. "Say ye true, what demands do ye place upon the powers of this land?"

"I demand nothing less than the safekeeping of my kingdom and my people," Lord Gavin replied, turning his head from side to side. His eyes searched through the rain soaked skies as he sought the source of the voice. Adrenalin pumped through his veins, driving his arrogance to overrule his apprehension.

"By what right do ye make this demand?" A strange-looking figure appeared in the mists. His long robe, the color of polished gunmetal, was belted at his waist by thick braided cords of black leather. Thick, dark hair with strands of silver hung in waves to his powerful shoulders, framing a long narrow face highlighted by piercing grey eyes.

Lord Gavin drew in a sharp breath. There was no mistaking the identity of this ghostly apparition. He was too familiar with the myths and legends told throughout his land to doubt that standing before him was Tazire, an ancient and powerful wizard.

Standing steadfast and proud, Lord Gavin held his head high and faced the wizard. "By the right of my birth," he replied. "By the blood of my father and his father before him. By the generations of my family who have ruled this kingdom in peace."

"Your birthright?" Tazire glared at him. "Do you really believe your *birth* grants you the right to seek control of men's destinies?"

"It's my birthright to seek control of this kingdom and all who live here." Gavin refused to back down. The reason for his birth, the very purpose of his life, was to rule his father's kingdom. He would do anything to secure his rule.

"How far does this birthright extend?" the wizard asked.

"I ask only for the control of Maninberg, my rightful kingdom."

"Your rightful kingdom? Ha! Tell me, how long does this birthright exist?" A wicked smile graced Tazire's lips, but his eyes remained hard.

"For as long as I have breath in my body." Gavin shifted his stance, raising his sword before him.

"And if you were to live forever, would this birthright still hold true?" Tazire's dark, grey eyes bore deep into Gavin, as if seeking his soul.

"Yes. Forever." Lord Gavin returned the wizard's steely gaze, inflexible in his demands, unyielding in his beliefs.

"Beware, young prince. Would you truly agree to accept immortality in exchange for total control of your kingdom – and only your kingdom?" A note of caution crept into Tazire's voice.

"I would accept nothing less," Lord Gavin stated confidently, ignoring the wizard's warning.

Tazire cocked his head, studying the young prince. "Such arrogance shall be rewarded." The wizard lifted his hands to the heavens. "Granted," he shouted, loud and clear. "Thy will be done." And with the wind, he was gone.

CHAPTER 1

Ninety-nine years later: The Duchy of Maninberg, 1791

Grand Duke, Lord Gavin Richard Montague III hardly noticed the stunning view of rolling countryside offered up by the glorious day bursting forth outside Wessington Manor. At the moment, he was nearly oblivious to nature's grand display shining through the dining room windows facing the morning sun. He was too focused on his reading to hear the chirping birds as they flittered from branch to branch in the nearby trees, or to fully appreciate the delicate pink and white blossoms scenting the breeze carried through the open balcony doors. Turning a blind eye and deaf ear to the spring-time celebration of nature, he stirred a dollop of thick cream into his freshly poured cup of coffee before reaching for another of the many foreign papers delivered to his breakfast table each day.

While he was not able to venture out into the world beyond his borders, he made a point of being well informed on its activities. Scientific discoveries and the latest inventions were his greatest interests. Whenever he learned of a new invention or innovation that piqued his interest, he endeavored to have it brought into his domain. However, he rarely, if ever, invited foreign heads of state to visit his palace. He'd grown weary of international politics long ago, being too far removed from their never-ending catalog of problems. His kingdom had been free of war, poverty, and rampant disease for several years; those issues no longer concerned him.

After scanning the headlines laid out before him, he checked his pocket watch. It appeared Rollins was running late with his report on the local news. While this was very unlike his royal secretary, Lord Gavin's wait was not long. Within minutes, Bruno Rollins opened the wide wooden door of the dining room and stepped inside.

"Pardon my delay, my lord." Rollins gave a slight bow as he entered. "I wanted to personally confirm the latest news before I released it to you." The duke's secretary set a thin stack of parchments before Lord Gavin.

Gavin set down his coffee and picked up the papers, his eyes scanning quickly over the page. "What news is that?" he questioned, looking up. They spoke in French, as was often the case in the few remaining duchies located near the ever shifting borders of France.

"The new owners of the Maynard Winery are expected to arrive later this week." Rollins canted his head toward the window, indicating the direction in which the estate was located.

"What can you tell me about these new owners?" Lord Gavin asked, knowing his royal assistant preferred to personally report the news. It added to Rollins' sense of importance, and Gavin had long ago recognized the man's need to feel valued. One did not live to be one hundred and twenty-nine years old without learning at least a thing or two about his fellow man.

One hundred years! Had it really been nearly a century since he'd lost his mortality? It seemed impossible. He was still mentally sharp, physically strong, and yet he keenly felt the passing of the years deep within his soul—a soul that had grown old while his body remained young.

"The old estate has been transferred to Maynard's granddaughter, Jeanine, and her husband, General Iain Gregerson. He's recently been released from service to the British Crown. They're expected to arrive along with their daughter, Marina, and her husband, Darren Metwick. I understand Mr. Metwick is a winemaker of considerable skill," Rollins said, sounding pleased.

"A general, you say? From England?" This was of interest to him. British subjects had little reason to visit his little kingdom, however England was spreading her wings across the globe with ruthless determination. Although he was well aware of the successful revolt against the rule of King George by the new colonies in America, the British Crown still had a growing presence in Australia, India, and the Middle East.

"Actually, I believe he's Scottish, Your Grace."

"Even better. I've always admired the fighting spirit of the Scots. It's a pity they weren't able to secure their independence." He rather liked the idea of having a Scottish general as a neighbor. "I believe this warrants a dinner to welcome our new neighbors." A reason to celebrate suddenly appealed to Gavin. He'd been feeling restless and in need of something new to occupy his time.

"Will this be a quiet dinner for you and General Gregerson's family?" Rollins asked.

"No, I think not. I believe we are overdue for a grand celebration. Arrange for a royal dinner – no, make it a formal ball. Invite all the usual people of importance," Gavin instructed his secretary, suddenly inspired.

Rollins pulled the ever present writing pad and charcoal pencil from his inside jacket pocket and began taking notes. "Have you a date in mind, my lord?"

Gavin glanced at his calendar and provided a date for Rollins. "Hopefully General Gregerson's family will have enough time to settle into their new home by then."

"Shall we announce the reason for the ball, to welcome your new neighbors?" Rollins asked.

"I would rather we didn't." He looked past Rollins, finally seeing the full beauty of the day. "We shall simply say it is in honor of the summer solstice."

"As you wish, my lord." Rollins nodded.

Gavin glanced back to Rollins. He could have asked him to call it the dup-de-dup ball and his secretary's answer would have been the same. It was always as he wished. It would be nice to have someone disagree with him once in a while, but that never happened.

The royal secretary completed his morning report and left to attend to his duties. Gavin stepped out to the balcony and breathed in the freshness of the crisp morning air. Lush rolling hills rose up to meet a freshly washed sky dusted with fluffy white clouds. Grazing sheep and milk cows meandered through the pastures, softly baying and mooing in the distance. Looking across the shallow valley, he set his sights on the distant villa sitting high atop the opposing hillside, just outside the border of his kingdom.

Stepping back inside, he retrieved a spy glass from its cradle near the doorway before returning to the balcony. He focused the eye piece on the villa's western façade. "Marvelous device," he mused as he studied the vineyard.

The villa had been nearly deserted since the passing of the elder Maynard. Only a minimal crew had been retained to maintain the working order of the estate while the executor sought its new owner. Unfortunately, old man Maynard had died without sons to take over his estate, and it had been months since anyone had been living in the large Spanish-style villa. With the arrival of the new owners, Gavin hoped the vineyard would resume business as usual. He looked forward to meeting his new neighbors and hoped they would provide an interesting distraction.

Lately, it had become harder and harder for Gavin to be truly interested in the world around him and he felt himself slipping dangerously close to the self-imposed madness of solitary confinement. Damn this immortality. He hadn't anticipated it would carry so many limitations. Then again, he hadn't really pondered the possibility of experiencing immortality prior to his conversion. One did not typically anticipate the improbable, much less the impossible.

Lord Gavin Richard Montague, Grand Duke of Maninberg, remembered all too well his life as a mortal man. He still carried the appearance of being a young man, in the prime of his life. His thick, dark hair did not thin or turn grey and his dark brown eyes did not dim or lose their focus. His strong warrior body did not weaken or stoop with the burden of age. Over the years, the sharp hollows of his cheeks may have grown more pronounced and the timbre of his voice may have deepened, but no other signs of age befell his being.

Time had passed, but his memories never faded. He'd been young, barely thirty years of age, proudly arrogant and supremely egotistical, when his father, the Grand Duke Richard David Montague, had died defending his kingdom. Focusing only on his desire to claim his birthright and gain ultimate control over his father's realm, Gavin had called upon the highest powers of the land to grant his wish. For better or worse, his wish had been granted, almost too willingly, by the wizard Tazire.

It seemed so simple, so amazingly simple. In exchange for accepting immortality, he had been granted complete and total control of his kingdom, the small but prosperous Duchy of Maninberg. At the time he had thought it the most magnificent blessing possible, the ultimate fulfillment of his grandest desire, to live forever with complete and total control of Maninberg.

However, he quickly discovered there was one stipulation he had not fully considered. He was absolutely, positively, and completely limited to inhabiting his domain and only his domain, always and forever, and not one step more.

Years upon years, decades upon decades, had given him ample time to repeatedly test this limitation. Countless times he had tested the power holding him confined to his land, and each time he had experienced the same disappointing results. He could not step one foot outside of his domain. He could not add one square inch of ground to his kingdom, nor could any be taken from him.

His kingdom had become his cage.

Some of his attempts had been comical, some nearly tragic, but none had been successful. With particular embarrassment he remembered the time he tried to catapult himself across the invisible border, only to fly face first into the invisible and impenetrable wall and crumple painfully to the ground.

Nearly as painful, both physically and to his ego, was the time he thought to disguise his exit by hiding in a coffin strapped to the back of a wagon. Surely the appearance of a dead body in a coffin would be allowed to cross the boundary. The driver, with horse and wagon, had proceeded across the border without incident, but the coffin in which he laid had become dislodged. The heavy wooden casket encasing his body had simply slid off the back of the wagon, and dropped to the ground with a bone-crushing thud. Once again, he'd been prohibited from making the crossing.

For all his efforts, he had finally learned to accept that he was a prisoner within his own kingdom. Anyone else could come and go as they pleased, but Gavin was held captive by an unseen force holding him ultimately and firmly within the confines of his allotted space. He often had an eerie feeling that the old wizard, Tazire, was somewhere watching his ridiculous attempts at freedom and laughing his ass off.

The blessing he had once so fervently sought had become the curse of his life.

It had not always been like this. In the beginning, his complete control had truly seemed like a blessing. In the years after his father's passing he built an empire of wealth, peace, and pleasure. His people planted crops yielding bountiful harvests, forests, grain, and produce grew plentiful on his lands. His people grew rich by the fruits of their labor and by extension so did he. Content in their lives, his subjects worked the land, raised their families, and year after year supplied him with the means to create a thriving and peaceful empire.

Over the years, a grand fortress had been built sitting atop the highest hill and surrounded by a thriving citadel. Merchants from far and wide came with their splendid wares to fill the vast rooms of his glorious palace. The results were grand, impressive, and very formal, everything he envisioned a royal palace should represent.

But those days were long past. Now, more often than not, he spent his days at Wessington, a grand manor located near the border. He had settled into a retirement of sorts, becoming a royal figurehead who no longer felt the need to manage every detail of his kingdom. Under the guidance of Ballistare, his trusted prime minister, it ran well enough with little attention from him.

It wasn't as though his subjects were slaves to his thoughts, they had their own minds, but if he made a request, they could not refuse. Even if he ordered them to refuse his demands, their refusal was at his behest. It was nothing less than maddening.

Anyone within the confines of his borders was compelled to comply with his demands. Even foreigners who crossed into his kingdom were under his command. Over time, he'd learned to choose his words carefully, asking for very little. He grew to understand that his words had the ability to change people's lives, and he no longer took this responsibility lightly.

Lord Gavin studied the rolling hillsides and the vast estate of the Maynard vineyard a moment longer before he lowered the spyglass. He was about to step back inside when a flicker of movement caught his eye. Looking about, he spotted a large grey and white owl that blended nearly perfectly with the bark of the poplar tree where it was perched. A nocturnal creature by nature, this owl was awake and alert to his movements on the exposed balcony, silently watching him as if hoping to go undetected. Feeling no need to disturb the bird further, Gavin went back inside to continue reading the local news, wondering what else he might soon learn about his new neighbors.

CHAPTER 2

Lady Tara Zanders of Cullenwood and her escort, First Lieutenant Loclyn Degraw, paused at the crest of the hill, considering their options.

"Time to decide. This is the last respectable inn before we reach your uncle's estate." Loclyn gestured towards the roadside establishment nestled near the valley floor. "We can either stop here for the night, or push on to the villa. I'm guessing we still have at least two hours of ride before us and less than an equal amount of clear daylight. So what do you say? Stop for the night or push on? Before you answer, I should warn you, the inn keeper's wife has a talent for setting a hearty and tasty supper. Having been down this road before, I'd welcome an opportunity to repeat the experience. The beds aren't anything to go out of your way for but her roasted pork stew is a mouth-watering pleasure."

"If I remember correctly, you said you knew this road well enough to find your way in the dark. Since we will be blessed by a nearly full moon to help light our way, it should pose no problem. My desire to see my cousin and sleep in a comfortable bed is far greater than my need for immediate rest. I vote for pushing on."

Unlike a proper English lady, Lady Tara sat astride her mount dressed as a squire in breeches and a greatcoat. Her long, blond hair was pulled back and tucked up tight in a tri-corner hat. If she could have it her way, she would never sit side-saddle again. It seemed to her a ridiculously inefficient position for riding long distances.

Loclyn acquiesced with a moan. "Perhaps you are right. A warm bed in the General's villa does sound inviting. However, we should at least stop long enough to refresh the horses and have something to eat. It will not serve us or our mounts to continue on empty stomachs, and the moon will still shine bright after a slight delay."

"I can see a compromise is in order. We will stop long enough to feed your belly."

"And the horses," Loclyn interjected.

"And the horses," Tara accepted. "Then we will ride on to my uncle's new estate. Is it agreed?"

"Agreed. You drive a hard bargain as always, little sister." There was no mistaking the smirking grin attempting to escape his lips as he acquiesced to her.

Tara laughed at the man she had known her whole life like a brother. "Don't you 'little sister' me. I know you're just as anxious to see Uncle Iain as I am to see Marina." Silently she acknowledged it pleased her to hear him call her "little sister," (a term of endearment he'd used since childhood) even though their blood relationship was that of distant cousins.

"Just because you happen to have the appetite of a bird and can travel great distances on a single crust of bread, doesn't mean the rest of us beasts should suffer from lack of sustenance." Loclyn patted the neck of his horse. "And you know, if we were in England, you wouldn't be allowed to sit astride, or dress as if you were my squire."

"That's one of the reason's I'm thankful we're not in England. You know I'll do whatever it takes to get where I'm going. But you can stop your teasing. I've already agreed to stop and rest. You shall get your meal and I shall sleep under my uncle's roof this night. I see no downside."

"You have a mighty strong back-bone for one so fair. An unjust advantage if you ask me."

"It comes with the territory, the burden of being an only daughter in a family full of men. One learns quickly how to deal with the male species, or risk being left behind. As you may have noticed, I tend to avoid being left behind." Even disguised as a man she knew she couldn't hide her natural beauty, but beneath her pleasing façade, she prided herself on having a sharp mind and a strong spirit.

"Left behind!" he scoffed. "It's my observation you're usually the one in the lead. Let us ride on, little sister, my dinner awaits."

The late spring sunset was giving way to the bright rising moon when Lady Tara and First Lieutenant Degraw rode into the courtyard of the Maynard villa. True to his word, Loclyn had known the way as he had been there a number of times before, acting as an emissary for Uncle Iain and Aunt Jeanine while they were busy settling the estate of Jeanine's grandfather and arranging to relocate to their new home. Jeanine's father, Maynard's eldest son, had died in battle, leaving the inheritance of the family estate to his daughter.

Having successfully reached an age and status that afforded him the luxury of retirement, Iain Gregerson left the care of his manor in the Scottish highlands his eldest son, Jared, and intended to take full advantage of his wife's newly acquired estate. The arrangement worked well for Tara's uncle. He felt it was past time for Jared to make a living for himself, and too many nights on cold battlefields had left him longing for warmer weather. He'd had his fill of battle and was looking forward to peacefully growing old with Jeanine, far removed from the near constant drizzle of the Scottish highlands.

Accompanying Uncle Iain to the newly acquired hillside villa was his daughter Marina, and her husband Darren. Tara knew her uncle was quite pleased with Darren as a son-in-law, especially since the Frenchman happened to be an accomplished winemaker. Marina and Darren also brought with them the greatly anticipated birth of another grandchild.

Roused from her bed with the news of her cousins late night arrival, Tara had barely stepped into the entrance hall of the villa before Marina rushed to greet her, overcome with excitement.

"Tara, Loclyn, it's so good to see you. How did you arrive so quickly? We've only been here a fortnight."

"I came as soon as I heard your good news," Tara said, accepting her cousin's welcoming embrace.

"We barely had time to pack," Loclyn offered as he too accepted Marina's embrace.

"But why are you dressed like this?" Marina asked, referring to Tara's manly attire.

"Don't look at me," Loclyn said, waving off Marina's concern. "It's not as if I had any say in the matter."

"Posing as Loclyn's squire allowed me to travel unquestioned," Tara explained. "It was faster, and certainly safer, this way. Too many rebels and bandits wander the French countryside and a woman, even one traveling with a man, is too great a temptation to pass unnoticed."

"You should not take such risks. I still cannot believe how your parents allow you to travel about freely as if you were a man." Marina clutched her night robe tightly at her neck.

"My thoughts exactly," Loclyn agreed.

Tara dismissed her cousin's concerns with a wave of her hand. "My parents have no more desire to restrict my wanderings than they would wish to cage a wild bird. Besides, being the youngest after seven brothers does have its advantages. They've grown too weary trying to corral my older brothers. It was simply a matter of wearing them down."

"There's no use arguing with her," Loclyn said with a shake of his head. "She insisted we push on to get here at our soonest. I feel tired, dusty and parched, and yet our cousin here looks as if she has just left a tea party."

"I am grateful for your escort, dear cousin, but you needn't make it sound so harsh. We did stop for dinner," Tara admonished him teasingly.

"Thankfully, I was allowed that small respite. Now, if you two ladies will excuse me, I'll go find the General to see if he's unpacked the good whiskey yet." Loclyn gave them a slight bow before heading out of the room toward the back of the house.

As soon as he was gone, Marina lowered her voice and drew her night shift tightly across her belly to reveal the barely noticeable swell. "I'm only in my fourth month, hardly showing." Marina dropped her night shift and grabbed Tara's hands. "Since you've arrived earlier than expected, you can go with us to the ball."

"A ball! Who would host a ball out here in the middle of nowhere?" Tara asked in a rapid burst of surprise. News of an invitation to a ball was the last thing she had expected to hear upon arriving at her uncle's remote villa.

"The Grand Duke of Maninberg is hosting a Summer Solstice Ball at his castle next Monday."

"So soon? I wish I could, but I'm not prepared to attend a ball. I'm sure my traveling trunks will not arrive in time. I have nothing suitable to wear." She allowed a short-lived pout to visit her lips. It was disturbing to think she would have to miss such a grand event.

"Oh Tara, come now. You know my talent for shopping. I have a bolt of some very fine fabric, just waiting to be made into a proper gown. My seamstress will be here tomorrow for my final fitting. It'll be easy to have her design something for you, especially since I know you always prefer simple gowns."

"Simple but elegant," Tara said, brightening. It was a joy to see her cousin's excitement, and an unexpected delight to think the problem was so easily solved.

"Of course. For you, nothing less than elegant will do. You even wear squire's breeches well," Marina said, laughing.

The two women embraced again with joyful affection. It was good to be reunited with her cousin. Having no sisters of her own, Tara looked upon Marina as the sister she had always wanted.

"I can hardly wait to show you the villa. I think you'll be surprised at how large the grounds are. Darren is anxious to begin overseeing the grapes and the winemaking. He calls it a true gentleman's pastime."

Tara only half listened to her cousin's words, knowing she would hear it all again in the morning when she was given the official tour. She linked arms with Marina as they headed towards the bed chambers, her mind wandering on a path of its own. It was quite interesting to hear that the Grand Duke of Maninberg was throwing a ball. Of course she had heard of the small duchy located near her uncle's estate, but knew very little about the kingdom or the man who ruled it. He was considered a recluse, rarely making public appearances, and never outside of his realm. An opportunity to visit his mysterious kingdom was more appealing than she cared to admit, and felt it was by the luck of the moon and the stars that she'd arrived in time to partake of the rare invitation.

~*~

The carriage carrying General Gregerson and his family moved slowly through the streets of Maninberg as they approached the end of their journey. Slowly, they wound their way up the final incline toward the wide stone gates marking the outer courtyard of the grand duke's castle, pushing through the crush of people and peddlers heading in and out of the fortress.

Entranced, Tara stared through the carriage window, absorbing the sight of the impressive castle. The fortress sat on the highest plateau in Maninberg, with thick stone walls rising high above the city, dominating the landscape for miles. Within the security of the outer fortress sat the wide expanse of the central castle. The main buildings rose four stories above the courtyard, with adjacent towers and wings joined together to create an image of royal elegance. Even though the building of the fortress had obviously spanned several decades of time and used a variety of architectural styles, Tara believed the resulting effect was one of powerful splendor. Soaring glass windows greeted them as they arrived at the wide sweeping entrance to the main castle, giving Tara a tantalizing peek into the grandeur awaiting them.

The courtyard, already crowded with activity from the onslaught of arriving guests, was the epitome of a well-run operation. A line of footmen stood waiting, ready to assist the visitors and unload their baggage as the carriages rolled into place at the wide castle entrance. Tara had traveled extensively to a number of countries and was well accustomed to observing all the finer details of her surroundings. She marveled at the finely-orchestrated attentions of the servants as they moved the arriving guests from carriage to castle with the efficiency of a finely-tuned music box, never missing a beat or note.

Tara was even more pleased when the chamberlain took them to their rooms in the newest section of the grand castle. Along the way, they climbed a wide curving staircase spiraling to the third floor of the wing, and then proceeded down a wide arched hallway lined with colorful tapestries hanging between the heavy wooden doors guarding each of the castle's many guest suites.

The chamberlain addressed General Gregerson as they came to stop in front of a series of ornately carved doors. "Since you have need of extra chambers, I've placed you in the Rosewood apartments. In accordance with your wishes, your niece will be staying in a chamber next to your daughter, across the hall from you. The Lieutenant's chamber is located only a few doors away, near the end of the hallway. I trust all is in order, however, if you should need anything during your stay, your chambermaid, Bonita, will be happy to assist you. Simply use the bell pull," he indicated the velvet rope hanging near the doorway, "and she will answer your call."

The chamberlain directed the porters where to place the traveling cases for each guest before he continued. "These rooms are slightly further from the grand hall, but they are quiet and have a fine view of the citadel. Is this acceptable to you?"

"Completely," Uncle Iain assured him.

"Very well then. Please do not hesitate to call for Bonita. She will do all she can to see to your needs." As if on cue a young serving maid appeared in the hallway and made a respectful curtsy to General Gregerson and his family.

"So it seems," General Gregerson remarked. "For now it appears we have all that we need. Bonita, if you would assist my girls with their unpacking, I'm sure my wife and I can see to ourselves."

Aunt Jeanine peered into her assigned chamber and whispered to Marina, "Do you have the feeling we've stepped into a fairy tale castle? I've never seen a cleaner or better run kingdom. Doesn't this all seem a little too good to be true?" Tara joined her aunt and cousin as they stood at the doorway scanning the room. A large four poster bed covered with a fluffy feather mattress and quilt dominated the room. A pair of lush upholstered chairs faced the fireplace, and the walls and carpets were decorated in a fine silver blue with deeper royal blue accents. For a simple guest chamber, it was quite luxurious.

Tara's uncle cleared his throat, drawing their attention away from his chamber. Tara and Marina moved aside to allow her aunt and uncle to pass.

"I've heard tell that the grand duke runs a prosperous duchy, but even the rumors have not done his kingdom justice. It's only fitting that we should avail ourselves of all the pleasantries the duke sees fit to offer, and to start, I believe we should test the comfort of that bed before we are forced to endure a sleepless night," Uncle Iain said.

"My darling, I've known you to be able to sleep on the hard-packed ground in the rain. I am fairly certain it will not be the lack of softness in the bed that will keep you awake this night."

"Och my fair lady, you know me only too well," he murmured as he raised his wife's hand to his lips and kissed the soft inner flesh of her wrist. With a knowing smile she welcomed his caress, as he pulled her further into their room before closing and latching the door behind him.

Turning away from the closed door, Tara smiled knowingly at her aunt and uncle's open display of affection. Loclyn and Darren exchanged wicked grins before Loclyn turned to follow the chamberlain down the hallway towards his chamber. Darren bowed graciously to Marina and Tara before slipping alone into his room, and the chamberlain, Tara noticed, acted as if nothing unseemly had happened.

The chambermaid followed Marina and Tara into her room to offer her assistance. Tara welcomed the opportunity to rest and prepare for the ball after the long carriage ride to the castle. The room was decorated in soft dusty rose tones and touted an overabundance of pillows on the large feather bed.

Marina quickly discarded her cloak and ankle boots, then flung herself into the midst of all those pillows, floating in a sea of billowing fluff.

"Bonita, please unpack the ball gowns first and brush them out to remove any wrinkles," she instructed the chambermaid as she settled into the comfortable bedding.

"Yes, m'lady," Bonita answered with a slight bobbing curtsey, and immediately set about accomplishing her tasks. From the traveling trunks she pulled out the two formal ball gowns and after smoothing out the folds, laid them out on a sofa in the room. When finished doing as she had been asked, she immediately began retrieving Marina's discarded clothing to properly store it in the available wardrobes.

Marina took a moment to admire her gown from the comfort of the overstuffed bed before she bounded up to fluff and fuss with the skirt. She stood there for a moment longer, admiring the liquid blue fabric, lightly touching the pale sea-green lace adorning the bodice and flounce.

Tara's dress hung in stark contrast next to Marina's elaborately designed jewel tone ball gown. Elegantly simple, the golden gown had a high empire waist, with delicate ivory lace gracing its rather modest neckline.

"Your gown is truly lovely," Tara remarked from the comfort of a well-padded settee. She watched her cousin delight in the feel of her exquisite garment. "The seamstress you found has remarkable skills."

"Finding someone of her talents was truly a bit of unexpected good fortune. I don't believe a London dressmaker could have done any better." Marina forced herself to stop with her fussing and returned to her place among the pillows to rest. It promised to be a long night, and Tara hoped her cousin would have enough energy to enjoy it all. "Did I tell you, I met her in the same shop where I found the fabric for your gown? I could never wear that color, it's too pale for me, but I was immediately drawn to it. It was too lovely to pass by, almost as if it was destined to be ready for your arrival. I tell you, I have the best luck when shopping. Darren says I find all the best buys."

"I hope he's not at risk of having you emptying his accounts," Tara teased her cousin.

"Not at all! I may love to look, but I only buy what I truly need," Marina assured her, cheerfully defended her spending.

"And yet, somehow you knew you would need a full bolt of gold fabric, a color you claim you could never wear yourself?" Tara gave her cousin a doubtful look.

"But of course, dear cousin, I must have been thinking of you. Let's just say I was inspired to buy it, and look how well it has all turned out."

"It is quite exciting to be going to a ball, but tell me, what do you know of the Duke?"

"Very little. Apparently he's a bit of a recluse, but my dressmaker told me he's very handsome. She saw him once while delivering fabrics to his castle. He's rather young and not married. Maybe he's using this ball to find a wife." Marina's eyes positively glowed, a sure indication of romantic dreams for her cousin.

Tara laughed. "Marina, you've always believed in fairy tales. Dukes hold balls all the time. It doesn't mean they're looking for wives."

"I hope we'll have a chance to actually meet the grand duke. Do you think he'll ask you to dance?"

"I'm sure there will be plenty of women from Maninberg to dance with the duke. I doubt he'll be in need of a stray partner."

"Tara, have you no romance in your soul?" Marina protested, as if she couldn't believe her ears.

"My love of travel fills my soul," Tara said. "I've no need for romance. I'll leave that to you."

Marina's expression drooped somewhere between a scowl and a pout. Either way, Tara knew she wasn't living up to her cousin's expectations. She wasn't sorry to disappoint her. She felt no need to play the role of Cinderella, or any other fairy-tale princess. She'd given up on fairy tales long ago when her fiancé deserted her before they ever walked down the aisle.

Tara had accepted Captain James Millhouse's proposal of marriage too young and too fast, without really knowing the man. Soon after announcing their engagement he had transferred to a position in India with the British Army, stating that he would soon return, or send for her. As it happened, he had done neither. She had waited over six months before finally accepting her parents' invitation to travel with them to France. When she learned that Captain Millhouse had returned to Scotland she had rushed back home, only to be told that her intended had been home for less than three weeks before he transferred out to Russia. He hadn't been able, or willing, to wait for her to return.

Eventually she learned that James had died somewhere in the Baltic, but by then it no longer mattered. Any affection or desire to marry she may have felt had already faded, and she had fallen in love with travel.

When she visited distant and exotic lands, she saw herself as more than just another richly entitled woman walking around with an inconsequential mind. She was an explorer embarked on the pleasure of discovery. She had learned early that men typically only saw what they wanted to see; whether it be a pretty, young woman seeking a husband or a gentleman's squire of little importance. Rarely did they look beyond her sweet smile to see her heart, her hopes, her dreams, or her brains, and that suited her just fine.

She never spoke of her ill-fated betrothal, preferring to act as if it had never happened. She no longer believed in happily ever after, and she certainly didn't qualify as anyone's innocent Cinderella.

Seeking to change the subject, Tara asked, "How did your father garner this invitation?"

"When the duke heard that Father had taken over the Maynard vineyard, he sent over a messenger. Apparently the duke had a fondness for Grand Papa and wanted to ensure Mother and Father felt duly welcomed. I'm sure it was a rather last minute invitation, but I really don't care too much why we were invited. I'm just glad to be here. This castle is divine, and I'm sure it will be a lovely ball."

"Yes, I'm sure it will be lovely," Tara agreed with a tinkling of laughter. "I'm sure we'll have a grand time at the duke's ball." Regardless of her circumstances, whether she was at a ball or simply strolling through a meadow, Tara made it a point to always have a grand time.

CHAPTER 3

Twilight was giving way to moonlight as the honored guests flowed toward the grand ballroom. Each in turn presented their hand printed invitation to the royal greeter and waited to be announced before being received by Lord Gavin Richard Montague III, Grand Duke of Maninberg. A wide sweeping staircase descended to the main level of the ballroom from the surrounding mezzanine. Large windows covered two sides of the expansive ballroom, reaching from floor to ceiling on both the upper and lower levels. Dazzling crystal chandeliers hung suspended from high above the guests, filling the space with the soft glow of dozens of candles. The domed ceiling was painted with celestial images, giving the impression of a view into endless space.

Lord Gavin listened to the announcement of each arriving guest, doing his best to not appear bored.

Conk, conk. The royal announcer struck his staff upon the wooden platform where he stood. "General and Mrs. Iain Gregerson." The announcer's deep baritone voice resonated throughout the large space.

"He prefers to be called General, and his wife's name is Jeanine." Rollins, the royal secretary, stood discreetly behind Gavin, whispering personal details for each guest into his ear.

The distinguished-looking military man and his wife proceeded down the wide stairs leading into the grand ballroom.

Lord Gavin sat up a bit straighter. "Is this the family that has taken over the Maynard vineyards?" he asked over his shoulder.

"Aye, my lord," Rollins whispered.

General Gregerson and his wife stood before Lord Gavin. His bow was just low enough to fall within the parameters of proper etiquette. She smiled sweetly and presented the perfect image of a loving, supportive wife as she curtsied before the grand duke.

"General Gregerson, I'm pleased to see you accepted my invitation on such short notice," Gavin greeted his guests.

"It is our pleasure to be here, Lord Gavin," General Gregerson replied.

"I hope we have the opportunity to speak later. I'd be interested to hear of your time in service."

"Ah, war stories. They're best for telling with a good mug of beer or a hardy shot of Scottish whisky. Wouldn't you agree?" General Gregerson replied in a friendly manner.

Gavin found the General's straight-forward humor slightly disarming, but he appreciated the old man's wit. It was something he rarely encountered from his subjects.

"I shall endeavor to keep that in mind should the opportunity present itself," Lord Gavin smirked. He gave them a dismissing nod and they moved on.

Conk, conk. "Mister and Mrs. Darren Metwick," boomed the announcer.

"General Gregerson's daughter, Marina, and her husband, the winemaker," Rollins whispered.

Gavin appraised the young couple as they began their descent down the staircase. They appeared well suited. Mr. Metwick wore a dark blue waistcoat with elaborate silver embroidery, which perfectly matched the blue of his wife's gown. While the husband appeared duly somber, his wife's anxious excitement was evident as she made her way to be received by the grand duke. When they stood before him, Mrs. Metwick curtsied low.

"Your Grace, my wife and I wish to express what an honor it is to be attending your ball." Darren Metwick spoke with a refined French accent. Obviously upper crust. He looked perfectly calm, but his wife appeared as though she would burst a seam with her giddy delight.

"The pleasure is ours," Gavin politely replied.

Mistress Metwick opened her mouth, as if to speak, but Rollins motioned for them to move along.

Noticing a break in the announcements, Lord Gavin looked over to the top of the ballroom staircase. The royal announcer was taking an inordinately long time to read the card presented to him. Finally he looked up.

Conk, conk. "First Lieutenant Loclyn Degraw and Lady Tara Luna Zanders of Cullenwood."

The couple took a step forward and Gavin's eyes locked on the vision standing at the top of the ballroom steps. A mass of flaxen curls cascaded down the young woman's back and over her shoulders. Her gloved hand rested lightly on her escort's arm as they began their descent into the ballroom. Her golden gown sparkled in the glow of the ballroom candles, highlighting the subtle radiance of her smooth, pale skin. To Gavin's mind she appeared as a moonbeam, wrapped in spun gold.

He waited, listening for Rollins' whispered introduction. Rollins was noticeably silent.

"Who is she?" Lord Gavin hissed under his breath.

Rollins choked and cleared his throat. "I do not know," he admitted. "They are not on my list."

"Not on your list? How is that even possible?" Gavin was sorely tempted to glare at his royal secretary, but he could not. That would have required him to remove his gaze from the vision making her way toward him.

"Lieutenant Degraw, Lady Zanders," he greeted the couple as they stood before him. Recalling the announcement of their arrival, he locked onto the only information momentarily available to him. She must not be his wife. But why was he her escort?

The first lieutenant bowed and Lady Zanders curtsied as they stepped before the grand duke. Her eyes were cast downward, as if studying the intricate marble pattern of the floor beneath her feet. When she finally looked up to meet his gaze, he was held captive by a pair of stunning ice blue eyes laced with ebony specks. The mixture of darkness and light, wisdom and innocence, created a hypnotic effect. Her enchanting eyes accompanied a pixie-like face graced with finely sculpted features, including a pert little nose and high cheekbones, but it was her serene smile that most strongly held his attention. An aura of sensual joy seemed to float in the air around her.

"Lady Tara," Gavin singled her out for acknowledgement. "Welcome to Maninberg." He reached for her hand, and touched his lips to her fingers.

"Thank you, Your Grace." Her voice floated like musical notes to his ears. She met his gaze unflinchingly.

General Gregerson stepped forward from the crowd, addressing the grand duke. "Your Grace, may I present my first lieutenant, Loclyn Degraw from Scotland. He was kind enough to escort my niece, Lady Tara, to our new home. She is my sister's daughter and arrived only two days past. Since your invitation was addressed to me and my family I took the liberty of including my niece and her escort. I trust this meets with your approval."

Lord Gavin suspected General Gregerson didn't really care whether or not it met with his approval, but apparently he knew royal protocol well enough to suggest that he did.

"Yes, of course, it's our pleasure to welcome your whole family to our kingdom." His words may have been addressed to General Gregerson, but his eyes remained fixed upon the woman standing before him, mesmerized by her golden beauty.

Conk, conk. The official announcer's staff alerted the duke of another arrival. "Cabinet Minister of Finance, the Right Honorable Jonas Millard, and Mrs. Jonas Millard."

General Gregerson withdrew from the royal circle and directed his family to join the other guests.

Rollins leaned forward to discreetly whisper into the duke's ear. "Her name is Julia. Their son, Simon, is enrolled in officer's training," The informative words were lost on Lord Gavin. His attention was still focused on Lady Tara and her family as they made their way into the depths of the grand ballroom.

When the introductions of the arriving guests had finally been completed, Lord Gavin sat alone on the dais, enjoying the music of the orchestra while observing the swirling movement of the dancers. In particular, his eyes followed the young woman with the golden curls and matching gown.

A distinguished older man in formal military attire approached the grand duke. His long grey hair was pulled back into a tight queue that hung down his back to just below his shoulders, however his formal dress uniform was absent of any military insignia of rank or display of metals.

"Tazire, my old friend. What brings you out of the woodwork?" Gavin's tone denoted an undercurrent of annoyance.

"Have you ever known me to miss one of your momentous occasions?" The old wizard grinned.

"There have been a number of momentous events when I have been graced by the pleasure of your absence." Gavin was not smiling.

"Then certainly those events could not have been as momentous as you believe," the wizard responded seriously.

Gavin turned to take stock of his ancient antagonist, not knowing whether Tazire meant it was his presence that made the occasion momentous, or if the wizard was aware of something greater afoot. Very likely it was the former, Gavin deduced, considering the wizard's tendency towards self-importance.

"I've noticed you watching the General's niece," Tazire slyly observed.

"She has caught my eye," Gavin admitted. "It's not often we are graced by such a pleasing outsider. They are few and far between."

"Why don't you ask her to dance? You know she couldn't deny you." As usual, Tazire took pleasure in taunting the grand duke.

"Do you delight in stating the obvious?" Gavin glared.

Tazire shrugged, nonplused.

Gavin latched onto an idea. "I would prefer it if you asked her to dance with me, as a favor to an old friend."

It was a risk to ask the wizard for a favor. Being the one who had cast the spell, Tazire was the only person in his whole kingdom who could refuse his request. But if he did agree to grant this favor, then Lady Tara would be free to accept or decline the request as she so desired.

"And if the lady should decline?" Tazire asked.

"Then so be it. She is free to decline," Gavin declared. He turned his gaze back to the crowded ballroom as if ignoring Tazire, though he watched the old wizard from the corner of his eye. There was a measure of nervous excitement to think she would be acting according to her own preference, if Tazire would only grant him this favor.

"Interesting. Does this indicate you are willing to relinquish your control?"

Gavin cast a scathing glance at Tazire. The old wizard was obviously trying to bait him. He refused to take the hook. "Believe it or not, I prefer truth over submission." Gavin rocked back on his heels, watching the dancers.

A dark grey brow lifted on Tazire's forehead. "There may be hope for you yet."

"Are you going to ask her for me or not?" Gavin fumed. He directed his attention back to the wizard with a glare.

Tazire held out a hand in supplication. "It will be my pleasure. How delightful to have the opportunity to experience first-hand her refusal of your desire."

"What makes you so sure she will refuse?" Gavin questioned, his brows knit with disdain. It was plain Tazire was having entirely too much fun at his expense, but he would begrudgingly swallow the sour taste of his pride in exchange for an opportunity to know Lady Tara's true reaction to him.

"What makes you so sure she will accept?" Tazire grinned, blatantly enjoying the verbal sparring.

"Forget it. I can see it was a mistake to ask you for such a petty favor."

"Calm yourself, lad. I said I would do it."

Gavin rolled his eyes with a shake of his head. He hated it when Tazire called him "lad". He was nearly one hundred and thirty years old and the term had long ago lost any appeal it may have once held.

He watched as Tazire moved with practiced stealth through the large crowded ballroom, quietly honing in on his intended target. The admiring horde of young men surrounding Lady Tara parted to make way for the wizard, then immediately closed ranks, concealing his actions from the duke.

~~

Her back was to him and yet she stopped her pleasant chatter and stood stone-still as he approached. She could sense him even before she saw him, the strength of his magic stroking her mind. She recognized his touch, for there was no mistaking the powerful pull of the high wizard, Tazire.

Turning, her face lit with an overflow of joy. "Grand Papa!" she rushed to embrace him. "How did you know I was here?"

"Tara, my little jewel, that's like asking if I can see the moon in the night sky, for surly you shine as bright as any star. How could I miss an opportunity to see my favorite great-granddaughter all dressed up and looking too lovely for words?" Tazire welcomed her into his arms.

"Your favorite great-granddaughter? I'm your only great-granddaughter." She kissed his cheek, taking a moment to linger in his embrace. "But seriously Grand Papa, why are you here? Is it only to give me such a pleasant surprise?"

"As much as I like to surprise you, I'm also here on a matter of business. I have a particular interest in an ongoing project and I like to check on its progress from time to time."

"Way out here in the middle of Europe? Why have I not heard of this before?" His revelation was decidedly intriguing.

"Come now, my little jewel, you don't really believe I would tell you everything, do you? Even my sons and grandsons are not privy to such details."

The grand wizard was the proud patriarch to seven sons, and each of them had several sons of their own, including Tara's father, Lord Tyrus Zanders, Earl of Cullenwood, the seventh son of Tazire's seventh son.

"Mysterious as always, I see," she said.

Tazire offered her his hand as the orchestra began a new piece. "Come, dance with me while we chat."

"With pleasure."

Tazire led Tara out onto the ballroom's large dance floor and with effortless grace led her through the steps of the dance.

"Are you not going to tell me what brings you to Maninberg?" Tara persisted. "Have you cast a spell over this castle? It certainly seems to have been pulled from the pages of a fairy tale, it's so perfect and polished."

"So you like the castle, do you?" Tazire asked.

"You must agree, it's quite impressive. A castle fit for a prince and his princess, although I hear there is no princess. Such a shame. The grand duke is a very handsome man, almost as handsome as you." She flashed him an impish smile to accompany her compliment.

"Do not waste your needless flattery on me, little one. I know very well that in your heart there are none who compare to me." With a twinkle in his steel grey eyes, he twirled her closer to the edge of the dance floor. "But I will grant you, the grand duke is an attractive man, if youthful charm appeals to you."

"You're quite right, Grand Papa. Your mature and powerful good looks have spoiled me for all others. I'm a lost woman, destined to compare all men to an unobtainable standard." She teased as good as she got, turning gracefully in step with the music.

"Perhaps, if you play your cards well and continue to ply me with flattery, I could arrange for you to dance with the grand duke. Would that please you?" He closely watched her face as he waited for her response.

She hesitated for a moment, keeping her thoughts to herself before she broke with a half-hearted smile. "Huumm, yes. Perhaps that would be nice."

"I detected some hesitation. Tell me why, before I put my reputation on the line to ask a mere duke to be trusted with my jewel."

She welcomed his tease, but answered in all seriousness. "It's true, he is handsome, but he looks so forlorn, as if he carries some great burden upon his shoulders."

"Do you think ruling a kingdom, even a small duchy such as Maninberg, is not a great burden? Perhaps that is why such things are better left to us men."

Her Grand Papa knew all her soft spots and apparently was willing to risk her wrath. She reacted quickly with a heated response. "You know better than to say such things. I can think of a dozen strong and powerful women who have ruled vast kingdoms throughout history. Some of whom you have known intimately, if I'm not mistaken."

"Let's not get too personal, young lady. You should have greater respect for your elders, especially an old man such as me."

"And I can think of many male rulers who have greatly benefited from having an equally strong woman by their side," Tara continued on with her argument.

"Speaking of which . . ." As the music came to an end, Tazire led her to the edge of the dance floor to stand before the grand duke of Maninberg.

"Lord Gavin Richard Montague, I believe you've met Lady Tara Zanders of Cullenwood."

Lord Gavin nodded, his lips curved into a slight welcoming smile. "Yes, of course. She was well received upon her entrance." He gave a slight bow.

Tazire turned to face Tara, staring intently, silently conveying his intentions. "Lady Tara, it has been my pleasure to meet you."

Tara raised an inquisitive brow at his comment. "The pleasure was all mine," she said, playing along with her Grand Papa's ruse.

"If it pleases you, and only if it pleases you," Tazire continued, "I would hand you on to the very capable hands of Lord Gavin. I have observed he is a fairly competent dance partner, and has been known to complete a whole dance without stepping on anyone's toes."

The look on her Grand Papa's face and the tone in his voice told Tara he wanted their kin relationship to remain private. She immediately understood his intentions and respected his wishes. The Zanders did not betray their family secrets. Being the descendant of a powerful wizard came with generous benefits, but it also carried substantial responsibilities. Apparently, in this regard, Tazire did not include Lord Gavin in his inner circle of trust.

With a nod of understanding, she accepted her great-grandfather's unspoken request, and placed her hand upon Lord Gavin's. Gazing up at him, she felt herself drawn into the depths of his dark brown eyes. His dark hair was brushed back away from his face and she noticed a fine, thin scar just above his left brow. She wondered how he had encountered such a wounding blow, and if the scar was recent or had faded with the passing of time.

His hair and eyes, both the color of dark chocolate, were perfectly suited for his dusty olive complexion and his strong, broad nose sat pleasingly above full sensual lips. He was taller than she had expected, beating her Grand Papa's height of six feet by at least an inch or two. She also noted with appreciation how well his broad shoulders filled out his finely tailored jacket. All in all, he made a perfectly respectable Prince Charming, if one was inclined to dabble in such frivolous fairy-tale fantasies.

~~

Gavin was nearly one hundred and thirty years old, and yet he felt like a school boy at his first cotillion. Except now, he was in greater control of his surroundings. With a wave of his hand,

Rollins was immediately at his side. "Instruct the orchestra to play a waltz," he ordered.

The royal secretary hurried off, and in less than a minute the orchestra was playing a waltz.

"Impressive," Lady Tara noted, "Ask and you shall receive."

"Being the grand duke does have its privileges." He indulged in a sly grin as he led her onto the dance floor.

"I'm sure it does. Your castle is quite amazing. It seems to have sprung from the pages of a story book. Do tell, what is your secret?" she asked in a casual manner, setting the tone of the conversation as she gracefully followed his lead.

He appreciated that she didn't address him in the stilted and formal manner so often adopted by fawning young ladies. Rather than be offended, he admired her confidence and comfort in his presence.

"For generations the Montague family has ruled this duchy, doing everything in our power to ensure its well-being. In return, we have been blessed by many years of peaceful prosperity."

He spoke the truth, but he had no intention of revealing his secrets. For generations *he* had ruled Maninberg to the best of his ability, and he took his responsibilities very seriously. Even as the years wore on, and the demands for his control lessened, he never let his efforts falter. He may have become less zealous over the years, but certainly not less sincere.

"It may not mean much, but my limited observations indicate your family has done a wondrous job. You and your forefathers are to be honored."

"You would be quite wrong," he interjected, leading her through a turn. Following his lead, she matched his steps with practiced poise. He appreciated her graceful style, along with how refreshingly stimulating it felt to hold her in his arms, even at a respectable arm's length away.

Facing him, she looked puzzled. "Why am I wrong?"

"Your opinion means much to me."

Flattered, as he had intended, she beamed a bright smile. "How can you be sure? Perhaps I have no basis for my opinion."

"My own limited observations tell me that you are well-read and well-traveled, which makes you worldly."

Expressing a look of surprise, she asked, "What makes you believe I am well-traveled?"

"It was announced that you are from Cullenwood, which, if I'm not mistaken, lies far to the north, in Scotland. You must have traveled from there to here at the very least. Much further than many I have known." *Including me,* he thought, as he effortlessly guided her through the steps of the dance. Each turn brought with it her scent of night roses, subtly strong and enticing.

"You're quite right, I do love to travel. When you've seen how life is lived outside a narrow range of influence, it broadens your viewpoint. Have you traveled much?"

"I can't say that I have, but not for lack of desire. Understandably, my duties keep me confined to my kingdom, perhaps more than I would like." Confined, imprisoned, very much the same, he mused.

Her bright smile darkened. "What a shame. The world has so much to offer." Before he could respond, she hastily added, "Of course, I respect the responsibilities that come with ruling a duchy, no small feat I am sure."

"Indeed. But even the most steadfast ruler may occasionally wish to shed the burden of unending responsibilities and leave it all behind, if only for a while."

He wondered how long 'a while' would be, if such an opportunity were to exist. If he were allowed to leave, would he return? Or would he turn his back on all he had accomplished and let it fall into ruin? And who could say if it would fall into ruin? There was no reason to believe his way was the best way, the only way, of ruling a kingdom. He had only done what he thought best, what worked for him. But yes, he would return. This was his home, these were his people. He would not abandon his responsibilities. Nor would he deny himself the pleasure of being able to leave it all behind, if only for a while.

"I have been blessed with the ways and means to travel extensively, and now, I cannot imagine my life without it." Her bright smile retuned, lighting her eyes.

He was thoroughly enchanted. "How very fortunate for you. That sounds quite interesting." The last strains of the waltz told him the dance would soon be ending. He had no desire to release her from his company, and wondered how he could prolong their conversation without making an outright request.

Lady Tara looked up at him through lidded lashes. "Fortunate indeed, for I can tell you, I have no love for the cold winters of northern Scotland. One of my favorite trips was a winter I spent in Egypt."

"You've been to Egypt? How very impressive, and rather exotic." It was one thing to think she had traveled from northern Scotland to central Europe, but a trip to the continent of Africa was truly extraordinary.

"I was traveling with a professor of ancient history and his wife. He was my teacher, and I was his wife's companion. We went to Alexandra and Cairo, and then returned through Greece and Italy. We went to see the birthplace of ancient civilization, the genesis of man's knowledge. It was fascinating. Rather hot and dusty at times, but magnificent, I can assure you."

"I imagine that to be a rather long and arduous journey for anyone to undertake, but especially for one so young." She had an impressive list of accomplishments considering she appeared to be no older than twenty.

"Oh, it was, but worth every moment, and actually, I believe my youth was in my favor. The older gents on the trip did not fare so well in the heat and could never be without a fresh supply of handkerchiefs to mop their brow." She gave a lighthearted chuckle, as if sharing a delicious secret.

With a final turn and a bow the dance ended. The only suitable action was to lead her off the dance floor and allow her to take her leave so she could dance with another.

He was just about to thank her for the pleasure of their dance when she said, "If you'd like, I can tell you more."

"Of course, as you wish," he replied. More than relieved, he was delighted.

He led her to a private alcove away from the dance floor and offered her a seat. She immediately continued on with their conversation, nearly breathless with enthusiasm. "We were gone for nearly eight months. The professor had commissioned his own sailing vessel for the trip. He is quite well known back in London, and we were accompanied by a number of other scholars and researchers. It was thrilling to be able to participate in such a grand journey." Her excitement for her subject was evident. Her passion for life surrounded her like the glow of a candle.

It seemed he had stumbled upon a topic she could discuss all night if given a willing audience, and he had every intention of being that audience. He had no place else to go, and no one he would rather spend the evening with. He admired her zeal, and the spark of passion she displayed when talking of her travels. More than once, he felt a twinge of envy as she described her adventures, but he pushed it aside, preferring to simply enjoy her company rather than dwell on impossibilities. She was an outsider, still young and passionate for life. She hadn't fallen prey to the dull stagnation that had come to define his kingdom. With her, it was as though the misty clouds covering his land had momentarily parted, allowing a moonbeam to descend into his presence.

It was more than an hour later when Lady Tara's escort, First Lieutenant Degraw, finally found them with their heads locked together in ardent conversation. In that time, she had taken him from the sands of Egypt to the blue seas of the Greek Isles, and was moving on to the romantic canals of Venice.

"Pardon my interruption, Your Grace. Lady Tara, your cousin, Marina, has grown tired and wanted to let you know she is going to retire for the night," Degraw addressed them.

"Oh, then I must accompany her." Lady Tara stood, as did Lord Gavin. "Forgive me, Your Grace, I didn't mean to monopolize your time with my ramblings. I have a tendency to get carried away when I talk of my travels. You've been a most kind and generous listener. I apologize for the abuse."

"I assure you, there was no abuse. It was my pleasure. I wouldn't have interrupted you for the world." He'd been too enamored with the pleasure of her company to notice the passing of time. It was the most pleasant evening he had enjoyed in years.

"If you will excuse me, I must go to my cousin. I have neglected her for far too long."

"Certainly, that is as it should be. Will you be staying at the castle for the morrow?" Lord Gavin looked from Lady Tara to Degraw, though he was careful to make it a question, not a request.

"I regret not. General Gregerson has informed me of his plans to return home quite early," the first lieutenant advised. "There is much to do at the Maynard vineyard."

"Then, should I not have another opportunity to do so, let me repeat how much I thoroughly enjoyed your company. You are welcome to visit Maninberg again at your leisure."

Her sweet smile grew even brighter. "I shall look forward to that," she replied. "It will be my pleasure."

No, he thought, the pleasure will be mine.

CHAPTER 4

Lord Gavin decided a visit to Wiltzer Park would make a fine distraction. Perhaps a stroll through the maze and rose garden would clear his head. It had been three days since the Summer Solstice Ball and his meeting with Lady Tara still lingered in his thoughts. He considered the public park along Maninberg's border to be one of the more agreeable escapes from his castle and his duties, if not his kingdom.

Within the park a hedge maze was maintained for the playful entertainment of the young and young at heart. The park, with its maze and expansive flower garden, straddled Maninberg's border with a wide path running through it. Maninberg lay on one side, the village of Larinda on the other. The maze was positioned in the center of the garden, fully within Lord Gavin's kingdom, allowing him the perceived pleasure of ignoring his enforced confinement. He could meander to the center of the maze, rest peacefully in the privacy of the six foot tall hedges, and then wander back out by another route. Although he never left his kingdom, it allowed him the indulgence of feeling lost in his own world, if only for a brief moment of time.

As Lord Gavin wandered through the hedge maze, he thought about his brief encounter with Lady Tara and the strong impression it left upon him. She was still vibrant and passionate about life, not yet disillusioned, he wanted to immerse himself in her youthful splendor. It had been years since he had felt this young. What a laughable notion.

It also intrigued him that a bright, intelligent, and obviously well-bred woman had found fit to wander into his kingdom. Though she was Gregerson's niece, she had been introduced as Lady Tara of Cullenwood, which implied some connection to nobility, or perhaps the aristocracy. Considering she came from England, the connection could be rather minor. The British tended to hand out titles as easily as generals handed out medals. They had barons, viscounts, earls, marquises, dukes and princes, whereas in his duchy, there was only him, the grand duke. And he was without a duchess.

Gavin exited the maze and wandered over to the expansive, formal rose garden. A recently planted varietal caught his interest. The fresh scent of the early blooms reminded him of Lady Tara, resulting in a form of self-imposed torture. In his mind's eye he imagined her as a moonbeam wrapped in gold dust.

He crouched to examine a single white rose in all its perfection, breathing in its fragrance. It was barely more than a bud, flawlessly formed, preparing to spread its delicate petals as it released its heavenly scent upon the earth.

From behind, he heard a voice. "That must be a very special rose to capture the attention of the grand duke of Maninberg." It was Lady Tara, announcing her presence as she approached the garden.

Surprised to see the woman of his thoughts suddenly appear, Gavin stood and turned to greet her with a nod and a smile. "It's a pleasing sight to see a moonbeam in the light of day."

"Is that what you call it, a moonbeam?" she asked gesturing to the rose.

"I do not know the rightful name of the rose but felt it a fitting term for one that shines so bright. Have you come to walk the gardens?" She was standing on the wide path running along the border, only inches outside of his kingdom. He hoped she would step across the border and join him.

Holding her ground, she explained, "My cousin, Marina, told me of a sculpture garden in the park that might be of interest to me. She and Darren are in the village visiting some of the shops. I grew bored and wandered here on my own."

"Your information is correct. There is a small but fine collection of sculptures located on the far side of the hedge maze." He pointed off towards the arched entrance to the area. "Would you like me to take you there?" It would be a pleasure to act as her escort through the sculptures since they were located completely within the border of Maninberg.

She hesitated, considering. "No thank you, not today. Your attention to the roses has sparked my interest. Many of the flowers are just beginning to bloom and it would be a shame to miss their glory. Today I think I would prefer a stroll among the blossoms."

"Of course, as you wish," he nodded.

"Truly?" she asked with a sweet half smile.

"I would have it no other way," he confirmed.

"Then a walk through the roses it shall be. We'll leave the sculptures for another day. But can you tell me," she lowered her voice a bit as she stepped across the border and into his kingdom, "are there any Roman statues included in the collection?"

He breathed deep when she placed her gloved hand upon his forearm, her scent more pleasing than the flowers at his feet.

"Perhaps one depicting a Roman god or goddess?" he asked. The provocative lift of his brow indicated he understood her meaning. He was cheered by the flash of pink that warmed her cheeks.

"It has been my experience that the Romans are quite talented at depicting the beauty of their gods." Her lips curved with devilish delight.

"I suppose that is something you will have to judge for yourself, perhaps on another day." He returned a sly smile, pleased by her innuendo.

"Yes, perhaps another day." She looked off towards the distant entrance, and then turned to study his face. His body warmed under the glow of her gaze, so intense and steadfast.

A moment later, when she turned to look away, it was if the sun had darted behind a cloud.

Directing her gaze upon a nearby rose bush in full bloom, she asked, "Do you think there can be such a thing as too much beauty?"

It was as if she had given voice to his thoughts. "Interesting question. One I have pondered myself recently." He offered his arm and they began strolling along the garden path.

"Do you think a rose, or any flower, knows when it has reached its peak of beauty? When there is nothing more it can do to improve upon its perfection? And if so, would it then be aware that this is the moment when it begins its descent towards decay?" Lady Tara asked.

"I dare say no. I doubt any flower is aware of its own beauty. It simply exists for the sake of existence. I cannot believe anything in nature is fully conscience of its own beauty." He strolled along beside her, taken aback by the depth of her comments.

"If that's true, I think it would be a shame." Lady Tara's lips turned slightly downward.

"Why is that?" Gavin wondered what it would take to make her glorious smile return.

"I would rather believe every living being is aware of its innate beauty, of the uniqueness it brings to our world, at least at some level." Her eyes followed a group of boys who had broken away from their guardian and were chasing a large dog across the lawns of the park, their playful laughter ringing in the air.

"Your observations are enchanting. Perhaps, at some level, you are correct," he acquiesced, declining to pursue the topic. "I really haven't given it much thought." He had no desire to disagree with her, and while he found her opinions rather interesting, they were completely unexpected. He wondered how they had gone from admiring flowers to discussing the deeper meanings of life.

She turned her attention back to him with a sharp look of dismay. It appeared as if his willingness to discount their topic of conversation disappointed her. "Enchanting! How quaint. And I suppose I should find your comments charming. After all, are we not blessed by this fairy tale encounter?"

He studied her, drinking in every detail of her appearance. Her pale blonde hair lightened in the sun, and her ice-blue eyes reflected her thoughts and emotions, much like a deep ocean pool bubbling with ideas begging to be released. "I agree, we are blessed," he said.

Lady Tara dropped his arm and began prancing down the path, stepping lightly from one rose bush to another as he followed. "You have an abundant supply of flowers, all of them quite lovely. If you would prefer, we can discuss my favorite color of roses. There are red, pink, and white roses, along with some very lovely yellow ones, which I have always favored. However, have you ever noticed that roses do not do purple very well? Morning glories, sweet peas, petunias, and even thistles have some lovely shades of purple, but roses seem unable to compete in that shade," she quipped.

Gavin watched as the moonbeam morphed into a butterfly, flitting from flower to flower as she danced among the petals. One moment she'd been all seriousness, and in the next, she feigned frivolous foolishness. It was an amazing transformation. "I believe I understand. We can have a polite, but rather pointless conversation about the color of flowers, or we can have a meaningful discussion of life's larger questions. It seems you have a preference for meaningful conversations."

Apparently satisfied she had made her point, she stopped and turned to face him. "Very observant. So, let me ask, where does enough end and too much begin? Can there be too much of a good thing? Too much beauty? Too much wealth or power? Too much love?"

"That would depend on what you determine to be too much. Eastern philosophers say true wealth is knowing you have all that you need, regardless of how much you have. According to their way of thinking, even a peasant could experience true abundance."

"I like their way of thinking," Lady Tara said. She once again took his arm and they resumed walking again along the garden path, side by side. "Although, it's hard to disagree with such thinking when I have been blessed with so much."

"When it comes to power," Lord Gavin continued, warming to their subject, "I believe that would be much harder to determine. For myself, I have observed that maintaining control over my power rather than letting it control me is the greatest challenge of all. But then again, I am the ruler of my kingdom. Small though it may be, here my power is unquestioned." Thanks to the wizard's spell, his power was indeed unquestioned, but it had been his own choice, his own resolve, that pushed him to conquer his absolute power and not let it rule over him.

"And what of love?" she asked, as they wandered further into the Maninberg gardens. "Can there be such a thing as too much love?"

Her question took him by surprise and he halted his steps. "On that I cannot speak. My experience is insufficient." His eyes no longer met her gaze.

"You are not unduly young, my lord. Surely you have experienced true love at least once in your life?" Her gently probing question was spiced with sweetness.

"I have loved," he answered honestly. "I married young; however, my wife died in childbirth, and my son, soon after. Since then, I have not found the desire to risk repeating the experience." His voice was flat, devoid of emotion. Without glancing her way, his steps quickened as they continued their walk along the garden paths winding further into Maninberg.

He had met and married Lenora well before his conversion to immortality, and he had known their love to be true. She became pregnant and he'd been elated to think she would bear him an heir. But that was nearly a hundred years ago, when medical knowledge was still crude and doctor's attitudes towards women and childbirth were even worse. Those so-called-doctors had been hopelessly unable to stop her flow of blood, or to save the child born too soon. She died a few days after giving birth. David, his son, had lived less than a year. He'd been too small to battle the harsh realities of life. The horrific and painful loss of his wife and infant son truly was an experience he did not wish to repeat.

Any hopes he had of finding true love again were dashed when he realized no woman could refuse any request he made of her. Because of that, he could never really trust if a woman truly loved him and was not simply acting under the influence of the wizard's spell.

"Forgive me for asking. It was too brash of me," Tara said in a low, soft voice. A look of compassion swept over her.

"There's no need to be sorry. It was a reasonable question and I provided an honest answer. Meaningful conversations would allow for nothing less. Perhaps you are better suited to answer that question. Do you believe there can be such a thing as too much love?"

"Love is the one thing there can never be too much of. True love gives one complete freedom. My parents have shown me that." A sparkle returned to her eyes.

"Your parents are truly blessed to have known such love. There are not many who can stake such a claim."

"It is not only their love for each other, it is also their love for me. I have also been truly blessed." She paused along the path to breathe in the scent of three blood red roses. Returning her gaze to Gavin, she continued. "Their unconditional love has always supported me. It's what allows me to travel so freely. To put it simply, they trust me. Trust that I'll act within reason, trust that I'll use good judgment, and most importantly they trust that I'll always return home."

"It is my observation that many are blessed, but very few are aware of their blessings. In this, you are truly unique."

"Is this a good thing?" she asked, a hint of flirtation slipping into her voice.

Her boldness was somewhat startling, but perhaps understandable. He realized he was being old-fashioned, being one hundred and thirty years old could do that to you. She had already demonstrated she was opinionated and outspoken. She conducted herself with the kind of confidence that came from a lifetime of being loved, appreciated, and encouraged. It was what set her apart from others less fortunate.

"It's a good thing if you're trying to impress me. Your thoughts and opinions seem to be well beyond your years. In truth, I had not expected to hear such thoughts so well expressed by such a young woman." Even as he spoke the words, he heard his unchecked voice of judgment.

Her sweet smile turned sour. "Thoughtful opinions are not exclusive to the elderly. And I may not be as young as you think."

He took a moment to study her face, considering her words. He, better than anyone, could understand the deception of a youthful face. He had already offended her, there was no reason to back-step now. "Perhaps your youthful beauty has deceived me. You seem wise beyond your years, which I admit to judging solely on appearance. I would place you at no more than one or two years above twenty."

As if pleased by his response, her smile turned sweeter. "I celebrated my twenty-sixth birthday months ago, on the fall equinox, September twenty-second. I'm over a quarter-century old. A confirmed spinster by most accounts."

Gavin bit his lip to avoid laughing. Did she really believe herself to be old? How preposterous.

"Then your appearance has deceived me. I cannot be held accountable." He felt relieved, believing he had dodged her anger. She seemed pleased by his answer, knowing it had not been his intention to insult her.

"It's both a blessing and a curse. I have learned to live with the benefits as well as the drawbacks."

"I believe I can guess at the benefits of appearing younger, but what are the drawbacks?" he asked, even though he'd already begun compiling a mental list of his own.

"Exactly as you indicated. Because I'm perceived as being younger, I'm often not respected or taken seriously. At times, I have been too easily dismissed."

"You mistake me. I take your opinions very seriously. I was simply impressed by the knowledge and experience they conveyed. In fact, everything about you impresses me, your beauty, your intelligence, and your love of life. I find it all very delightful."

Pleased, and perhaps slightly humbled by his comment, she turned her attention back to the gardens. "This is a wondrous park with lovely gardens. Does this all belong to Maninberg?"

"The land is shared by Maninberg and the village of Larinda. I believe it was less than a dozen years ago when this strip of land lying along my border was commissioned to be Wiltzer Park. The desire was to provide public grounds for everyone to use. Much of the labor and expense was borne by my kingdom, but the park is open to be enjoyed by all. The hedge maze in particular has always been a favored attraction for young and old."

"Have you ever considered building a gazebo?" she asked, studying the layout of the park.

"A gazebo? Frankly, no. Why do you ask?"

She pointed at the open section of lawn running along the Maninberg border. "A gazebo here by the flower garden would give the ladies a shady place to rest while they admire the flowers, without being undone by the sun. It would serve as shade for the elderly, or a meeting place for lovers and friends. Would you not find that appealing?" As she spoke, her smile took on an impish glint.

"Your suggestion has its appeal. I will pass your recommendation on to my master gardener. He oversees the maintenances of this park." Not only would he pass along her recommendation, he would insist it be put into place. Encouraged, he had not missed her reference to lovers and friends.

"Ah, it appears Marina and Darren have tracked me down," Lady Tara said, looking over his shoulder.

He turned in the direction she was looking and saw the couple making their way toward them from across the park. Together, Lord Gavin and Lady Tara walked back along the garden path to meet the approaching couple. Marina looked a little winded by the time the couple reached them. Lady Tara led her cousin over to the nearest garden bench, instructing her to rest.

"It would be nice if the park offered some suitable shade, like a gazebo, perhaps." Her eyes darted to Lord Gavin's with a mischievous twinkle. "For now, this will have to do." Lady Tara

51

sat down next to her cousin and took hold of Marina's parasol while turning a sly grin towards Gavin.

"You need not worry about me," Marian protested, even as she pulled a fan from her handbag and waved it in front of her face. "I'm fine, but it is nice to rest. I brought this on myself. Too much time lingering over shop windows on our way here. Darren does indulge me so." She cast a generous smile at her husband standing by her side.

He bent to brush a kiss upon her cheek. "As if I could deny you anything," he whispered into her ear, his eyes dark with seductive mischief. His wife giggled with pleasure. Such a loving relationship was to be admired.

"If you wish, we can arrange to have your carriage brought here to the park and save you the walk back into the village," Lord Gavin offered. It would also serve to cause a minor delay to Lady Tara's imminent departure.

Darren looked to his wife. "Would you like that, my love?"

"Yes, that would be very kind, if it's not too much trouble."

"No trouble at all, I assure you." Gavin lifted his hand to signal the boys tending horses tethered near the edge of the park, and one of them came running. Together Lord Gavin and Darren instructed the boy where to locate the carriage and the lad was off, running toward the village.

As they waited, Darren asked Lord Gavin about the hedge maze. "Perhaps you can enlighten me as to the function of that large hedge row?"

"It's a game, a maze. There are four entrances, one at each corner, with twists and turns that eventually take the players to the center if they take the right path. Sometimes there are competitions with rewards stashed in the center ring. The goal is to see who can arrive there first."

"The hedges appear quite high. They must easily be six feet tall." Darren observed. "What does one do if they become lost?"

"They can continue to wander until they find their way out. Usually, by trial and error, one is able to find which way to go. Eventually we all find our way out. If they are truly lost, they can cry out and hope someone will find them and come to their rescue. I suppose that is what we all do when we're lost, in one way or another," Gavin mused.

Darren looked to the ladies. "Which would you prefer?" he asked.

"I rather like the idea of being rescued," Marina said, smiling at her husband.

"I would prefer to find my own way out. It would be far more rewarding and in keeping with the spirit of the game," Lady Tara stated.

Gavin was not surprised by either of their answers. It was as he expected, but he was pleased to hear Lady Tara confirm her preference for self-determination. A helpless woman didn't appeal to him, and she appeared to be far from helpless.

"Perhaps we can arrange a challenge someday. We could ask Loclyn and General Gregerson to join us. The women could oversee our game to ensure we follow the rules. What say you, Lord Gavin, would that interest you?"

"Are you saying we wouldn't be allowed to participate, but only observe?" Lady Tara questioned, sounding not at all pleased with that idea.

"You could certainly join them, but it wouldn't be of interest to me," Marina remarked.

Before Darren could respond further, the carriage pulled up on the nearby lane running along the Maninberg border. A footman dropped from the back-board to attend to the door and pulled out the carriage steps. Darren personally assisted his wife, seeing her settled into the carriage.

"A moment more," Lady Tara addressed Darren as he held the door for her. He nodded his acceptance and entered the carriage.

Turning to Lord Gavin, she asked, "Do you think Friday would be a good day to view the sculpture garden?"

"I think Friday will be a perfectly fine day. The morning light is often quite favorable."

"Then I will plan to return on Friday morning. I hope your offer to escort me on a tour is still available." She was standing on the road next to the carriage, a road that ran just outside the boundaries of his kingdom.

"Nothing would please me more," he assured her. He was very much aware of her exact location and it pleased him to think she was speaking freely. He was perfectly willing to follow her lead and respond to her requests. He'd accept only what she wanted to give, asking for nothing more.

She extended her hand, a tentative search for his. He instinctively moved to take her offered hand, but stopped at the last possible moment, acutely aware of the invisible wall that would block his movement. A moment of panic consumed him. To refuse her hand would be a cutting insult, and yet she was just beyond his reach. He held his breath.

In his brief moment of hesitation, she took two steps forward, standing fully inside his kingdom. Her fingers touched lightly upon his outstretched hand. He breathed again, releasing the air trapped by his fear of discovery.

A kiss, he thought, just a taste of her lips against his was all he wanted. But he would not take what she did not offer.

Her eyes held his gaze, unblinking. Was it his wild imagination wishing to believe she would welcome such an intimate gesture, or was he reading her thoughts? He detected her movement forward, a small step, ever so slight, yet so full of intention as she leaned into his touch. He leaned forward slowly, giving her ample opportunity to pull back.

Instead, she her ground, and merely offered her hand, as was proper. Accepting her actions, he bent his head and raised her hand to his lips. His lips lingered upon her fingers and he breathed in the scent of her skin. It was only for a moment, the merest touch, and yet the taste of her was exquisite. It was a brief, public, and very proper kiss, but for one magical moment the rest of the world fell away, as if it no longer existed.

Then he felt her pull back, again only the slightest gesture, the smallest movement, but it was enough to alert him to her thoughts, her feelings. *This is all that is proper – all that can be allowed.*

Pulling back, he collected himself. Rarely had he felt such awareness, or been so immersed, in one single moment. Looking up, he met her gaze, and it seemed her eyes promised so much more. It was tempting, oh so tempting. He wanted to pull her into his embrace, to hold her within his kingdom. With a simple command, he could steal her away and keep her forever, but he refused to utter the words. He would take no more than she wanted to give.

Stepping back, he released her hand, breaking their connection. "Thank you for a lively conversation."

"You're welcome," she answered, her voice hushed, filled with meaning.

She lingered a moment longer, and then turned and allowed the waiting footman to assist her into the carriage.

Once she was settled inside, the footman hopped onto the back-board and knocked on the coach's side alerting the driver that they were ready to go. With a flick of the straps, the driver engaged the horses and the carriage rolled down the lane towards the village. Within minutes, it had turned down the main street of Larinda and was carried out of sight.

Gavin stood there a moment longer, grinning like a school boy, before he headed back to his horse with a bounce in his step. She had left him for now, but she had also promised to return.

~*~

Overcoming her weariness, it seemed Marina was keen on describing every shop and window display in Larinda to Tara before they reached the front gates to the villa. "I know you don't share my love of shopping, but you must believe me, there are a number of lovely shops I think you would find interesting. The village of Larinda has developed a rather thriving shopping district for such a remote locale, so far removed from London or Paris. One of the shop owners told me it's well favored by the grand duke, and that he often has samples sent to the castle or other estates for his appraisal. I understand one of his manors is located not far from here. Of course, he doesn't visit the shops personally, but many are favored to supply the essentials for his various homes," Marina rushed on with her telling.

Tara listened with amused indulgence to all her cousin was saying, enjoying the level of excitement Marina displayed. Glancing at Darren, he appeared grateful there was someone else to accept his wife's attentions as he settled in, relaxing quietly on the seat beside his wife.

"I may not enjoy shopping as much as you, my dear cousin, but I certainly enjoy your excitement in the sharing of your discoveries. If I had accompanied you, we'd be missing this delightful exchange."

"This is true, but still, I hope you will agree to accompany me to at least a few choice shops. I would so like to receive your opinion on their wares."

"Perhaps, to a few," Tara accepted. "Now that you have scouted out the best I'm sure you'll make the outing well worth my time."

"It will be hard to choose, there are so many. You must sample the wares at the sweet shop. Their chocolates melt in your mouth. And the dressmaker's where I found the fabric for your gown, that's not to be missed. Of course it would be lovely if we could take tea at the French Salon. The décor there is simply luxurious." Marina ticked off a few of her favorites.

"Perhaps you can choose a day when I'm busy in the vineyard and you both are in need of feminine distractions. It will afford you a day completely devoted to following your whims," Darren said. Tara knew Darren loved his wife, and he had willingly agreed to accompany Marina while she visited the shops, but he would be just as pleased to pass the honor on to her.

"That would be perfect," Marina smiled broadly. "I can hardly wait. We must pick a day sometime soon."

"Of course, dear Marina, someday soon," Tara agreed, knowing she couldn't disappoint her cousin. However, today's outing had been much more satisfying for her than any stroll along the shopping district could ever hope to be. Tara smiled indulgently as Marina prattled on and on about the sights and shops of Larinda, while her thoughts were focused on her own unique experience.

She had welcomed the opportunity to explore the village of Larinda by herself, being especially interested in seeing the main road leading into Maninberg. She was quite curious about the neighboring kingdom, and Marina's day of window shopping with her husband had provided the perfect opportunity for her investigation.

Her wanderings, which included her visit to Wiltzer Park, had interestingly confirmed what she had already suspected. The flash of light she'd seen as they entered and exited the kingdom of Maninberg was not a fluke. Nor was it her imagination. It was, in fact, a very real manifestation in the realm of magic.

Tara thought back to the day of the Summer Solstice Ball when she had accompanied her Aunt Jeanine and Cousin Marina as they journeyed into Maninberg. She was quite certain she had seen a momentary flash of sparkling light as they crossed over the border into the duchy. At the time, she had accredited the effect to a fanciful glint of sunlight hitting the interior of the carriage. But when she experienced the same flash of light during their early morning departure, at a time when the sun was still obscured behind a cover of clouds, her suspicions regarding the nature of the phenomenon increased considerably. She had definitely seen something, causing her to wonder what it was and, more importantly, why was it there?

When she went to Wiltzer Park, knowing it lay along the border of Maninberg and the frontier village of Larinda, she had gone there with the singular intention of exploring the unusual phenomenon. What she discovered exceeded her expectations. The visit answered some of her questions, while at the same time, creating even more. It was quite amazing to realize that every time she touched the border of Maninberg she experienced a flash of sparkling lights. She noted that touching, or even passing through the veil, caused neither pleasure nor pain. In fact, there was no perceptible physical sensation at all, just the glittering light. She had held her hand up to the thin, invisible veil, and watched in wonder as sparks of light danced around her fingers. Testing the effect, she had moved them back and forth along the magical wall, up and down, in and out. It was delightful, and wondrous, and truly magical.

And that's exactly what it was, an invisible, magical wall suspended all along the Maninberg border. After seeing her Grand Papa at the duke's Summer Solstice Ball, she had no doubt as to who was responsible for the potent spell. Which left her to wonder why. There was no reason to believe it was a mere coincidence that her great-grandfather, a powerful wizard, just happened to be in Maninberg and had decided to attend the ball. It wasn't like him to favor a remote gala with his presence. It showed a strong interest in the duke and his kingdom. He had indicated as much at the ball when he told her he was working on a particularly engaging project.

What surprised her even more was discovering who else was affected by the magical wall. By the end of her visit she realized she was not the only one who could perceive the invisible boundary. There was one other person who was notably aware of it; the Grand Duke, Lord Gavin Richard Montague. Marina, Darren, and all the other visitors she had observed at the park had appeared to be completely oblivious of the exact location of the border, or even if it existed, but the duke was not.

It was truly an unexpected pleasure to find Lord Gavin at the rose garden, and Tara was grateful for another opportunity to spend time in his presence. It wasn't long before she realized he was also keenly aware of the invisible barrier. When he avoided making any contact with it, she immediately understood its significance. The Maninberg castle and its owner were living under a wizard's spell. From what she could see, it didn't appear to be a violent or malicious spell, but she understood all too well, all was not as it seemed in the kingdom of Maninberg.

More than once she had tested her suspicion that Lord Gavin was affected by the invisible boundary, and each time he had acted in accordance with her expectations. She had been able to step back and forth across the border at will, but Lord Gavin had remained steadfastly on his side of the boundary. Not once had he stepped a foot beyond it. The final test had been at their parting. She had endeavored to impress upon him that she would accept a parting kiss, that he need only to step forward to receive it. But he had remained frozen, locked behind the wall.

To the casual observer, his actions might have indicated a reluctance to press his suit beyond acceptable public etiquette, but she had detected so much more in his inability to close the final few inches separating them across the thin expanse of the magical wall. Not wishing to embarrass the duke, or more importantly, reveal her understanding of his unique situation, she had quickly stepped forward to close the gap between them.

His chaste, lingering kiss had been her reward.

She had been impressed by the sublime splendor of his appearance and had taken her time to study subtle clues imbedded in his features. His finely sculptured face carried the hard-edged beauty of a mature, yet still young man. But within the depths of his dark brown eyes there simmered a wisdom and maturity that belied his youthful appearance. It was intriguing and disconcerting to see such contradictions present in the appearance of one man. Few wrinkles graced the corners of his eyes, and the clean shaven skin of his face was nearly flawless except for a crescent moon scar that hung faintly over his left eye. Such immortal beauty seemed almost godlike.

He was also uniquely charming. She wondered if it had come from years of practice or if it just came naturally. She guessed it to be a bit of both. She allowed herself to laugh remembering his initial reluctance to take her seriously, and to his reaction when she began flitting through the flowers. The look on his face was worth her flirtation with foolishness. It had taken a bit of pushing on her part, but he had finally engaged her in meaningful conversation. Years of intense debate with her parents, older brothers, and attentive teachers had left her with an attachment for stimulating conversation, and as such, she censured herself very little when expressing her thoughts and opinions. Even though she was very much aware Lord Gavin was the grand duke of his kingdom, she tended to look upon everyone with a level eye, seeing no one as grander than another.

Her travels had exposed her to some very regal peasants, and some very lowly rulers. Though still young, she easily understood that everyone shared a common need to be seen, heard, and cared for. She was grateful for the freedom and privilege her parents had given her to travel wherever she wished. Being their only daughter, they loved her dearly. Their love had supported her through her disastrous engagement, and their inspiration had set her free upon the world. They treated her no differently than her brothers, allowing her to slip past the silken ropes of female restraints placed upon most women her age, a privilege not usually bestowed upon young women of high-ranking birth. Most were chaperoned and caged behind the high and confining walls of proper etiquette and decorum.

She had also detected the sadness underlining many of Lord Gavin's comments. At the ball, he had impressed her as someone who felt as if he carried the weight of a serious burden. More than once she had hesitated as they spoke, wanting to probe further, but not wishing to offend, and yet she had been too curious to let it go. When he shared the story of his wife and child, it had touched her heart and filled her with a desire to comfort him and take away his pain, but she knew life's disappointments were not so easily soothed. He had seemed resigned to his fate and they had moved on to other subjects.

She was now certain there was an invisible wall surrounding the duchy of Maninberg, and she suspected her great-grandfather, Tazire, was responsible for casting the spell. Apparently, Lord Gavin was captured by its power, but *why*? Why had her great-grandfather created a magical barrier to hold the grand duke captive? What could Lord Gavin possibly have done to deserve such a punishment, if it was indeed a punishment? Perhaps it was merely a form of protection. If so, from what was he being protected? And more than that, she wondered if there were any other aspects of the spell of which she was unaware.

The Grand Duke, Lord Gavin Montague had intrigued her from the moment she saw him, and the more she learned, the more intriguing he became.

~*~

Upon returning to his castle, Lord Gavin immediately called for Rollins. "Have the master carpenter and gardener report to me.

Tell the gardener to bring his maps and plans of Wiltzer Park with him. I'll be in the library."

"Yes, my lord, right away." Rollins hurried off to fulfill the duke's request.

Several minutes later, Lord Gavin was joined by Hugo, the master carpenter, and Hector, the royal gardener. Spread before them on the large central meeting table were maps and landscaping plans of the large public park. After pulling a number of books from his extensive library portraying the art and architecture of buildings from distant lands, Lord Gavin began sketching rudimentary designs of gazebos and these lay scattered amongst the maps. Gavin knew Lady Tara enjoyed traveling to foreign countries and he wanted to create something unique, something she would find interesting, and hopefully pleasing in appearance. Not just any gazebo would be good enough for Lady Tara.

After numerous sketches meeting with varying degrees of success, and an intense consultation with the carpenter, he decided on a design he felt was sufficient for his intentions. It was based on a temple in India, unusual and exotic, with rounded arches and a domed roof. It appeared strong yet distinctively feminine, in a way he found pleasing. It reminded him of her.

"Here, I want the gazebo built on this section of lawn." Gavin pointed to one of the detailed landscaping plans provided by the gardener. While the raised structure would be fully contained within his border, one set of stairs leading to the gazebo would connect to the pathway that crossed into Larinda village. His sudden focus on a public gazebo might seem frivolous and beneath his position, but of course the master carpenter could not refuse, or even question, his request. It would be as he ordered.

"As you wish, my lord," Hector and Hugo said, speaking as one.

"How long will it take you to build this gazebo?" Gavin asked Hugo.

"I will need at least a fortnight to gather the needed materials and have them properly assembled into this design."

"Begin immediately, use your best men. Be quick, but don't rush the work. I want it done well and done right, only the best for this project." Gavin didn't care if these men thought him impractical or crazy. He hadn't indulged in such a blatant use of his power for several years, and as far as he was concerned, he was long overdue.

Turning to Hector he continued, "As soon as the building is finished I want you to begin planting new landscaping around the gazebo. You should begin your designs now. Lay out paths to connect the gazebo to other sections of the park. And I want you to improve the grounds on the village side as well. They're shabby compared to the Maninberg gardens. I want them brought into balance with the rest of the park."

"It'll be my pleasure, my lord," Hector affirmed with pride. Gavin knew nothing pleased Hector more than being able to design new gardens and plant fresh flowers.

The Larinda side of the park, while well enough attended, had never received the same level of attention as the royal gardens. Since Gavin couldn't venture outside his kingdom to enjoy those grounds, they paled in comparison to the efforts lavished upon his lands, but that was about to change. It was part of his gift to her. Lady Tara wouldn't be forced to venture into his kingdom to enjoy the benefits of a bountiful garden. He would also have the horse trails and foot paths improved, lined with flowering trees and shrubs to provide shade and enjoyment for the people of Larinda. It was time to share his abundance with his neighbors, and if it also pleased Lady Tara, it was all the better. He had her to thank for inspiring such generous thoughts. These improvements would benefit the people of both Maninberg and Larinda, but in his mind the gazebo would always be his gift to Lady Tara.

~*~

Tara lay in her bed, lightly sleeping, with thoughts of Lord Gavin running through her dreams. The day had been splendid, and it would be even grander to see him again. She couldn't resist a peek.

After seeking him out through the mists of slumber, she cast herself into a dream and stepped into his room. It was very much as she expected, masculine and elegant and very royal. In the warm summer night, Lord Gavin lay with his bedcovers draped across his waist, leaving his fine muscular chest daringly exposed. The tantalizing view of his hard sculptured torso was more provocative than Tara expected, but not unwelcomed.

As yet unaware of her mystical presence, his eyes moved beneath his lids and she knew he was dreaming. It was tempting to join him in his dreams, to see what his unconscious mind was creating, but that wouldn't be right. It was much too soon to take such liberties uninvited. Besides being inappropriate, the results were unpredictable, but still, it was oh so tempting.

As she watched over him, his eyes slowly opened, still drowsy with sleep. She smiled. Even if he saw her, most likely he would think she was only an image of his dreaming mind. Slowly she stepped away, breaking their connection, and faded from the room. Her visit had been short, but quite pleasant. If nothing else, the vision of his nearly naked chest had been reward enough.

CHAPTER 5

The following Friday, after Tara mentioned to Loclyn that she was planning another visit into the village to meet with Lord Gavin, he insisted on accompanying her. "I wouldn't want you going there unescorted. It wouldn't be proper, even if you are meeting with the grand duke of Maninberg," he teased as they headed toward the carriage house.

Tara accepted her cousin's taunting with a gracious smile. "That might be true if I were still a young lass wanting only to find a suitable husband, but since I've long ago given up on marriage, I feel my reputation is not at risk." Tara wrapped her thick, sage green cloak about her shoulders. The sun was shining, brightening the day, but a lingering chill weakened its warmth.

"Your youthful looks do not support your position. Any man who sees you will believe you are a young maid ripe for picking rather than an old spinster ready for the shelf." Loclyn motioned for the footman to bring the carriage around.

Tara couldn't resist laughing at her cousin's remark. "Oh cousin, you bruise and smooth my ego all in one fell swoop. Perhaps I should rethink your company."

"Too late," he countered as the carriage pulled to a stop before them. "You're going and so am I. It's been decided. Besides, I plan to visit George Ebert, the president of the regional bank. If I play this right, I may be lucky enough to garner an invitation to tea." A rise of his blond brows accompanied a conspirator's grin.

"What could possibly be so appealing about having tea with a banker?" Tara asked as they settled into their seats.

"Why, his daughter Patrice, of course! Have you seen the lass? She's as pretty as a spring day, a breath of fresh air, and as slim as a willow." His grin stretched wide across his face.

"I've seen the banker. I'm surprised to learn he has an attractive daughter. Surely you've noticed his paunch. It's only exceeded by the bushiness of his eye brows and the thinning of his hair. Perhaps he spends too much time going over ledgers and numbers."

"Tara, how unlike you to be so harsh." Loclyn appeared taken aback by her remarks.

"I know it sounds harsh, but you cannot deny that it's true. However, you are right. I should keep my opinions to myself, or at least soften my words, especially when they are less than pleasant. It's a bad habit of mine, I know, but often times I speak too freely," Tara admonished herself. She was capable of presenting the perfect image of proper manners should she feel the need or inclination, which she usually did, but she could also blister the skin of a seasoned sailor if she felt it was justified. She'd traveled too long and too far to be satisfied being a mellow wall-flower, and there were times when she rather enjoyed releasing the full extent of her opinions upon an unsuspecting world.

"It's not that I disagree with you," Loclyn offered, lessening the blow, "But his daughter is fair of face and slim of figure. She takes after her mother's side of the family I believe. Apparently Mrs. Ebert was a real beauty in her younger days, and has actually been able to hold on to most of her looks. As you noted, such kindness has not been blessed upon her husband. Perhaps in his youth he held superior looks, but they have failed him through time. It happens, you know."

"Only too well. There's an injustice in the fickleness of fate which leaves some of us looking much younger than our years," she touched a finger to her cheek, "while others age far too quickly. It seems there is no magical cure for the dictates of one's heritage."

"All of the Zanders age much too slowly, if you ask me," Loclyn scoffed. "Even your mother, who is only wed into the family, seems to have inherited the trait. It's not fair, I tell you."

Tara chuckled lightly at her cousin, knowing very well his boyish good looks had often served him well, and would probably do so again today. "Cousin, you are every bit as much a Zanders as I am, even if you were birthed on the wrong side of the sheets. Your father never denied you. It was completely your choice to keep your mother's name. After all, Uncle Sebastian did eventually marry Matilda and make her an honest woman." Besides being distant cousins, Tara's mother and Matilda were lifelong friends, and Tara and Loclyn had grown up together.

"I'm quite pleased with my parents, thank you very much, but by the time the name was available I'd grown too fond of Degraw to change. Besides, there are far too many male Zanders already running around the countryside. I lose count, is it twenty-one or twenty-two male cousins?"

"Twenty-three."

"Can you blame me? With so many Zanders running about it was a never-ending state of confusion, and one I was happy to avoid."

"Even if you do not carry the name, you've always been like a brother to me." Tara smiled fondly at her cousin, knowing she could always depend on Loclyn to take care of her. She valued their friendship more than she could say.

"Tara, you have more than enough older brothers, but you are my only little sister. Now, tell me, why should you be allowed to wander a sculpture garden alone?" His tone sounded light but she saw the serious concern in his eyes.

"I won't be alone. I told you, I'm expecting to meet Lord Gavin," Tara said, hoping to reassure him.

"Alone with the duke? Very impressive, but not necessarily reason enough to be left alone with him."

"I find him intriguing. Besides, it's the middle of the day in a public park. A tour of his sculpture garden can hardly be considered scandalous," she argued, dismissing her cousin's concerns.

"I suppose if you've been allowed to travel to Egypt and back, a morning stroll through a public park should be fairly harmless. But still, I can't help but voice my reservations. You hardly know the man, duke or not. Your father . . ."

"My father isn't here, and I can assure you, I'm quite capable of taking care of myself. However, if you insist on joining me, I'll have to insist on joining you for tea with Patrice. It seems only fair. I'm sure she'd enjoy hearing how you nearly drowned when your raft went over the falls at Cullenwood. Or even better, how you nearly lost your breeches when you were finally pulled from the water." She knew he was only trying to protect her, but it really wasn't necessary. She had learned her lessons long ago.

"You drive a hard bargain, little sister. Too much like your father." His scowl was only half-hearted.

"I've learned from the best." She raised her brows, flashing a wicked grin.

"We're nearing the park. Where do you want to be let off?" Loclyn asked, surrendering the battle.

"There, near the rose garden, will do fine," Tara informed him.

Loclyn informed the driver to pull up, and stepped down to assist Tara when they came to a stop. "When should I expect to return for you?" he asked as she stepped out of the carriage.

"Take your time, have tea with your banker and hopefully his daughter," Tara encouraged her cousin, brushing down the folds of her cloak. "I have no idea how large the sculpture garden is, but I'm sure Lord Gavin will find some way to amuse me if you are delayed," she grinned.

"Yes, no doubt." Loclyn agreed. He bowed and gave her a light peck upon her cheek before stepping back into the carriage. "Do behave," he admonished her through the open window. "I have no desire to fight a duel on your behalf, especially with a grand duke."

"Take care for yourself," she said with a smile. "I shall expect a full report upon your return."

"I'll share if you share," he grinned as he rapped upon the carriage to alert the driver to move on.

When Tara turned to walk in the direction of the sculpture garden, she saw Lord Gavin was already at the park, waiting. He was standing near a new building project, consulting with the foreman as he watched her arrive while workers unloaded stacks of lumber and other building materials. It was too soon to identify what the structure would be, but she couldn't help but wonder if he had taken up her suggestion to build a gazebo. She was touched and impressed to think he had taken her idea seriously and had acted so quickly.

~*~

Friday had not come fast enough for Lord Gavin Montague. It took an act of significant self-restraint not to rush to the Wiltzer Park well before the appointed hour. Thankfully, he had the excuse of checking on the progress of the gazebo to justify his early arrival. Anxious to see her, his watchful eyes were well aware when Lady Tara's carriage came into view. Before he could step away to greet her, she was assisted out of the carriage by a man he recognized from the ball as First Lieutenant Loclyn Degraw. Even more disconcerting, the man then issued a very friendly kiss upon her cheek which she accepted as perfectly natural. Gavin didn't know the full extent of their relationship, but he was sure he didn't like it. He knew Degraw was General Gregerson's his right hand man, but who was he to Lady Tara? Was he simply a protective and overly friendly escort, or something more? Either way, he believed Degraw was a man well worth watching.

Pushing aside any unpleasant thoughts for the moment, Gavin greeted Lady Tara with a warm and welcoming smile as she stepped briskly into his kingdom. "Lady Tara, I'm pleased to see you could keep our appointment."

"The pleasure is mine, Lord Gavin." Giving a little bobbing curtsy, she returned his greeting with a bright smile of her own. "I'm looking forward to seeing your sculpture garden. The pleasure of your company and the beauty of this spring day only add to my delight."

Her casual acknowledgement of her anticipation of their meeting was a pleasant boost to his esteem and went a long way towards soothing his earlier concerns. Regardless of anything else, it was her choice to meet with him as planned. This was an entirely new experience for him, to desire a woman while relinquishing all control. He was allowing her to take the lead, and she was proving to be quite capable in the role. He hadn't imagined a young woman could be so strong minded and independent, and yet so completely lady-like. Granted, his courtship skills had been honed over one hundred years ago, and much had changed in that time, but still, he had the distinct impression Lady Tara lived outside of the norm.

"Shall we proceed to the sculpture garden?" he asked, offering his arm.

"Aren't you going to tell me about this building project?" she questioned, indicating the construction workers.

He glanced in the direction of the work site, knowing it was too soon to truly guess at the final results.

"Not yet." He took her hand and linked it in the bend of his elbow. "We'll leave that for later." He liked creating a little mystery although he was quite sure she suspected what was in the works.

Lady Tara raised her brows and smiled, but said nothing, apparently accepting his desire for suspense.

The moment they reached the sculpture garden, Lady Tara stopped and stared, displaying a mixture of awe and appreciation. Although he maintained a serene façade, Gavin felt the swell of pride puffing his chest. He believed his collection was quite impressive and hoped she felt the same. Some of the pieces were commissioned reproductions of the originals, but many were unique works of art she would never have seen before.

Unexpectedly, Lady Tara pointedly ignored the largest statue taking center stage of the collection, and instead, began by examining the delicate beauty of two smaller statues closer to the entrance, both depicted females. The smaller of the two held a bow in her hands, and the hounds at her feet indicated the statue to be of Diana, goddess of the hunt. She was also associated with the moon and virginity. Next to her stood Venus, the goddess of beauty and love, with her delicately carved hair flowing smoothly over her unclothed marble body.

"They're beautiful," Lady Tara stated, circling the statues. "Such lovely renderings of the female form. I see you've chosen two of the most favored goddesses in mythology." Her approval pleased him.

"What collection would be complete without Diana and Venus?" Deeper in the recesses of the collection were a number of other statues depicting the female form in various stages of dress or undress, but none were of the quality, nor held such a high place of honor in his collection as these two.

71

"I think Diana is the more beautiful, or perhaps the more appealing, of the two, even though Venus is considered the goddess of love and beauty," Lady Tara remarked as she examined the statue.

"Beauty is very subjective, wouldn't you agree? Perhaps this artist was more talented, or simply more inspired by his subject. Perhaps he was intimate with the woman who posed as his model." Gavin was fairly certain it was the latter, which explained much about how the goddess was depicted.

"All good points," Lady Tara agreed, glancing at him over her shoulder. "I hadn't considered how much the model could affect the final outcome."

"If the artist is drawing from the beauty he sees around him, then much depends on how he sees such beauty. In the case of Diana, I've always felt there was a close, personal connection between the artist and his model. I believe he shows the light of love in her face which we, as outside observers, see as beauty." Looking up, he focused on the face of the moon goddess.

"Lord Gavin, you surprise me." Lady Tara turned her focus on him. "You're leading me to believe you're a romantic." While her voice was playful, her comment was heavy with meaning.

"Is that so surprising? Are grand dukes not allowed to be romantic?" he quipped, keeping his voice light, almost teasing, while he earnestly awaited her response.

"Images of dukes, kings, princes, and even gods, are often romanticized, especially in the minds of impressionable young women, such as me. It's rare when the reality lives up to the expectation."

Her comment was outrageously flirtatious, and the allusion that she found him romantically appealing was not lost to him. A pleasant warmth spread throughout his veins, settling in the area of his chest.

"Do you really see yourself as an impressionable young woman?" he questioned, somewhat surprised by her self-assessment. "From what I have seen, you're an independent and strong-minded woman with rather well-formed opinions." Traveling around the world as she did, she was far more independent than any other woman he knew.

"To be honest, I cannot argue with you. I've been known to express my opinions quite freely. It's a flaw I must own." She looked away, returning her gaze to the statues.

"I would not judge it as a flaw, more like a strength that needs to be well tended," he countered knowing he shared a similar trait.

"You're too kind. However, I believe Mr. Degraw may have cause to disagree with you."

"What makes you say that?" he questioned, forcefully trying to avoid any display of resentment towards a man he already mistrusted as being too familiar with Lady Tara.

"On the carriage ride here he commented that my opinions tend to be too harsh, and in the moment, I had to agree. There are times when it would serve me well to be more thoughtful in my choice of words." As if uncomfortable with the direction of their conversation, she directed her attention to the largest piece in the garden. Leaving the goddesses behind, she walked over to the Poseidon.

Centrally positioned in the collection was a larger-than-life, white marble statue. Sitting flush upon the ground, its sculpted base represented the agitated surface of an ocean with a naked man rising up from the sea. His upper torso was fully visible above the churning waves, which barely concealed his genitalia. The oversized figure was intended to signify the grandeur and strength of this ancient god.

Lady Tara eyed the sculpture with curiosity. "Is it Neptune or Poseidon?"

"You're asking if he's Roman or Greek. The myth stays the same, only the name changes. I believe this artist was partial to the Greek gods and has called him Poseidon. Which would you prefer him to be?"

"Interesting question, but I don't believe I have a preference. Roman or Greek, a god by any name still creates an impressive image. May I touch it?" she asked with her hand halted in mid-air.

Gavin appraised the work through her eyes, knowing the artist had done a fine job of sculpting the marble, rendering it almost life-like. Hard, stone skin depicted a god-like male in minute detail, down to the throbbing veins pumping blood through the muscular body. It called out to be touched, even caressed.

"Certainly, if you wish. They're not fragile. It won't break."

After removing her glove, she raised her hand to the statue. "I can almost imagine the artist running his talented hands over the stone, polishing it to this fine finish." Reaching up, she graceful drew her hand lightly across the statue's torso, lightly tracing a line from Poseidon's broad chest down to his taut stomach. "It's almost as if it's a living thing. It deserves to be enjoyed and appreciated. Not just by sight, but by actual physical contact, a tactile delight. This artist has truly depicted a god, magnificent in his proportions."

A shudder raced through Gavin. All too easily he imagined the sensation of her fingers touching his heated skin instead of the cold, hard statue. It had been too long since he'd felt such an affectionate embrace and he wondered if she had any idea what effect her caress of the statue was having on him.

"You seem pleased," he remarked, reigning in his emotions. He had to say something, anything, to break her spell and recover his senses.

"It certainly is impressive. It's the center-piece of your collection, no doubt. Am I correct?" A subtle mixture of innocence and womanly guile graced her features.

"It's also the largest. Spacing alone would dictate its centralized location. However, I agree, the surrounding statues cannot compete." Pointing towards the two smaller female statues, he continued, "Venus and Diana, while they depict immortal beauty, are each too delicate to command center stage." Moving to his left, he indicated another large male statue. "And while Jupiter, or Zeus as the Greeks called him, is considered the king of the gods, this artist has not rendered an image that can compete with the Poseidon."

She smiled at his explanation. It was logical of course, but he couldn't deny the pure physical appeal of the Poseidon. She released an audible sigh as she stepped behind the statue to appreciate the view of its backside.

"Oh my, he is rather impressive," she said as she circled the statue. Her smile widened into a mischievous grin as she clasped her hands to her chest.

"You certainly surprise me." He blurted out his rather blunt remark before he could check his words. Too many years devoid of the unexpected had taken their toll on his usually impeccable manners.

She gave him a quizzical look. "I'm not sure I understand what you mean."

"You are a unique woman. You're like a fresh breeze that blows away the clouds and brightens the air around you. How did you become so free, so open? There are not many young women who would openly display an appreciation for the nude male form. Most would rather feign offense than admit to such appreciation." Upon hearing his words he rather regretted his choice of phrasing, fearing he sounded unkind, as if he was questioning the very nature of her character.

Her reaction relieved his fears. The smile that lit her face was brighter than a moon beam piercing the darkness of night. "I have my parents to thank," she gushed. "I've been blessed by superior, loving parents. From them, I've been given the ways and means to travel. I have seen more of the world than most women of my age, and it has broadened my perspective in ways few are privileged to experience. I believe my parents are uniquely enlightened."

Lord Gavin appreciated the love she expressed for her family and tried as best he could to ignore her reference to her travels.

"They have sought out the company of some very forward thinking men and women," Lady Tara continued. "If you see me as unique, I can only thank my parents."

Not many would give credit to their parents for their blessings. It was far more common to hear people complain of the burdens inflicted upon them by the people who raised them and loved them. "Not many are so appreciative of their parents. Another remarkable trait you possess."

"I would say not many are blessed to have parents as kind, and loving, and considerate as mine. I am six and twenty, and yet I can assure you, I am not in need of a husband as if my only lot in life was to secure a safe future. My father comes from a wealthy family and I'm his only daughter. I know I have been pampered and spoiled, but I'm well aware of my blessings and am always thankful. My parents would have it no other way. They have never allowed me to take anything for granted. Theirs is a contrary philosophy in a society that values entitlement over enlightenment. Far too many do not appreciate what they have. Instead of being thankful, they often seek to only take more. My parents believe wealth is an energy that flows through our lives, not something to be captured and stockpiled away from others. The more we give the more we receive. I have seen it to be so."

Her little speech was so impressive, he almost felt like clapping. "Your enthusiasm is remarkable. Poor Poseidon shrinks in comparison. It is you who now takes center stage of this garden." He leaned against the base of Jupiter to better enjoy her presence, delighted to hear her thoughts.

"Oh, I'm sorry. I do tend to run on. I don't mean to monopolize the conversation." As if suddenly aware of the spotlight she had created, she took a few steps towards the nearest statue and focused her attentions upon it.

"You're not monopolizing the conversation. I willingly submit myself to the mercy of your wit." He enjoyed every minute of her presence, watching her face as she spoke. She was like a flower blooming before his eyes, or a powerful bird spreading her wings preparing to take flight.

She turned to him again. "You see, this is what I mean. I am blessed to be here with you, to see this garden and these sculptures. To meet the grand duke of Maninberg and spend a day discussing Greek and Roman mythology with you, I am nothing less than blessed."

"You honor me, but I believe you overstate the value of my acquaintance. It is I who am pleased by your company. I have far too many subjects who would prefer to agree with every word I speak rather than share such unconventional thoughts as you freely express. It is truth when I say you're a breath of fresh air to my stale existence."

She captured his gaze, perhaps searching his eyes for evidence he was speaking honestly. She seemed unconvinced, or at best, unsure. But there was something else he sensed, possibly a longing. He shook it off, not wishing to misinterpret her intent.

They continued to wander through the collection of statues and came to one of the smaller statues depicting a smooth-faced youth holding a bow. A lyre sat at his feet.

"This would be Apollo, if I'm not mistaken," Lady Tara ventured a guess as to the statue's identity. She paused to study the sculpture.

"You are correct. It is indeed Apollo, son of Zeus and Leto." Lord Gavin smiled, enjoying the extent of her knowledge on the subject of the ancient gods.

"Why do you think Apollo is typically depicted in the diminutive? I don't believe I've ever seen a life size statue of him." Lady Tara stood nearly eye level with the miniature male as it sat perched upon a low pedestal.

"I have rather limited knowledge of other statues depicting this particular Greek god. I liked this particular statue so I added it to the collection." The image of a youthful boy had appealed to him and in his mind it served as an anonymous memorial to his son, the child he was denied.

"How do you go about finding statues to add to your collection?" she asked. "You mentioned you don't travel much."

Her gaze was innocent yet probing. He could see she was genuinely interested, but he was a man of strong reserve and firm control. He'd spent decades perfecting the art of deception to avoid offering up details of his life.

"Often I am presented with sketches of statues that are available for purchase and I make my selection based on what appeals to me. Sometimes, if I am aware of a particular statue that interests me, I secure a broker to determine if it is available. That's how I obtained the Poseidon. But it was the youthful appearance of this Apollo that first drew my interest."

"A youthful god. I suppose it's not unexpected. I can see the appeal," she said.

"Apollo is considered to be one of the more diverse of the Olympian deities. He's accredited with being the god of light and the sun, the god of truth and prophecy. Interestingly, he's also known as being the god of archery, which is a killing sport, as well as being a god of medicine, with the ability to heal. A rather contradictory set of attributes." Gavin realized he had allowed himself to become lost in his admiration of the statue's image, and the god-like characteristics he would have bestowed upon his son if the child had lived. Regaining his composure, he sharply pulled himself back to reality.

Lady Tara remained silent for a moment, her sensual lips slightly parted with a stunned expression of awe. Then, blinking as if roused from a trance, she said, "I think I recall hearing similar stories from the professor I studied with when I toured the Mediterranean. I hope to revisit there soon."

He instantly recalled from their conversation at the Summer Solstice Ball that she had gone on an academic tour of Greece and Italy. "Oh yes, your travels," he sighed. It was a deflating blow to once again be reminded of her unfettered freedom.

Lady Tara continued speaking, clearly unaware of his inner turmoil. "I have already been to more places than most will visit in a lifetime, and so much more awaits me. Oh, the places I shall go. I feel as if the world is an open book, no, a library of open books, just waiting for me to choose the next grand adventure." Smiling, her eyes sparkled with delight. A true look of rapture graced her face as she spoke.

In contrast, Lord Gavin became acutely aware of the deep frown settling across his face.

It was a bitter reminder. She was free to move about the world, but he was not. He had no business pursuing something so far outside of his reach. He was enchanted by her, as any man would be. Her beauty alone was enough to entice, but the unchained flight of her mind was even more appealing. Perhaps, if she knew the truth of his existence, she would agree to visit him from time to time, to grace him with her bright presence, but he knew such fleeting visits would never be enough, not for him. Nor would she ever willingly agree to being caught within his cage. No matter how attractive his kingdom might appear, it was still a cage.

Melancholy settled over him like a heavy cloak engulfing his being. It was an uncomfortable feeling, but one he had felt many times before. The women of his kingdom could deny him nothing, and yet they held no appeal. Here was a woman to whom he would deny nothing, and yet he knew he lacked the one thing she valued most of all, freedom. She had license to move about the world and experience life, while he was confined to less than a thousand square miles of earth.

He could ask her to stop her talk of worldly travels, even force her to remain within the borders of his kingdom, but that would be breaking the vow he had so recently made to himself.

Stiffening his stance, he sharpened his resolve against the whetstone of his reality. He needed to end their dance, for he knew they could never leave the dance floor together. He needed to end this charade immediately, here and now.

He would return to his castle high upon the hill, far away from his borders and all that reminded him of her. It was imprudent to have allowed himself such a foolish flight of fantasy. It was time to resume his role as sovereign.

"I hope you have enjoyed the tour, but unfortunately I must now end our visit," he spoke rather abruptly. "I have duties that require my attention back at the castle." It was a rather vague excuse, but he knew she wouldn't question him. No one in his kingdom ever did.

Her flashing smile slid quickly from her face and she took on the look of a deflated doll. "Oh, I didn't know. I thought we would have more time together. Isn't there still more to see?" she responded hastily.

"I'm pleased I was able to keep our appointment, Lady Tara. I have enjoyed your company, but now I must return to Maninberg castle." He told himself it wasn't a lie. He needed to end this pretense for her sake as well as his. "Of course you are free to stay and explore the gardens as long as you wish. If you need anything, simply ask for Hugo. He is the master carpenter. I will leave instructions for him to see to your needs."

"Thank you, but that won't be necessary," she countered curtly. "It's best if I also leave. Loclyn is in the village having tea with Mr. Ebert, the banker. He invited me to join them. I wasn't sure if I would be there in time, but since our visit is over, I shouldn't keep them waiting."

"Please, by all means, do not keep the gentlemen waiting. Do you need a carriage to take you back to the village?" His voice was terse. It galled him to be reminded that Degraw had accompanied her here and Degraw would be the one escorting her home.

"No, I believe I would prefer to walk," she replied, her tone equally terse.

He wasn't surprised. She was smart enough to know she was being dismissed. And while he admired her ability to stand up to him, it didn't change anything. He needed to end this flirtation before his desire for her got the best of him. He had made a promise to himself that he would not ask her for anything, and that included asking her to stay. She was free to come and go as she pleased and now it was best for her to go.

~~~

In silence, they walked the path back towards the park's entrance near the border of Maninberg. She had seen how strongly Lord Gavin had reacted to her talk of traveling to far-flung countries and she could kick herself for being so thoughtless, but she was determined to hide her emotions. She refused to question his motives or beg for forgiveness. Instead, she kept her eyes focused on the gardens, the flowers, the hedge row and the trees, anything to avoid looking at him. She didn't trust her ability to fully hide her emotions, and she'd be damned if she'd allow him to see any sadness or disappointment in her eyes. He was being a royal cad. She would not plead for his company.

As her eyes scanned the gardens, she noticed a smoky grey owl perched in one of the tallest tree, watching their movements. She took advantage of the delightful distraction, focusing her attentions on the wild owl instead of the man walking beside her. Such a magnificent bird was an unexpected pleasure seeing it nestled so close to the village.

Darting a covert glance at Lord Gavin, she considered for a brief moment if she should confront him about his inability to leave his kingdom, or challenge him to step beyond the boundaries of Maninberg. It was a tempting thought, but she quickly decided against such abrasive actions. Her reckless talk of travel had already caused enough trouble, it would serve no purpose to be intentionally rude or mean-spirited. He was choosing to maintain his secret, and the least she could do was be kind enough to honor his decision. After all, she had secrets of her own.

It was agonizing to recall how excited she'd been when she told Marina about her time with the duke. The ball had been a grand evening and seeing him again at the Wiltzer gardens had exceeded her expectations. She considered herself to be well-traveled and worldly wise, but she was still impressed by the duke's charm and good looks, if not his royal lineage.

Their tour of the sculpture garden had started off so well. The statues were quite impressive and she had been enjoying his company, perhaps too much, considering she had allowed herself to become lost in the clouds. Now she was being pulled back to reality and her spirit returned to earth with a painful thud. Like an unthinking fool, she had offended him with her ramblings. Would she never learn to control her words?

Telling him she was meeting Loclyn and the banker for tea had been a blatant manipulation of the truth, but she didn't care. It was obvious he wanted to dismiss her and she had no desire to linger in the gardens without him. She might be acting like an indignant mule, but in her mind it was better than retreating like a wounded pup.

When they reached the workers at the building project, Lord Gavin made his formal good-byes and sent her on her way. Their parting was brief and to the point. The presence of his workers was enough to dash any hope for a kind word or friendly gesture at their parting.

She was annoyed by the turn of events but she hid her frustration behind a forced, polite smile and slipped away with hardly a word. *Have it your way*, she thought. She knew why his feathers were ruffled and she refused to care. She would not beg for his attentions.

She stalked off, hoping the brisk walk back to her carriage would relieve some of the pressure building in her chest. Regardless of what she told Lord Gavin, she had no intention of joining Loclyn for tea, it was too intrusive. She much preferred to sulk alone while she waited for Loclyn to return.

As she walked from the park to the village stables, her emotions rolled through her with varying degrees of intensity, swinging from being furiously angry at the duke to being sadly disappointed with herself. By the time she reached the parked carriage, the tension in her chest slowly began to dissipate. Even so, she wasn't ready to completely release all of her anger, not just yet. Now, instead of being directed at Lord Gavin, her indignation was directed at herself.

In all honesty, she knew she had no one but herself to blame. Just because she found the duke attractive, intelligent, and pleasing company, didn't mean he shared her feelings. More likely, her impetuous nature had allowed her to leap to thoughts of an attraction that simply did not exist. It was one of the reasons she had gotten engaged too young to a man she barely knew. She had thought by now she would have learned from her past mistakes.

She admonished herself for being an idiot, babbling on about faraway places to a man who had spent his whole life in one tiny duchy. It was only natural he would take offense, how very thoughtless of her. And she couldn't very well ask him about his restrictions since it was only because of her connection to a powerful wizard, a wizard who just happened to be her Grand Papa, that she was even aware of his enchantment in the first place.

They each had their secrets, and she had to respect his privacy as much as she valued her own.

He had sent her away, done in by her relentless talk of travel, and there was no reason to believe he would ask her to return. Furthermore, it was obvious he wouldn't be calling on her anytime soon.

Tara returned to the carriage and climbed inside. What else was there to do but wait for Loclyn to return? Drawing her cloak around her, she settled on the large padded bench, trying to relax. It was a relief to know it would be some time before Loclyn would return. She needed time to calm her emotions and set her mind at ease before she faced her cousin. Closing her eyes, she forced her mind into silence, dispelling Lord Gavin from her thoughts. Eventually she fell asleep, escaping into a peaceful slumber.

The sound of the latch on the carriage door startled her from her nap.

"You're here early," Loclyn greeted his cousin through the open carriage door. "From the looks of it, you've been here long enough to take in a nap. Was the sculpture garden really that dismal?" he asked as he climbed in and took the seat across from her. Rapping on the carriage roof, he instructed the driver to return to the villa.

"The sculpture gardens weren't dismal, the duke holds a very impressive collection," Tara answered. She sat up in her seat and smoothed the folds of her skirts. "Did you enjoy tea with Patrice, or were you limited to the banker's pleasant company?"

Loclyn ignored her question. "Are you sulking?" he asked.

"Yes, if you must know," she answered as she slouched against her seat.

"Why?"

"It went badly. The duke sent me away, and justifiably so. I talk too much, and I say all the wrong things. You said so yourself." She allowed herself to sink even lower as the carriage swayed down the road.

"Come now, you don't expect me to believe that. You're just being harsh on yourself. This isn't like you."

"It doesn't matter. For the most part, it's true. I'd much rather hear how your day went. From the looks of it, it was better than mine."

"Apparently so. Patrice was able to join us for tea, or rather I should say, I joined her for tea. Ebert took me over to his house to have tea with his wife and daughter. It was all very friendly. Ebert may not be a looker, but he is a spirited conversationalist. He had many fine stories about the finance minister of Maninberg. Ebert facilitates much of the duchy's finances through his bank, and I got the impression he is well paid for his services. A nice little set-up. He also let it slip that Patrice has a plentiful income of her own, from an existing trust. It turns out she's a woman of beauty *and* means."

Just being in the presence of her cousin was enough to ease Tara's mood. His high spirits were evidence of his pleasant afternoon and she was happy for him. A near smile returned to her lips. "I'm happy for you, Loclyn. I wish you only the best." She gave him her standard good-luck wish, wondering what was best for her.

"That's not all," Loclyn continued. "I have reason to believe there are new visitors to the villa who will be of interest to you." A sly smile graced his lips.

"Really? Who?" She perked up immediately, anxious to hear the good news.

"Not so fast. I can't be certain. Besides, I think the suspense and surprise will be good for you."

"Well, it must be someone I know. Is it someone we met at the ball?"

"Patience, little sister. We all have our secrets." His grin was mischievous. He looked quite pleased with himself and she knew better than to attempt a full confession. From their childhood together, she had learned such attempts usually ended in failure. Instead, she huffed and indulged in a pout, which was accompanied by internal grumbles. Secrets, she stewed, was what had gotten her into this pickle in the first place.

CHAPTER 6

There was no mistaking her father's carriage. Tara spied it the moment they pulled into the villa's courtyard. Her parents' trunks were still being unloaded from the back of the large black traveling carriage with the crest of Lord Tyrus Zanders, Earl of Cullenwood, embossed on each door.

"Loclyn, how could you be so mean?" She swatted at his knee. "I had no idea Mother and Father planned to visit." She had thought Loclyn's reference to secret visitors were simply people from town and had paid it little mind. While the suspense had done little to lift her spirits, this surprise was more than enough to make up for a truly bad day. "You're only allowed to live because I'm so happy to see them."

Loclyn chuckled with a cocky grin, happily accepting her friendly flogging.

Tara could barely wait for the carriage to come to a stop before she unlatched the door and leapt to the ground. Picking up the hem of her skirt, she dashed across the courtyard and up the front steps of the villa. Rushing into the grand marbled entrance of the villa she was met by Parker, Uncle Iain's butler.

"My parents, Lord and Lady Zanders, have you seen them?" Tara asked, as she came skidding to a halt across the highly-polished black and white marble floor, barely able to catch her breath.

"Your parents are in the front parlor with the General and his wife," Parker informed her. "I believe they're anxious for you to join them, however, I dare say, no more than you appear to be."

With his hand outstretched, the butler stood ready to accept her cloak. Tara rushed to oblige him, shedding her outer garment, and nearly dropped it to the floor as it she thrust it in his direction. Only a quick reaction from Parker allowed him to catch the flying garment.

"Young people," he grumbled under his breath. "Always rushing." He shook out the folds of her cloak and laid it over his arm before turning to properly greet Loclyn as he made his way into the entrance hall behind Tara at a far more civilized pace.

Tara flashed a ready smile over her shoulder at the disgruntled butler. She believed Parker rather enjoyed the lack of proper etiquette displayed in her uncle's home, even when he pretended otherwise. Hardly slowing her pace, she crossed over to the front parlor and dashed into the room. The sight of her parents sitting comfortably on a settee together warmed her heart. When her father stood to greet her, she nearly flew into his arms. His welcoming embrace soothed her bruised ego, giving her much needed comfort.

"Papa," her voice was nearly crushed into the lapels of his coat by the strength of their embrace as she lingered in his arms.

"Tara my love, your greeting overwhelms me. Has our absence been that deeply felt?" he asked rubbing her back.

"Should I not be happy to see the most important man in my life?" she teased, knowing her father always enjoyed a bit of flattery as she hastily brushed away a tear that threatened to spill down her cheek.

"Then I am a fortunate man indeed." He pulled her back for another crushing embrace before brushing a kiss upon her cheek.

Her mother, who had remained seated awaiting her turn, now moved to accept her daughter's embrace.

"I can't believe you're here." Tara burst with happiness. "I had no idea you planned to visit Uncle Iain. Why didn't you tell me you were coming?"

"We wanted it to be a surprise. It's more fun this way," Lord Tyrus said.

"And more mysterious," Aunt Jeanine said, raising a brow.

"You didn't think I would allow the news of my brother becoming a grandfather to go unnoticed did you?" Lady Chandra smiled serenely at her daughter.

Tara offered a quick greeting to her aunt and uncle before returning her attentions to her parents. It had been more than two months since she had last seen them at their home in Scotland. From there she had gone to their London town-home for several weeks before she sent word of her plans to travel with Loclyn to Iain and Jeanine's new villa.

"I'm sure I don't need to remind you, this will be my fourth grandbaby," Uncle Iain broke in. "Jared has already produced an heir and a spare, and Finley's daughter is nearly two now." Uncle Iain was obviously a proud grandfather, and had no qualms executing his bragging rights. The large, barrel chested man relaxed comfortably in his favorite oversized brown leather armchair, flanked by his wife and daughter on either side.

Tara sat next to her mother on the pale yellow settee, displacing her father who moved to a wingback chair. "Mother, I'm so happy to see you," she gushed, thinking how much she could use the wise counsel and comforting care of her mother. "You couldn't have come at a better time,"

"Is your father not also cause for celebration?" Tyrus half-heartedly teased his only daughter.

"Oh Papa, you know I'm happy to see you. I greeted you first didn't I? And I expect to enjoy a long detailed discussion about your recent travels at dinner tonight," she countered.

"But first you need to speak with your mother, am I right?" It seemed her father's loving gaze probed right past her silver blue eyes and straight to her wounded heart.

"You are right, and wise, and so very understanding, as always." Tara's smile dimmed for only a second before she quickly recovered. "You must remind me to tell you about seeing Grand Papa at the ball in Maninberg," she added, knowing it would spark his interest.

"Tazire? What's the old man doing out here?" Tryus questioned, raising a fine, dark brow. At nearly sixty years of age, he still retained his striking good looks. The silver gracing the temples of his black hair and the sun lines touching the corners of his deep green eyes only served to enhance his allure. Far from appearing old, he projected the image of a charmingly handsome man. Like all the Zanders men, he carried the blessing of a youthful appearance that belied his years.

"That's a good question. I'll look forward to discussing it with you later this evening when we share stories of our travels," Tara replied with an mischievous grin.

"I shall wait if I must," her father conceded. "However, I expect to be well rewarded for my patience."

"Most certainly, Father," Tara smiled, knowing she held his love in her heart.

Sooner than polite manners allowed, Tara dragged her mother away from the company of the other family members, to the privacy of her bedchamber.

"Daughter, what has you so anxious for my attentions? I know you can be impetuous, but you're usually not rude." Her mother's stern words were somewhat tempered with a note of humor in her voice.

Tara understood her mother's desire to lighten the mood. Over the years, her mother had surly become well acquainted with her outbursts of emotion. However, Lady Chandra tended to avoid undue drama and had limited tolerance for her children's theatrics. Her mother's tone, as well as her choice of phrasing, had its intended effect of bringing Tara back to earth. Tara often thought of herself as a high-flying kite with her mother as the earthly anchor to which her tenuous line was tethered.

"I'm sorry, Mother, but I wanted to tell you, I've met a man," Tara began in a quick rush.

Lady Chandra cocked her brow, her smile pressed into a thin line. "How very interesting. Should I be concerned?"

"A rather unusual man," Tara emphasized.

"Do go on," her mother encouraged.

"He's the Grand Duke of Maninberg, Lord Gavin Richard Montague. I met him at the ball, the one I mentioned to Father. He's wickedly handsome, highly intelligent, and rather amusing. I find I'm extremely attracted to him, although I fear it's a lost cause." Tara stopped to take a breath of air as her mother smiled indulgently.

"This is a new one for you. It's been years since . . ." After a moment of thoughtful hesitation, Lady Chandra asked, "Are you trying to tell me you've fallen in love?"

"No, of course not." Tara quickly disputed her mother's mistaken impression.

"I should hope not. You've been here for no more than a week."

Tara recoiled for a moment, and then blinked. Her mother's comment was abnormally blunt.

Lady Chandra's face softened and she lowered her voice. "Why don't you start at the beginning, and please go slow so your old mother can keep up?"

Tara understood her mother's meaning. Since her childhood, she tended to move swiftly. It seemed as if she was always rushing from one place to another, always looking for the next grand adventure. It was one of the reasons she refused to seek a husband after Captain Millhouse deserted her. Since his abandonment, no man had been able to keep up with her or slow her down long enough to capture her heart. At times she wasn't sure if she was running away from her past or rushing headlong to her future. Either way, she felt best when she kept moving forward.

"You're not old – you're beautiful," Tara lovingly informed her mother.

"Thank you, dear," Lady Chandra graciously accepted the compliment. "Now do go on, and please, start at the beginning."

"Loclyn and I arrived here a little more than a week ago, as you so rightly pointed out. As soon as we arrived, Marina informed us of an invitation to a ball they had received. The ball was held at the Maninberg castle by the Grand Duke, Lord Gavin Richard Montague. I was quite surprised, but happy, to see Grand Papa there. However, he didn't seem surprised to see me."

"You should know by now, nothing surprises your Grand Papa."

Tara nodded with a shrug, anxious to continue her tale. "Later in the evening, Grand Papa encouraged me to dance with the duke, which I happily accepted. He's a fine dancer, extremely handsome, and he lives in a beautiful castle. How could I not accept? After we danced, we sat together and talked for much of the night. I told him of my travels. He was so polite. He listened to me as if I was the most interesting person he had ever met." Glowing warmth spread through Tara as she recalled her first meeting with Lord Gavin.

"Tara, I don't mean to be harsh, but he's a man. Every beautiful woman is the most interesting person they've ever met. And you, my dear, are a very beautiful woman. It's the Zanders' curse."

Tara laughed lightly. "I guess I was being naïve, or maybe muddled. I didn't take that into consideration." She blithely accepted her mother's rebuke. "But here's the interesting part. On the road into and out of Maninberg, I thought I saw a flash of light. When it first happened, I thought it was a trick of the light, but the second time, on the way home, I became suspicious, so I went back to the village a few days later with Marina and Darren to investigate." Lowering her voice, Tara leaned towards her mother, her tone becoming solemnly serious. "Mother, I found an invisible wall. A magical, invisible, wall. I think it surrounds the Duchy of Maninberg, right at the border. It's not really a wall, more like a veil or a boundary. Anyone can pass through it, I can't even feel it, and I can only see it when I touch it. Then it gives off sparks of light. I don't believe anyone else can see it."

"My word, Tara. That is interesting. But what does it have to do with Lord Montague?"

"From what I can see, I believe he's trapped or imprisoned behind this magical wall. No one else seems affected by it, but Lord Gavin seems unable to cross over it. I think Grand Papa has something to do with it. That would explain why he was at the ball. And why I can see it when no one else can."

"You haven't talked to the duke about this, have you?" Lady Chandra asked, looking slightly worried.

"Of course not. What could I say? 'Pardon me, Lord Gavin, I happen to be the great-granddaughter of a powerful wizard, and am able to see the magical wall surrounding your kingdom. Would you mind telling me why it's there and why you fear going near it?' I'm sure he would love to hear that," Tara quipped.

"You didn't tell him about Grand Papa?"

"No, Mother. I know our rules," Tara replied, somewhat miffed.

"Do you truly believe Lord Gavin is afraid of the wall?"

"Not so much afraid, but I know he's aware of it. I don't know if he can see it, or just sense it, but he acts very guarded whenever he's near it. He seems to know exactly when I am standing inside his kingdom, and when I am not. He'll walk right up to the invisible wall, and then stop, without even ever touching it. Yes, I'm quite sure he's aware of it. What I want to know is why? Why does this boundary exist in the first place, and why is he being held captive?"

"You don't know if he's being held captive. Perhaps it's there for his protection. I agree, it would be interesting to know more about his situation; however, as your mother, I would much rather know how this concerns you. Why has this gotten you so upset, other than your own innate curiosity?"

"That's just it. After the ball, when I went back to Larinda to investigate and found the invisible wall, I also happened upon the duke. He was at Wiltzer Park walking in the rose garden. It's very lovely there. That's when I noticed how much he avoids any contact with the wall. He always stays inside his kingdom. You see, the park spreads across his border. Most of it lies within Maninberg, but there's a road running through the park that's located just outside the border. It didn't take long after I discovered the wall to realize Lord Gavin refuses to even touch it. While I was there, we had a lovely conversation. He's really quite charming and I was . . ." Tara hesitated a moment, searching for a correct wording.

"Besotted," her mother offered.

"I was going to say impressed, but yes, besotted also works." Tara nodded with a shrug. "All I could think of was being able to see him again. When he offered to show me the sculpture garden, of course I accepted. That's where I was today. We had agreed to meet earlier this morning. It all started out so lovely. He really does have an impressive collection of statues. You should see the Poseidon. I know you'd love it."

Lady Chandra nodded and smiled obligingly, but looked anxious for Tara to continue.

"Everything was going so well until I started talking about how much I love to travel. Then it was as if a light had gone out and darkness had descended. He couldn't get rid of me fast enough. I felt like a blooming idiot. If he truly is stuck behind that wall, as I suspect, then the thought of me traveling freely around the countryside must be really upsetting for him."

"You can hardly blame him. I'm sure you let him know how much you love to travel, it's part of who you are. It's in your blood, and in your bones. To deny that would be to deny your very self. If he truly is unable to leave his kingdom, as you believe, he may have no desire to ask you to give up your travels. I suspect he sent you away for your sake as much as his. Perhaps he feels there's no benefit in pursuing a relationship that has no future."

"Why do you say it has no future?" Tara asked with trepidation.

"Are you willing to give up your freedom to travel? A wife can't very well leave her husband to go traveling about the world. It looks to me as if he wants to avoid putting you, or him, in such an unpleasant position."

"His wife?" Tara's voice was shrill. "I'm not looking for a husband. I'm not thinking that far ahead."

"That doesn't surprise me," her mother said, shaking her head. "You rarely think two steps ahead of where you are standing. Those who know you, and love you, may find it endearing, but it appears Lord Montague has a more forward looking view of his world."

"Then there is no hope." Tara sighed, feeling deflated.

"If I may ask, what did you have in mind?"

"Honestly, I don't know. It's as you say, I wasn't thinking two steps ahead. I only know that every time I see him my heart swells in a manner that is both painful and pleasant at the same time. I just wanted to spend more time with him. I wasn't thinking where it would lead."

It was true. She hadn't been thinking, she'd been feeling, which wasn't all that unusual for Tara. However, it was extraordinarily unusual for her to be so affected by the attentions of one man. Even Captain Millhouse had not affected her like this.

At the time of her engagement, her desire to be marred was much greater than her love for Millhouse. In the end, the engagement and the man had both thoroughly disappointed her. Since then, she hadn't felt particularly interested in any one man, and she certainly had no desire to marry.

As she thought about it, her attraction to Lord Gavin, a man she had known so briefly, was actually quite disturbing.

"Oh my word," Lady Chandra said. "This is one area where a mother's love cannot save you." She drew her daughter near, embracing her with comfort. "I'm not sure what I can do other than give you my love and support, although it may not seem like much."

"Oh no, Mother. You've been very helpful. I knew I could count on you. Just talking to you has done me a world of good. You've helped me see this from a new perspective. And you're right. If Lord Gavin is uncomfortable pursuing a friendly relationship because it holds no potential, it appears I have no other choice than to honor his wishes. I'll be honest, I find it a little frustrating to have him deciding our fate, as if I have no say in the matter. But what can I do? I refuse to force my attentions upon him."

Lady Chandra looked skeptical. "Are you sure? Will you be alright?"

"Yes, Mother. I'm sure." Tara's words held much more confidence than she felt.

Her mother still seemed unconvinced. "It was a long carriage ride. I had hoped to refresh and change before the evening meal, but I'll stay if you need me."

"Please Mother, go see to your needs. I also need to change before dinner." Tara looked down at her traveling gown, recalling the anticipation she had felt earlier that morning while she was dressing. Now it was all drained away.

Standing, Lady Chandra paused to ask, "Should I send your father in for a private exchange of stories before dinner?"

"No, his tales can wait until the dinner table when he'll have a larger audience to amuse." Tara smiled at the thought of her father holding court at dinner, as he was often known to do.

"I'll see you at dinner then." Lady Chandra brushed a kiss upon Tara's cheek and swept from the room, leaving a wake of lilacs and love.

Surprised by her mother's insightful observation, Tara sat for a moment in quiet reflection. She wasn't ready, or willing, to admit she was falling in love with Lord Gavin. It was much too soon for such intense feelings, even if they did sit begging at the doorway of her heart like a love-starved puppy. For now, the puppy simply needed to be ignored.

~*~

Lady Chandra left Tara's chamber and released a sigh. She wasn't at all fooled by her daughter's show of bravado. Deeply concerned about the emotional landscape her daughter was passing through, she knew this was one journey Tara would have to navigate on her own. This was so like Tara to underestimate the consequences of her actions. She had waited years to meet the man of her dreams, not just another fantasy, and now her heart was diving into dangerous waters without looking.

Lady Chandra could easily recall when the roles had been reversed. She wondered how often her daughter had squashed a young man's romantic endeavors, merely by her own notable lack of interest. For years, her daughter had soared above the fray, too absorbed by her forward momentum to look back. Chandra doubted Tara was aware of the broken hearts she had left in her wake. Now it appeared the consequences of her actions were coming home to roost.

Lord Tyrus entered the bed chamber only moments behind his wife. Lady Chandra paused in the midst of her evening preparations to greet him. They'd been married for nearly thirty-three years, and yet every time she looked at him she still felt their love. She knew the loving would never stop, nor the joy of being with him.

Lord Tyrus greeted his wife with a kiss. "After traveling all day with you in that confined carriage, I'm of a mind to strip you down and take advantage of you before dinner." Playful lust was evident in his voice.

"I believe we think alike. However, I fear we will scandalize my brother if our lovemaking delays us to his dinner table." Lowering her lashes, she gazed at her husband with loving desire. This was a game they often played, and it never grew old.

"You must be kidding. Given the opportunity he would do no less, if Jeanine would allow it."

"Of that I have no doubt, but I don't believe he expects such lustful behavior from his little sister." A mirthful chuckle escaped her lips. As a young woman, she'd always been the prim and proper one in her family, but since falling in love with Tyrus, all that had changed.

"Then isn't it well past the time we set the record straight?" Tyrus ran his hand along his wife's bare shoulders, pushing the sleeves of her dress down along her arms. The heated reaction of her skin was immediate.

"If that was my only concern I would already be disrobed, but surely, you do not want to alert our daughter to the lustful nature of her parents." It was a good-humored tease, one they'd played out many times before, in various scenarios.

"Good point. If she isn't aware by now, we shouldn't spoil our image. On the other hand, do you really think our children are not aware of my desire for you?" He was already raining kisses along the smooth contours of her shoulders, his hands slipping lower into the bodice of her dress to caress her breasts, freeing them from her stays.

"They may be somewhat aware, but still, I do not believe we should force the image into their heads. Offspring tend to find the thought of their parents actually enjoying their sexuality to be somewhat disconcerting." She tipped her head back to better receive his attentions.

"Yes, right as always. I will have to stow my lust until a more reasonable hour, when I can properly ravish your body by candle light. But I can assure you, my dear, it will be a heavy load to bear."

It was a comforting thought. Even if she made him wait, it would not lessen his desire.

"Which will make it all the more satisfying to unleash," she said. A sigh of pleasure escaped her lips, produced by thoughts of delights to come as well as the momentary pleasure of her husband's caresses. It was followed by a moan of longing when he left her side to take a seat near the fire in order to remove his boots.

By the time he had taken off his waistcoat and white linen shirt, she knew she would succumb to his seductions. She was simply unable to resist him. This was all part of their seduction, their test of wills to see who would hold out the longest. While it appeared she would be the first to give in, she was far from being the loser.

Loosening the buttons of her traveling dress, she let it slip from her body and fall to the floor in a puddle of dark blue fabric. She stepped out and away from her garment then turned her back to him so he could unfasten her corset. She had dispensed with chambermaids years ago in favor of her husband's assistance. The arrangement worked quite well for them both.

She glanced at the bed and then over her shoulder. She knew she had his attention. His eyes raked over her with undisguised lust.

"We will need to make it quick," she remarked with a mischievous smile, dropping the corset.

"It may be quick, but I can assure you, I will not disappoint." His voice was husky with lust as he hastened to remove his breeches, revealing his aroused form for the pleasure of her viewing.

"Of that, I have no doubts."

Quickly discarding the rest of her undergarments, she raced to the bed and pulled back the large feather comforter, exposing the crisp white sheets. Her husband was right behind her, tumbling her onto the bed even as he reached for her naked body, enjoying the smoothness of her skin and the moisture pooling between her legs. She turned into his embrace, welcoming him into her body as she had so many times before, fully aroused by the love he gave and the pleasure she received.

They may have started with good intentions, but their lovemaking was rarely quick. It was always satisfying, but rarely quick. By the time they had resumed their grooming for the evening meal they were in a rush to finish. From years of experience born from necessity, Lord Tyrus helped to dress his wife's hair, which thankfully she preferred to wear in a simple coiffure. When he was finished, she expertly knotted his cravat.

"Now that we're presentable, can you tell me why our daughter required your immediate attention?" Lord Tyrus asked. He checked his appearance one last time in the looking glass before preparing to exit the chamber.

"It seems Tara has fallen for a man, although she is reluctant to admit the full extent of her feelings." She joined her husband waiting at the door, taking one last moment to smooth the folds of her creamy gown, and draw a deep rose colored shawl about her shoulders. She had a tendency to be overly chilled and had learned to be prepared. Her collection of evening wraps, Kashmir shawls, and cloaks was extensive. When packing for their travels, she often claimed there was always room for one more wrap.

"At six and twenty we cannot exactly say she has rushed this experience. What do you know of the gent? Is he reasonable, respectable, and proper? In other word, all the things I will require in a husband for my only daughter?" He took his wife's hand and linked it in the crook of his arm as they headed down the hallway towards the main staircase.

"In that regard, I believe she has chosen well. He is the grand duke of Maninberg."

"Ha! Nothing less than the best for my darling daughter," Tyrus said with a self-satisfied grin.

"However, there are complications," Lady Chandra began to explain, registering her husband's raised eye brow. "Tara has reason to believe he's subject to a spell, one possibly cast by your grandfather."

"A spell cast by Tazire? Well now, isn't that an interesting little thought? What makes her think that?"

Pulling her husband aside at the top of the stairs, Lady Chandra quickly repeated all Tara had told her about the grand duke; her discovery of the invisible wall, her visits with the duke, and how she believed Lord Gavin was trapped inside his kingdom. As she spoke, she caught her brother's eye as he entered the front salon from the foyer below and was relieved to know they wouldn't be arriving unduly late.

"How keen of her to figure this all out on her own," Lord Tyrus remarked with fatherly pride as he started down the stairs. "The situation certainly is intriguing. Many questions, but few answers. I'm sure this has created a great deal of curiosity for her.

What a perfect little puzzle Tazire has presented to our Tara. Somehow this makes perfect sense. Tazire has set-up his great-granddaughter with a man who is incapable of deserting her."

"You think he has arranged this intentionally?" Lady Chandra glided her free hand along the polished banister.

"Oh come now, have you ever known Tazire to act without intention? He's given his great-granddaughter the opportunity to choose between her love of travel and the possibility of being with a man who can never leave her. Quite a fine little dilemma, if you ask me."

Lady Chandra paused for a moment before they entered the dining room. "It does help to explain why she saw him at the ball but you must admit, it doesn't necessarily bode well for happily ever after."

"Who are we to say? That's something only Tara can decide," Lord Tyrus replied.

~*~

True to Tara's expectations, her father regaled the dinner guests with stories of his travels from Cullenwood to Larinda. One of the highlights was his description of the Dutch seaside village of Scheveningen along the northern European coast.

"Beautiful stretch of shoreline they have there, but still too cold this time of year to fully do it justice. The wind can blow fierce, and you know how Lady Chandra shuns the cold. The artist colony there is starting to show promise. Thanks to their efficient fishing fleet we were able to enjoy one of the best dinners I've had in years. Fresh fish right off the boat," Lord Tyrus said. He took another sip of wine before finishing off the last bit of seasoned roast beef and potatoes from his plate.

"Of course their cook had much to do with that, my dear," Lady Chandra clarified for her husband, setting aside her silverware and reaching for her wine glass. "We stayed with Ambassador Cadbury and his wife, a lovely couple.

"What took you to Schving . . . Scheveningen?" Uncle Iain asked, stumbling over the pronunciation of the town. "I'm familiar with the place, but it's a bit off the beaten path, wouldn't you agree?"

Tara's parents briefly exchanged knowing glances. "A bit of a fact-finding mission you might say," Lord Tyrus replied, remaining vague. Everyone at the table knew he was often engaged by the Crown for various 'fact-finding missions,' as he liked to call them, but none were privy to exactly what sort of information he might be gathering or exactly how he went about gathering it. Tara suspected her mother was a significant aid in his endeavors. She had once come across them dressed as an aristocrat and his courtesan. They had passed it off as a way of gaining access to a certain military officer, but of course, neither would discuss the matter further.

"Perhaps you should take your fact-finding skills into Maninberg," Uncle Iain offered. "Find out what makes that place run as well as it does. That should be of some use to good King George."

"What do you mean?" Lord Tyrus questioned, finishing off the last his wine. When one of the wait staff moved forward to refill his glass he motioned him off, indicating he was done drinking for the night.

"It's not normal, I tell you," Aunt Jeanine broke in. "It's like they've taken a fairy tale castle and plopped it down in the middle of Europe. The place is clean and tidy and the servants seem happy to serve." She instructed a nearby servant to clear away the dinner plates and bring out the fruit tarts for dessert.

"It's more than that," Uncle Iain continued. "I've never seen a kingdom with so little discord. I didn't hear a word of discontent from any of the subjects. From the highest ministers to the lowly chamber maids, all seem to be truly enchanted by their ruler, the grand duke."

"Enchanted? A fairy tale? Those are not descriptions usually applied to any kingdoms I have visited. Drafty, disorganized, and with a propensity for petty gossip are far more usual observations," Lord Tyrus remarked.

"I agree," Jeanine said. "Most courts have an abundance of dysfunctional courtiers. London, Paris, Salzburg—they all have their fair share of power-hungry, gossip-mongers. Which makes Maninberg all the more unusual."

"Didn't you have a good time at the Maninberg ball?" Marina questioned her mother. "I found it delightful. I was glad the grand duke sent us an invitation."

"Yes dear, the ball was lovely." Jeanine agreed with her daughter, "Almost too lovely, don't you think?"

"Perhaps I haven't been to enough balls to judge correctly, but I could find no flaws. The music was divine and the castle is simply stunning. The people there were beautiful. Everyone was so nicely dressed," Marina said, praising the event.

"Exactly, that's what I mean," Jeanine countered. "It was a little too perfect."

Tara couldn't resist any longer. She had to come to the defense of Lord Gavin, whether he deserved it or not. "I'm sure the duke simply arranged to have everything looking perfect for the event," Tara said. "Certainly that's to be expected. He was hosting a ball for hundreds of people, after all. Any good host would want to impress his guests."

Although she had also noticed how the castle and kingdom appeared to have sprung from a fairy tale, she didn't feel comfortable hearing such observations from others, not when they used them to criticize Lord Gavin.

"Still, perhaps it wouldn't hurt to take a look around. What do you say, my dear?" Lord Tyrus asked his wife. "Interested in taking a trip into Maninberg for some fact-finding?" The look of glee on his face made it evident his mind was already busy with ideas and schemes.

"What do you have in mind?" Lady Chandra asked, setting down her wine glass. Her lips curved ever so slightly as a spark of intrigue lit her eyes.

Tara had seen that look before. She wasn't sure if she should be worried or grateful. She knew once her mother set her sights on a mission there was no turning back.

"Nothing too elaborate, just a Lord and his Lady paying their respects to a royal neighbor on behalf of the Crown. What do you think? Is it worth the effort?" Lord Tyrus cocked an inquisitive brow.

A sly smile lit Lady Chandra's face as she silently joined her husband in considering various schemes. "Of course, when you put it that way, it would be nothing less than rude for us not to pay a visit to our brother's new neighbor. I'm sure King George would have it no other way."

Tara could almost imagine what they were thinking. Besides being able to see the kingdom of Maninberg, such a visit would allow them to personally scrutinize Lord Gavin as a possible suitor for her hand. At her age she hoped they had moved beyond such considerations, but she had few doubts about their ulterior motives. Still, she was secretly pleased to think her parents were taking an interest in the duke. If anyone could learn more about this elusive man, it would be Lord and Lady Zanders.

~*~

The hour was late when Tara finally retired to her bed chamber, yawning as she entered the room. She felt much better after spending the evening with her parents, surrounded by her extended family. It was quite impossible to remain depressed, her cousins had seemed determined to lift her spirits. Marina and Loclyn had made it their personal mission to make her laugh, giving her no time to focus on her earlier disappointment. There had been a fair amount of joking about princes, fairy tales, and enchanted castles, all done with good intentions and light humor.

Rather than being sad or gloomy, she decided to focus on cherishing the experience of meeting such a charming man and the pleasant times she had enjoyed in his company. As her mother often said, "Look for the good, find the good. Look for the bad, find the bad. It's all a matter of where you're looking." Also, if she knew her parents, and she believed she did, she had reason to believe she would be seeing the grand duke again sometime soon.

Her parents rarely let momentary circumstances get in the way of ensuring their children's happiness. She trusted if there was a way for her parents to arrange a meeting with Lord Gavin they would find it.

After changing into the new night shift her mother had brought her from Belgium, Tara prepared for bed. Taking a moment to fully appreciate the long, white, flowing gown, she did a little twirling dance in front of the wardrobe mirror. The night-gown was fit for a princess, adorned with exquisite lace at the cuffs, hem, and neckline. With a happy sigh and a sweet smile on her lips, Tara settled beneath the comforting warmth of the feather quilt, preparing to enjoy dream-filled sleep. At six and twenty years, she wondered if she was too old to dream of a charming prince and his fairy tale castle.

CHAPTER 7

After leaving Lady Tara at Wiltzer Park, Lord Gavin returned to the all too familiar surroundings of his castle and headed straight for his study. He poured himself a generous dose of brandy and downed it in one hard swallow. Savoring the heat of the liquor spreading through his body, he drank a second, and then a third equally generous dose before taking a seat in the well-worn leather chair behind his desk. Remorse, an emotion he was quite familiar with, washed over him. Far too often, he had experienced generous portions of the bleak sensation during his exceptionally long life.

Unbidden and undesired, his mind dredged up old aches as if searching for a replacement to his current pain. Regrets, mistakes and wrongdoings swirled through his brain. Eventually, the dark, horrid months he spent indulging in sexual debauchery rose to the top, twisting his gut as the memories surfaced too quickly to be stuffed back into their little black hole.

Too easily, his mind dredged up memories of what he had come to refer to as his long dark years of desperate affairs. He had encouraged, no *demanded*, a number of women in his kingdom to engage in every sexual fantasy he could imagine. One after another, he had pursued every woman in his kingdom that caught his eye. Of course they all succumbed to his attentions, they'd had no choice. Each in turn had fallen under the spell of complete obedience to his wishes.

After the death of his wife and infant son, he had spent years maintaining a celibate and exceedingly boring lifestyle, until he had become worn-out by his self-imposed restrictions. In a burst of self-indulgence he had rebelled in the most extreme manner imaginable, seeking available women to satisfy his needs. Each new mistress had complied with gusto, wallowing right beside him in the muck of his sexual greed. He had fooled himself into believing he was only taking his passions to a higher level, freeing himself from the confines and restrictions of polite, acceptable society.

At first, the initial thrill of the new and untried had held his interest, but all too soon it gave way to endless submission, until the relationship deteriorated into nothing more than a constant replay of "Yes, my lord" from his compliant, spellbound mistress. Once, he even fooled himself into believing he had found the one woman whom he desired above all others at his disposal. He'd been thrilled by her sexual appetite and her desire to please him, returning to her bed night after night to delight in the pleasures she heaped upon his body. But like all the others, she eventually became stale and repetitive, becoming merely a body, without a mind to challenge his intellect.

Now, years later, he couldn't even remember her name.

Finally, after the seventh—or was it the eighth—affair he become too weary of the predictable cycle to pursue the pretense any longer. Like the poisonous after-effects of over-indulgence in strong whiskey, Lord Gavin had felt the emotional consequences of his guilt-induced hangover. His desire to find true love was thoroughly squashed, trampled, and shattered to bits. He was surrounded by willing subjects, and yet he was totally alone.

He shuddered at the memories, forcing them back into the far recess of his mind, hiding them from his conscience. It served no value to dwell in a place he no longer belonged. The past was regrettable, but he had moved on, taking the painful lessons he had learned along with him.

Mercifully, as painful as they were, the agonizing memories reminded him not to wish for things outside of his reach. His life had become a lonely existence, holding very little hope for future contentment. The best he could hope for was satisfaction in knowing that all he had achieved would survive, and his kingdom would continue to thrive. He had staked his life upon this, even his freedom, the ability to create a truly peaceful and prosperous kingdom.

Unfortunately, he was also well aware that for far too many years it had ceased to be enough.

Eventually the gloom of the evening gave way to the darkness of night and still he sat slumped in his study. He'd had too much to drink and nothing to eat. Thankfully, Rollins was there to ensure he wouldn't spend the night sleeping in his clothes. Not that it would be the first time.

With his secretary's assistance, Gavin made his way to his bed chamber and recovered enough of his senses to get ready for bed. After Rollins helped him change out of his clothes and into his night robe, he ran a cold wash cloth across his face and rinsed from his mouth the foul taste left behind by an excess of brandy.

"Once again, I am quite grateful for your assistance," Gavin thanked his royal secretary. He felt considerably better but still needed to make a concerted effort to stand upright without leaning.

"You're quite welcome, my lord," Rollins assure him. "Happy to be of assistance. Is there anything else I can do for you?"

"No. I believe I can take care of myself now. You're dismissed for the evening." Doing his best not to bob or weave, Gavin made his way to the open window, hoping the chill of the night air would help chase away the effects of over-indulgence and refresh his brain.

Rollins looked less than convinced but offered no argument. "As you wish, my lord." He exited the room, leaving behind a single lit candle on the bedside table.

The drapes at the windows were pulled back, giving him a clear view of the half-moon sitting low in the sky. Interestingly, the semi-circle of light was accompanied by a shadowy outline of its dark, hidden side. Together, the two halves, light and dark, mystically completed the nighttime orb, and yet it was merely a pale reflection of the sun's true brightness.

Closing the window on the cold night air, Gavin took a seat in an overstuffed chair near the fireplace, not yet ready to retire to his bed. The light of the low burning fire in the hearth combined with the solitary candle to bathe the room in a soft golden glow, causing shadows to dance in dark corners and fade into nothing.

It was distressing to think he had damned himself to a life of solitude for the sake of his desire to rule his kingdom, this small, little duchy. Such folly was laughable. His dreams of grandeur were only an illusion, a diversion he had created, and much like the moonlight shining through his window, were merely a pale reflection of a life truly lived.

What was I thinking to have sent her away in such a fashion? It was rude and inexcusable. Why couldn't I simply enjoy the pleasure of her company without constantly considering the consequences? Yes, I know she will leave. There's no reason to doubt she will soon return to the travels she so dearly loves, but couldn't I at least have given her one pleasurable day? Have I truly experienced too many broken tomorrows to refuse myself the simple pleasure of her company for even one day?

Gavin leaned his head against the back of the chair and closed his eyes, intending to rest for only a moment before taking himself to bed, but quickly gave in to the heaviness of sleep and the escape it provided.

Within moments, a vision appeared before his eyes. It was Lady Tara dressed in a virginal white gown adorned with ribbons and lace. A sly smile played at her lips.

He gazed at her in wonder. "What are you doing here?"

"We're having a dream," the vision replied. "Isn't it lovely?"

"A dream? How can that be?" Surely his mind was still full of mist and fog from the brandy, resulting in this sleep induced fantasy.

"Yes, a dream. I'm dreaming of a prince and princess and a fairy tale castle. Would you like to join me?" she offered.

"My darling, Tara, if only I could," Lord Gavin whispered, feeling weary and sad.

"Of course you can," she assured him. "In dreams you can do whatever you want." She floated and twirled as if moving to music only she could hear. "Come, dance with me, my prince." She opened her arms, beckoning him to join her.

Again he repeated, "If only I could."

"Come," she demanded. "This is my dream. You cannot refuse me." Effortlessly she dragged him from the chair, pulling him into her embrace. "Do you not hear it?"

"Hear what?" Gavin questioned.

"The music of the night," she murmured. "Listen to the sound of moonbeams splashing upon your windows and the rustle of the wind through the trees. Listen to the hooting of an owl in the darkness, the songs of the crickets, and the crackling beat of the flickering flames. Listen, my lord, and you shall hear the music they produce."

Much like the music she described, her voice floated through the night air. Joy spread across her lovely moonlit face as she moved to her night music. Effortlessly, they began to dance in step to some far off love song only she could hear. In silent harmony, their bare feet slid across the polished wood floor.

She seemed so real, the sound of her voice, the taste of her skin as he lowered his head to brush his lips across her neck. He studied her face. Her eyes were half closed as if in peaceful repose, her sweet smile unfailing.

"Yes, I will dance with you, my love," he said, giving in to the magic of the moment. "I will dance with you and hold you close until the moonbeams take you away." Together they glided across the floor in a lover's waltz until his feet grew tired and lost their rhythm.

"Stay with me a moment more," she pleaded as she twirled in his arms.

The weight of deep sleep grew stronger, pulling him from the dream. "If only I could. If only I could live this dream instead of the life I have created. If only I could awake and find you here. If only I could choose again. But I grow weary, my dreams are fading."

"Believe, my fair prince. Believe." She swayed in his arms as he melted further and further into the deep, deep slumber of dreamless sleep.

"Come, lay with me," he urged. "Let us resume this dream. Let me not awake to find you gone. Take me with you, but do not leave me." They crossed to his bed and he laid her gently atop the thick feather quilt. Lying down beside her, he held her in his arms as she curled against him seeking his warmth. "If only you could take me with you."

"If you wish, you may see me yet again," she whispered, slipping further away as he sank deeper and deeper into dreamless sleep.

~*~

The rising sun flowed through the open drapes, filling the room with its soft morning light. Gavin awoke to find he was lying alone atop his bed covers, hugging a bunched-up section of quilt. Memories of an all-too-vivid dream reappeared, refusing to be denied. Looking about his bed chamber, he half expected to see some remnant of his midnight encounter, but there was nothing. She had arrived and departed on moonbeams, leaving only memories. There was no glass slipper or sprinkles of left-over fairy dust, only the morning sun dimly shining through the windows.

The recent days of sunshine and fair weather had given way to misty spring showers. Dark, rolling clouds blocked much of the sun's rays, leaving only a few patches of bright blue sky.

Gavin dragged his stiff body from the cold bed to relieve himself using the chamber pot in the adjoining dressing room, and then set about restarting the fire that had grown cold in the hearth. Once the blaze was lit he returned to his bed. This time he crawled beneath the covers. He was tempted to indulge in a long rainy morning in bed, but sleep would not return. He picked up the book resting on his bedside table, one he had started reading several days ago, but found he no longer had any interest in the subject. Tossing the book onto the floor beside his bed, he burrowed into the covers and waited for the fire to do its job of dispelling the morning chill from his room. Boredom and brooding gave way to stark introspection.

His attempt to escape back into sleep wasn't working. He needed to come up with a better plan. Something more original than running away from Lady Tara and the desire she inspired in him. He needed to meet this challenge head on.

He had hidden out in his castle for long enough, nearly a century. It was time to invite the world to his door. The Summer Solstice Ball had been a fine beginning. He couldn't quit now. Formulating a plan, he rang for his valet. Within minutes, Neil Harper was at his door looking neat and pressed, as usual.

"How may I be of service, my lord?" Harper inquired in his usual respectful manner.

"Tell Rollins to send an invitation to General Gregerson and his family to join me for dinner this Sunday afternoon at Wessington. Have it delivered immediately and have the messenger wait for a reply," Lord Gavin ordered. "Make sure the invitation requests the presence of the General and his family, his entire family. I want everyone at the Maynard villa to know they are welcome."

It was a bit of a risk, but hopefully Lady Tara would know she was included in the invitation, even if she wasn't mentioned by name. To single her out would seem improper, and all things considered, perhaps a bit too forward, but surely she would know she was included. If she refused, at least he would know where he stood.

"Yes, my lord." Harper replied. "Will there be anything else?" The valet was already in the process of straightening the bed chamber, setting it to rights. After attending to the fire, adding another log to the blaze, he picked up the discarded book from the floor and placed it back on the bed side table.

"Tell Rollins to include Millard, the minister of finance, and his wife and daughter." He seemed to recall from the ball that General Gregerson's wife had spent some time chatting with the finance minister's wife. Hopefully, the additional guests would help keep the evening interesting for the General and his family.

"As you wish," Harper confirmed.

Gavin hopped out of bed and began pacing his chamber. "I'll be returning to Wessington today. I expect you to join me there," he instructed the valet, referring to his manor located near the village of Larinda.

"Of course. As you wish, my lord." The valet began fluffing the pillows and straightening the bed. When that task was finished, he moved to the wash room to prepare the duke's bath.

Filled with a sense of anticipation, Gavin paced about the room fiddling with the tie of his robe. It was a sign of nerves he didn't usually display. He couldn't expect the messenger to return with an answer before late afternoon or early evening. Until then, he had things to do.

He fully expected to receive a positive response. After nearly a hundred years void of rejections Gavin had a tendency to forget such a thing was even possible. He also had great faith in his plan and believed General Gregerson was interested in returning to Maninberg. The General impressed him as a man with a strong sense of inquisitiveness coupled with a fair dose of intrigue. It was unlikely he would decline the invitation.

Harper informed him that his bath was ready and Gavin moved quickly to take advantage of the tub of hot water. Slipping into its relaxing warmth, he began to wonder about the young woman who had him tied up in knots in such quick fashion.

I'm acting as though I'm a young man, touched by the excitement of first love. He chuckled at the thought and then corrected himself. *No, I'm feeling like a young man again, and I'm allowing myself to act on those feelings.* Though the difference seemed slight, he readily understood the significance. Feelings and emotions he had believed to be lifeless and buried were reemerging with unexpected strength.

He tried to remember the last time this had happened. He came up blank. Nothing in recent memory could compare to the effect Lady Tara had on him. It was quite possible he'd been isolated from the outside world for much too long and was simply enamored by the first fresh face that came along. Even if that was the cause for his recent rising interest—which was currently making itself known in a rather obvious and physical way—he believed he owed it to himself to fully explore the full extent of his feelings.

In the past one hundred years he had experienced more than enough missed opportunities, moments of regret due to a lack of initiative on his part. Over time, he had become comfortable with playing it safe. It was time for him to take action, no matter how frivolous it might seem. What was the worst that could happen? That she would reject him? While it might be a hurtful blow to his ego, he'd have years to recover.

He wondered when he had gone from being an arrogant young man demanding complete control of his kingdom, to a wimpy old man fearful of his own emotions. It angered him to think he had become a cold old man hiding beneath the façade of a younger man's face.

It was difficult to pin-point exactly when the change of emotional seasons had occurred, going from promising spring and glorious summer, to cold and lonely winter. But somehow, during his long, lonely winter, his feelings had turned to ice. He was well past due for a warming spell to thaw the frozen landscape of his old and lonely heart. Lady Tara carried the promise of long sunny days, moonlit nights, and a return to the evergreen blossoms of spring.

A tentative half smile crept across his features. This was an opportunity to renew himself. He hoped he would be so lucky.

CHAPTER 8

When Tara awoke the next morning, she took a moment to linger, snuggled in the warmth of the large feather quilt, as she recalled the most delightful images of her midnight adventure. As misty images of her dance with Lord Gavin replayed in her head, she breathed deeply and sighed. Cherishing her memory of the dream, she smiled a wickedly mischievous grin. Casting dreams was a wonderful way to pass the night, and feelings they evoked were a delightful way to start the day.

After taking a moment to enjoy a long, limbering stretch, she jumped from her bed, ready to greet the dawn's breaking light, but when she pulled back the drapes from her windows, she was greeted by a rain-filled sky. Grey clouds did their best to block the light of the sun, but to her it was still a beautiful day. She knew that above those clouds the sun was still shining, the sky was still blue. The rain only served to scrub the sky while it refreshed the green earth. For no good reason, other than the lingering effects of her delightful dream, she was filled with a sense of anticipation for the day ahead.

Dressing for the day, she changed into an ivory-colored day dress and added a colorful Kashmir shawl artfully draped over her shoulders. Besides adding a dash of brightness, it would help to fend off the chill of the rainy day. Like her mother she had a strong dislike for the cold and made a point of dressing warmly, as much for comfort as for fashion.

By the time she reached the breakfast room, her parents had already taken their places, along with Uncle Iain and Aunt Jeanine. Greeting her parents, Tara kissed each of them lightly on their cheeks before taking a seat beside her mother.

"It looks as if this drizzle of rain is going to last throughout the day." Uncle Iain commented on the weather as he cut into one of the plump sausages heaped on his plate.

"Not exactly fine weather to go calling on your neighbor," Lord Tyrus replied, reaching for the jam pot. He spread a thick layer of the sweet preserves upon his toast. After serving an additional heaping spoonful onto his plate, he neglected to return the pot to the center of the table.

"I must agree. It would not bode well to present ourselves to the grand duke looking like drowned rats." Lady Chandra spoke with a hint of disappointment as she reached for the teapot to fill Tara's cup.

Tara helped herself to a thick slice of freshly baked bread and asked her father to pass the jam pot deposited at the front of his plate.

"I hope you will not be too disappointed my dear, but I believe we must delay our visit to Maninberg," her mother said, before taking a sip of tea.

"I'm not worried at all. Don't you always tell me if I look for the good, something good will happen? And it nearly always does." Tara replied with a happy smile.

Lady Chandra raised her brow, giving her daughter a skeptical look. Tara continued to smile, thinking how it must please her mother to know her often spoken words had actually been taken to heart.

"You seem rather chipper this morning. Is there any particular cause?" her mother asked.

"I had the most delightful dream last night," Tara confessed. "Even the rain cannot derail me from this pleasant mood."

From behind her tea cup Lady Chandra whispered to her husband. "That must have been quite a dream."

Lord Tyrus looked suspiciously at his daughter. "Were you weaving dreams, or casting them?"

"Perhaps a little of both," Tara admitted gleefully, unable to hide her guilty pleasure. Her parents knew about her ability to cast dreams, to conjure up a dream of her choosing for herself or another. She could cast out a suggestion for a person to dream about white horses, and upon waking they would report that they had imagined riding a great white horse along a white sand beach.

She also had the ability to weave others into her dreams, stirring them in their slumber to join her in her dreamscape. Often, as a young girl still developing her extraordinary skills, she would weave her parents into her dreams, beckoning them to play whimsical games with her in her magical made-up worlds.

"It looks as though we shall be confined to the villa today. Can I interest you in a game or two of backgammon?" Lady Chandra asked. Tara's mother had discovered the board game on one of her travels and had brought it home when Tara was still quiet young. It had become a regular source of entertainment for them as they engaged in heated competition, playing the game of dice and stones.

"I would love to, Mother. If I recall correctly, last time you took me three games out of four before I accepted defeat. Hopefully luck will be on my side today." Tara paused a moment to recall a few snippets of her dream as she brushed stray bread crumbs from her smiling lips.

"Perhaps later, when Marina is able to join us, you can give us a lesson or two on how the game is played," Aunt Jeanine requested, setting down her tea cup. Marina had recently developed a tendency to sleep late most mornings, owing to both the fatigue from her pregnancy and her affinity for lazy mornings, even when in the best of health.

"I would be happy to. It's always nice to have a new opponent to play against," Lady Chandra replied. The devilish sparkle in her mother's eyes led Tara to believe she was seriously contemplating her next victim.

"I'll wish you beginner's luck," Tara offered. "However, I'm not sure what good it will do. I don't know if she's just lucky or blessed with devious skill, but Mother is known for winning more games than she loses." Happy to be surrounded by the love of her family, coupled with the lingering effects of her dream, Tara took a moment to enjoy the scent of her tea before sipping the hot, dark brew.

"I have a chess board we can set up in the parlor if you care to join the ladies," Uncle Iain addressed Lord Tyrus. "Or if you prefer, we can hide out in my new billiard room. I've recently acquired a perfectly level table and had it installed. Tested it myself." Her uncle's slightly snide remark was part of a running joke he shared with Tara's father, referring to a previous trouncing Uncle Iain had received at the hands of his brother-in-law. Since then, he claimed billiard tables had the uncanny ability to tilt in the Earl of Cullenwoods' favor.

"Billiards, I believe. How can I pass up the opportunity to beat you on a perfectly level table in your own home?" Lord Tyrus accepted his brother-in-law's challenge.

When Iain rose to refill his plate from the serving table, Lady Chandra took advantage of the moment to gently admonish her husband. "Tyrus, kindly remember that we are guests in my brother's house." She raised her elegant brow.

"I shall endeavor to behave myself," her husband replied with chagrin.

~*~

It was nearly tea time when Tara's uncle came into the parlor looking for the female occupants of the villa.

"My word, will you look at this? Just when you start making plans, the world conspires to give you exactly what you want. We have just received an invitation to dine with the grand duke of Maninberg," General Gregerson announced to the ladies as he stepped into the parlor.

Marina had since joined her mother and now the four women had two games of backgammon going on between them.

Tara looked up from her game with a happy smile, "Really, Uncle Iain?"

Lady Chandra took one last look at the game board to assess her position before she turned her full attention toward her brother. "Now isn't that interesting?"

"Yes, truly," Uncle Iain replied. "And for tomorrow eve, no less. The messenger is at my door waiting for a reply to send back to the duke. He wants to know if we accept, and how many will attend. It's addressed to me and my family. What should be my answer?"

"Why, yes, of course," Lady Chandra answered for them all. She gave Jeanine the benefit of a questioning glance. "Don't you agree?"

Aunt Jeanine spoke to her daughter, "Will you and Darren want to attend?"

"Oh yes, very much so." Marina replied. "I feel perfectly fine to travel, and I'm sure Darren will agree, another trip into Maninberg would be quite enjoyable."

Lady Chandra turned to her brother. "Tell him to expect eight. That should set his mind to wondering, wouldn't you agree?" She cast a sly smile to the women in the room.

"The addition of two more guests will be somewhat puzzling, I agree, although not without precedent. It seems I have a tendency to expand my family each time we visit." Uncle Iain crossed the room and stood near the fireplace.

"Tomorrow eve, dinner with the duke," Lady Chandra mused. "Yes, life does seem to provide exactly what we need exactly when we need it. What do you think prompted him to make such a request?"

Tara could almost see the wheels of thought turning in her mother's eyes. "Mother, do not get ahead of yourself."

Lady Chandra ignored her daughter's warning. "You did say the invitation was addressed to you and your family, didn't you?" Lady Chandra looked to her brother.

He nodded.

"Clearly a sign he wishes to include your niece, if you ask me."

Tara didn't like it. Her mother looked far too pleased with herself.

"So it would appear," Uncle Iain agreed. He stoked the fire, more from habit than for need.

"Is the dinner being held at the castle?" Jeanine asked.

"Oh, I do hope it's at the castle," Marina said, leaning forward in her chair.

"No, the invitation is for a private dinner at Wessington Manor. I believe it's the duke's summer home, the one nearest to Larinda, across the valley from here. Perhaps not today, but on a clear day you can see it from the backside of my villa, up on the far hill-top. Why do you ask?"

"The distance of course. Since the castle is nearly three hours drive from here, a call to dinner would require an overnight stay. But a visit to his summer home is a much easier commitment on our part."

"Yes, quite right," Uncle Iain agreed.

Unlike Marina, Aunt Jeanine was not overly impressed by the grandeur of the duke's palace. Most likely, she dreaded a long ride more than she desired another visit to his estate.

"Tara, didn't Lord Gavin tell you he planned to return to his castle?" Marina asked, looking hopeful.

"I'm sure we have no reason to doubt the messenger." She knew Lord Gavin had returned to his castle, she had seen it in her dream, but something must have happened to change his mind. Feeling serenely smug, she wondered if her dream casting had anything to do with it. Either way, the prospect of dining with the duke held pleasing possibilities. The advantage of having her parents there for moral support was a comforting bonus.

"How very accommodating of him to return to his summer home," Uncle Iain said.

"Yes, very accommodating indeed," Lady Chandra agreed.

"Then it's settled. I'll send word back for the duke to expect us tomorrow for an early dinner. Being eight of us we'll need two carriages. I'm sure Tyrus will want to use his own. I'll arrange to have Loclyn ride in your carriage, if that's not a bother." Iain addressed his sister. Like any good general, he was already strategizing on how to move his troops to the duke's home.

"No bother at all," Lady Chandra replied.

With a nod of acceptance the General left the room to advise the messenger of their reply before returning to his billiard game with Lord Tyrus.

Uncle Iain had hardly exited the room before Lady Chandra moved closer to her sister-in-law, the backgammon game with Tara momentarily forgotten. "Jeanine, you've met the duke, what is your impression of him?"

"Charming and handsome, I would say. However, I must admit, my encounter with him was rather limited, little more than the introduction in the receiving line at the start of the ball, and one other brief meeting when we departed. It was Tara who occupied most of the duke's time."

As her mother's assessing gaze turned to her, Tara feigned indifference, though her skin heated pleasantly as she recalled her dance and prolonged conversation with Lord Gavin.

"Charming and handsome, you say," Lady Chandra echoed her sister-in-law's words.

"Mother, I can tell you're scheming. Should I be worried?" Tara asked.

"No, not at all, my dear. I'm just looking forward to meeting this man with such high recommendations. I take the duke's invitation to dinner very seriously and have every intention of conducting this meeting with all the importance it deserves. Now, we'll need to consider what to wear. I don't suppose you brought a very extensive selection of gowns with you."

Years of traveling had taught Tara how to pack well for most occasions, though for practical reasons, she preferred simple, elegant gowns.

"Not an extensive selection, but I'm sure I have something suitable. In fact, I think my lilac dress and plum colored cloak will suite just fine." Tara mentally scouted through her limited wardrobe, and while she was suitably pleased by her selection, she suspected her mother would have her shopping the stores of Larinda in the coming days.

"I can offer you a look through my wardrobe, if you wish; however, we would probably need the skills of the village seamstress for a proper fit," Marina offered. She was obviously excited by the prospect of once again dressing her cousin for a special occasion. Marina was happiest when she was surrounded by lovely gowns and accessories, and wasn't at all opposed to sharing her treasures with others.

"The only way to be certain is if we take a look. Enough of this backgammon, let's go check on your wardrobe." Lady

Chandra was already on her feet, anxious to get the question of a suitable dress settled.

Tara knew there was no stopping her mother once she had a notion in her head and stood to join her. "You only say this because I'm about to beat you three games of five."

"Don't be so sure of yourself, young lady. I could still recover the lead."

Tara glanced at the board and felt confident such an upset was highly unlikely. She had all of her pieces on her home board section and nearly a third of them in the goal box, while her mother had not yet sent any of her pieces into the goal box.

"If there's time, we can return to this game, or start a new one," Lady Chandra offered.

Tara knew her mother preferred the second option. It would give her a fresh chance at another win.

Not more than an hour later, Lady Chandra stood back to admire her work. Lying across the feather bed in Tara's room was their final selection, including slippers, a wrap, and appropriate jewels to complete the ensemble. In the end, they settled on the lilac gown, as Tara had first suggested, but only after examining every gown Tara had brought in her trunks, and taking a good look through Marina's wardrobe as well.

The neckline of the lilac gown dipped low enough to expose a flash of Tara's creamy white neck but was modest enough to comply with an image of innocence that suited Lady Chandra. Tara wondered if Lord Gavin would notice her efforts. There was no denying he had captured her curiosity, and maybe, if she was being honest, a piece of her heart.

~*~

Throughout the rest of the day, talk of the upcoming visit to Wessington Manor would occasionally resurface, keeping Tara in a constant state of awareness. It was agreed that Lord and Lady Zanders would travel in their carriage along with Tara and Loclyn.

They would follow her uncle's carriage carrying Marina and Darren along with Marina's parents. It was reassuring for Tara to think she had the support of her cousins, just in case the situation proved to be more difficult than she anticipated. Considering how quickly he had reacted when she had thoughtlessly revisited the subject of her travels while at the sculpture garden, Tara wondered how he would react upon seeing her again. While his reaction in the garden was not unfounded, it did make her think.

Recalling her mother's comments, Tara wondered if she would willingly forgo the pleasures of travel in exchange for a relationship with Lord Gavin. While she had earlier dismissed the idea as being too premature—she barely knew the man—she also knew her mother was right. It was a serious question, worthy of serious consideration. However, she wasn't sure if she had a ready answer.

What would it be like, she wondered, to live your whole life confined to a limited area of land, even one you loved as much as your own kingdom? She didn't know. It wasn't in her experience. Even as a child, she had often traveled with her parents. By her sixteenth summer, she had already traveled extensively through Scotland, England and parts of Europe, and by two and twenty she had begun to travel on her own. She was always accompanied by companions of course, but after being abandoned by her fiancé, she no longer felt she required the permission of her parents or anyone else to do as she pleased. By society's standards, she was seen as a jilted lover, tarnished, and destined to become a spinster. She saw no reason to correct society's image. It served her too well.

What a grand day it had been when her parents finally gave their approval and financial backing for her trip to the Mediterranean with the professor and his wife. The focus of the trip had been scholarly research, but the thrill of adventure was still vivid in her memory.

After that trip she had sailed to a British colony in Jamaica, acting as governess for the young son of a baron and his wife. That had turned out to be a tedious adventure, and one she had no plans of repeating anytime soon. Besides the long, boring sea crossing, the colonies in Jamaica were so underdeveloped as to offer very little excitement other than an unending exploration of raw, savage, wilderness. She much preferred the exotic splendor of Egypt, the historical grandeur of Greece, and the dazzling architecture of Italy.

If she continued to travel, choosing to forego any possibility of a relationship with Lord Gavin, would she someday discover that the freedom to travel the world had become a shallow replacement for a truly loving relationship? Or would she easily find another who stirred her emotions as strongly as he did?

Had she not been free to travel, she might never have visited her uncle's villa in central Europe, which in turn, provided an opportunity to meet Lord Gavin Richard Montague. Still the question remained; could she relinquish her freedom to travel to stay with a man she found more and more intriguing with every moment she spent in his company? To be honest, she did not yet know the answer. While the idea seemed appealing now, ten years from now, would it still be so?

She wondered if there was a way to break the spell holding Lord Gavin imprisoned within his kingdom. She suspected Tazire was the one who had cast the spell and wondered if she could convince Grand Papa to break it and release his hold on Lord Gavin. It seemed unlikely. Spells were cast for a reason. They weren't a willy-nilly thing her Grand Papa went about casting for the sport of it. Whatever his reasons, the spell would most likely need to run its course. It made her wonder about the purpose of the spell, and what outcome it was meant to achieve.

She wanted answers to her questions but she wasn't going to find them sitting alone in her room. She needed to see Lord Gavin again. Thankfully, she would soon be dining with him in the comfort of his home, surrounded by her supportive family, giving her another opportunity to learn more about this mysteriously intriguing man, and hopefully answer some of her questions.

CHAPTER 9

Tara had seen it before, the look of pride exhibited by her father as he sat looking at the two most important women in his life, his wife and daughter. Her mother, who was somewhat of an expert on the art of proper attire—or disguise—for any occasion, had done a marvelous job dressing Tara's hair and choosing the most appropriate jewels for her dress. The lilac gown and plum colored shawl served as a dramatic background to her ice blue eyes and pale wheat-colored hair, cascading in waves down her back. The lace-trimmed bodice highlighted the flawless beauty of her neck and shoulders without being too revealing. Tara liked the effect.

Sitting across from her, Tara's mother looked young and vibrant in her silver blue gown topped by a deep, royal blue cloak. The color of the cloak had a way of making her mother's smoky grey eyes seem more alluring. Draped artfully across her shoulders was a woolen shawl in the same dark, rich, blue.

"Iain tells me you were quite valuable in helping him relocate to the Maynard villa," Lady Chandra said, directing her comment to Loclyn.

"I made a couple of scouting trips for him," Loclyn confirmed. "The General, of course, had some very specific concerns about this estate. He wanted to be sure it was truly a country home, far from any major cities. He's hoping to avoid encounters with foreign governments. I believe he's had his fill of military life. He also wanted it to be somewhat removed from the crush of holiday crowds. He was quite pleased when I reported his wife's inherited estate met all of his requirements."

"Yet he's nearly camped at the doorstep of Maninberg and has already met the duke. How is that?" Lady Chandra asked.

"Keep in mind, Lady Chandra, Maninberg is a small duchy and the duke's castle is a good three hours ride from the border. I didn't believe General Gregerson had any reason to expect an immediate acknowledgment from the grand duke. It was really quite unexpected," Loclyn explained.

"But Wessington, the duke's summer home, is less than an hour's ride across the valley from him. They're practically neighbors," Lord Tyrus remarked.

"True, but how much time do royals really spend outside of their castles? Country homes are more often for show, rarely visited by their owners. I had no reason to think the General would garner such immediate attention." Loclyn replied, sounding undaunted.

Tara admired Loclyn's display of self-confidence. It wasn't unusual to see men wither under the bombardment of questions her parents had a tendency to inflict upon unsuspecting acquaintances, but her cousin seemed to be holding his own against their combined enquires.

The gentle sway of the carriage had Tara rubbing shoulders with Loclyn sitting next to her and his presence comforted her. At one time, when they were much younger, she had gone through a brief phase of infatuation for her cousin, following him around like a puppy seeking attention. Thankfully, the phase was short-lived.

As soon as Loclyn began noticing other girls, and other boys started noticing her, they had quickly returned to their friendly and familiar relationship of brotherly and sisterly affections.

"You bring up a good point," Lord Tyrus noted, referring to Loclyn's comment. "I wonder what brought General Gregerson to the duke's attention. Didn't Iain say the family had only just arrived when they were invited to a ball at the castle?"

"Correct. I consider it to be the luck of timing more than anything else. The duke was planning a grand ball and extended his invitations to every noble family in his duchy, as well as many of the leading citizens of Larinda. That was how I first met Patrice, the banker's daughter. She's a lovely dance partner." A sly smile graced Loclyn's lips. "I danced with her at least twice, maybe three times, during the ball. Unlike someone I know who monopolized her dance partner's attentions after only one dance."

Tara knew the jest was directed squarely at her. "I started talking about my travels and he asked me to tell him more. I couldn't very well deny Lord Gavin, he is the grand duke and we were his guests at the ball." she defended herself. However, now that she thought about it, she realized Lord Gavin hadn't actually asked her to talk about her travels. She was the one who encouraged the conversation, he had simply continued to listen as she had rambled on, seduced by the lure of a ready audience. It was as her mother had said: a man will listen to anything a woman says if he finds her attractive. Silently, she vowed not to bring up the subject of travel during their visit, or even comment on the topic if it should arise.

"I wouldn't think to suggest such a thing, however, considering it was a ball, I wouldn't be surprised if there were other women who had hoped to dance with him. That is one of the reasons for attending such a ball, is it not?"

Tara glared at her cousin. "If the duke wished to dance with another, he should have said so."

"Maybe he was too polite to interrupt," Loclyn countered.

"Maybe he enjoyed my company."

Mother tapped Tara lightly with her fan. "Enough bickering. I expect you both to behave properly."

Knowing better than to dispute her mother, Tara answered. "Yes, Mother." Although, under these unique circumstances, she couldn't help but wonder what exactly was considered proper behavior. Should she try to seduce the duke into further conversation, or sit quietly on the side with her hands folded primly in her lap waiting for him to acknowledge her? Since she was not known for keeping her thoughts to herself, it seemed highly unlike it would be the latter.

A moment later, the two large traveling coaches made their final turn onto the long drive leading up to the duke's summer home. To Tara's eyes, it was as grand as any manor she had seen back in England. The impressive broad façade with its bank of tall, narrow windows was well balanced by two large, circular towers anchoring each wing of the square central building. Wide manicured gardens flanked the manor, surrounding it with flowering trees and well-tended shrubs. The scent of blossoms and fresh cut grass floated in the air. The broad, gravel-covered drive led them to the grand front entrance where the carriages came to a stop.

A slumbering flock of butterflies suddenly decided to take flight inside her stomach, no doubt aroused by her prickly nerves. Tara clasped her hands over her stomach, attempting to force them into submission. As she took deep, steady breaths, she reminded herself they were only answering a neighbor's invitation to dinner. This was nothing more than an ordinary social call, something she'd done dozens of times before. Unfortunately, her butterflies didn't seem convinced.

Rollins, the royal secretary, ushered General Gregerson and his extended family to the grand salon. Acting as her escort for the evening, Loclyn took up his post at her side and together they followed her parents into a large, elegant room adorned with deep gold and dark red accents. Pale, rose-colored walls, covered in silk complimented the polished, blond wood floors. An oversized, decorative rug defined the seating area in front of the large man-sized fireplace, while an odd collection of chairs and settees created a comfortable atmosphere within the formal room.

~~

Lord Gavin stood as the troop of visitors entered the salon, watching as the General's ranks continued to swell. First there had been four, then six, and now eight. Since receiving General Gregerson's reply, he had been wondering about the additional family members. He had even questioned Rollins for any information he might have, but his secretary was of little assistance. Rollins knew General Gregerson had two sons, but it wasn't known if either of them had traveled to the Maynard villa.

Rollins ushered in the new arrivals and formally introduced each of them to Lord Gavin and the other guests, which included the Minister of Finance Jonas Millard, his wife Julia, and their daughter Brandie. Lord Gavin was particularly pleased when he learned the latest additions were Lord and Lady Zanders. While unexpected, their presence presented an opportunity to learn more about Lady Tara's fabled parents.

"Lord and Lady Zanders, how nice of you to join us," Gavin greeted them with a bowing nod.

"The pleasure is ours, Your Grace." Lord Tyrus stepped forward to accept the greeting. "It was very kind of you to include us in your invitation to General Gregerson."."

"You did ask me to bring my whole family," General Gregerson broke in. "Since they are guests at my home, I naturally included my sister and her husband." His grin was only a shade shy of being a smirk.

"Of course. I'm grateful you could accept on such short notice," Lord Gavin replied. "Come, sit," he motioned to a grouping of chairs near the large fireplace. "Lady Tara has spoken highly of you. Although I was not informed you planned to visit, this is quite an unexpected pleasure."

"Their visit was a surprise for all of us," General Gregerson explained.

Gavin turned a quizzical eye toward Lady Tara. She met his gaze but remained serenely silent, while Degraw stood rooted at her side. Gavin was less than pleased to see General Gregerson had once again included his first lieutenant in the invitation. It made him wonder about the nature of their connection and what kept the man continually in their company.

Sizing up Tara's parents, he could see where Lady Tara received her good looks, however he would never have guessed they were old enough to have sired Lady Tara and her seven older brothers. These new visitors were more interesting than Lord Gavin had expected.

General Gregerson and his wife took seats near the finance minister and his wife, while Gavin motioned for Lord and Lady Zanders to sit next to him. Lady Tara, he observed, maneuvered to sit slightly outside his conversational circle as she took a seat next to her cousin, Mrs. Metwick. He wasn't surprised she was avoiding him, not after the way he had dismissed her at the park. His only consolation was seeing the first lieutenant take a seat next to Miss Brandie Millard, the finance minister's daughter. It pleased him to see the pretty young lady draw Degraw's attentions away from Lady Tara.

Focusing his attention on Lord Zanders, Gavin asked, "What brings you to our part of the world?"

"We were traveling to Scheveningen for business. A detour to see the General's new villa seemed perfectly logical." Lord Tyrus replied.

"Scheveningen? I've heard of it. I understand it's a fishing village along the British Channel, and something of an artist's colony. What type of business would take you there?" Gavin asked in a polite show of interest.

"Just some fact-finding for good King George, a minor issue that needed some clarification. All very boring, I can assure you," Lord Tyrus said.

"When I heard the news that my brother is to become a grandfather again I wanted to come and congratulate him personally," Lady Chandra offered.

"This isn't my first grandchild," General Gregerson interjected. "My two older sons have already bestowed that honor upon me."

"Yes, but this is Marina's first child and she deserves our support, perhaps more so than you, dear brother," Lady Chandra replied, maintaining her polite smile. Turning to Gavin, she added, "I understand my brother and his family were quite impressed with their visit to Maninberg castle. Tara tells me you have a very impressive sculpture garden."

The reference to her daughter brought a wave of pleasure rolling through Gavin, swelling and cresting in an area near his heart. "I'm honored." He glanced over to Lady Tara. She looked in his direction and held his gaze for a brief moment before returning her attention to Mrs. Metwick. "My family has worked for generations to maintain the castle and this kingdom."

"The family of Montague has served our duchy well," the finance minister offered. "A Montague has been at the helm of Maninberg for several generations, nearly two hundred years, I'm pleased to report."

Lord Gavin had chosen well by inviting the finance minister. Millard prided himself on being a bit of a historian, making him a perfect candidate to relay the history of Maninberg. It was an artificial history of course, one which Lord Gavin had created himself, but it served perfectly well for the outside world. It included his reigns as Lord Gavin Richard Montague I, II, and III, the title he now wore. Over time, the duke had created the impression of a succession of rulers by turning over the rule of his kingdom to himself, as his own son. The ruse worked quite well, since no one within his kingdom was able to question his authority.

"Two hundred years of Montague rule. That's quite an impressive record," Lord Tyrus said.

"With each generation, the duchy has passed peacefully from father to son," Millard said.

Lord Tyrus raised a brow. "No violent upheavals, no mass rebellions?"

"None in recent memory. Lord Gavin rules a peaceful kingdom," Millard replied.

"Passed from father to son. How fortuitous to always have a ready heir." Lord Zanders remarked in a low voice.

After raising a brow at her husband, which seemed to go unnoticed, Lady Chandra asked, "I understand you're presently not married. Is that correct, Your Grace?"

"That is correct. I was married years ago, but my wife died in childbirth and my son did not live out the year," Lord Gavin replied, repeating the story he had recently told Tara. Although the event had actually happened several decades ago, he doubted anyone outside his kingdom was privy to the exact timing. One of the few benefits of his condition was the ability to completely control any information released to the world beyond his borders.

"I'm sorry to hear of your loss." Lady Chandra's smoky grey eyes took on a remorseful look. "How terrible for you."

Lord Tyrus reached for his wife's hand. "You have our sympathies. I can't imagine life without my wife by my side."

"It has been some time now. I have learned to put the past behind me," Gavin assured them. He hoped the mournful look on his face would be enough incentive for Lady Chandra to drop the subject. Unfortunately, she failed to heed his intention.

"Surely, as the ruler of your kingdom, are you not expected to marry again someday and produce an heir like your father?" Lady Chandra asked.

"Perhaps, someday. I am still young. There's plenty of time." His response was curt, indicating the subject was closed. As a rule, he purposefully avoided any discussion of his son who had died as an infant.

"You say you're familiar with Scheveningen. Have you ever been there?" Lord Tyrus asked.

"No. I tend to not travel outside of Maninberg. My duties require me to stay close to the castle. I believe my forefathers have done quite well in their service to this kingdom. It's up to me to carry on their tradition." After years of practice, he had learned how to deflect unwanted questions, but the Zanders were proving more difficult than most. Rather than request they cease with their questions, Gavin changed the subject. "General Gregerson, I don't believe you ever told me what prompted you to take on the Maynard estate. Has wine making been in your family for long?" Lord Gavin asked, turning his attention to the General.

"We've inherited the estate through my wife's family. The Gregersons have always been military men. It's my son-in-law, Darren, who has the knowledge of wine making. But I'm done with my days of fighting. It's time to relax with grandchildren at my knees."

"I can assure you, it wasn't easy to lure him away from Scotland," Mrs. Gregerson commented smiling at her husband.

"It wasn't all that hard. I've grown weary of the cold northern winters. I need a place to warm my old bones. Besides, it's time for my eldest son, Jared, to take a greater interest in our family home. I can't agree with these old goats who want to wait until they're dead and buried before they release the reins of their estates to their heirs. What kind of nonsense is that? How's a man to know his worth if he's not given the chance to prove himself on the battlefield? I was in charge of Windermere for years while my father was off fighting for the Crown. It's only right I should give Jared the same opportunity."

"So you have moved here to stay?" Gavin asked, impressed by the general's philosophy.

"Don't you worry, I plan to be back for the summer months to keep an eye on the lad. Last I heard they're having a cold, wet spring. I'm happy to bide my time here in the sunny hills of Maynard for a while longer."

"I, for one, am happy to have you as a neighbor," Gavin said. "It would be a shame if the old Maynard estate had been allowed to fall into ruin. I'm glad to see you taking on the place."

Lord Gavin couldn't help but admire the General. He seemed to have a well-grounded sense of himself. He was right, there weren't many men who were willing to relinquish their command of the family's estate while they were still alive. For many, the idea of a gentile retirement seemed tantamount to admitting defeat. General Gregerson didn't seem like a man who readily accepted defeat. Instead, Lord Gavin saw him as a leader who knew when to lead his troops, and when to allow his seconds the chance to cut their teeth.

Maybe if Gavin had had more experience with ruling a kingdom, he wouldn't have been so arrogant during that fateful meeting with Tazire. Maybe he wouldn't have made demands that carried such dire consequences. It did little good to remind himself that he had been a relatively young man, living in the shadow of a beloved and successful ruler. All he could see was his desire to take control and hold on to something he believed was rightfully his – his birthright.

For the last ten decades—it seemed like lifetimes—he had built up his kingdom until there was nothing left to build, nothing left to create. Legacies should be passed on to one's children so the next generation could be allowed to rule. But in Maninberg, there was only Gavin, he had no one to pass his legacy to. Of course, there were always outsiders waiting in the wings, foreign nobles who viewed his position with envy, but their cravings for power were not a threat. In his kingdom, he was god, and his word was law.

Though she sat a slight distance away, far enough to respectfully avoid engaging in direct conversation with the duke, she kept her ears tuned to her parents' conversation with Lord Gavin. She was neither surprised nor disappointed when her mother and father began directing subtle, and some not so subtle, questions his way. It seemed they were doing their utmost to garner as much information about the duke as polite conversation would allow. Also not surprising, he offered up very little more than she already knew while he attempted to charm her parents, winning them over with his regal manners.

It helped to remember he had grown up in a castle, a house of royalty. It also made her wonder if perhaps he was too far removed from her social position, and out of her reach. Though she was the daughter of a Scottish lord from the noble house of Zanders, she had never courted royalty before. Due to her parents' influences and wide circle of friends, she had encountered everything from high born royalty to common country folks. She had traveled with learned academics, and conversed with everyone from staunch military men to unruly peasants. Her experiences crossed all manner of social strata, and yet never before had she considered the courtship of a royal. Then again, since the loss of her fiancé, she had not seriously considered a courtship of any kind. While she didn't believe she would always remain unmarried, becoming a true spinster, she also had no desire to rush into marriage simply for the sake of convenience or security.

It didn't surprise her when Brandie, the finance minister's daughter, became the recipient of Loclyn's attentions. She loved her cousin and valued his friendship, but their close relationship did not blind her to his true nature. Like most men, it was his nature to flock to a lovely woman like a moth to a flame, either fearlessly, or foolishly, unaware of the potential for getting burned.

She wondered if Loclyn was already losing interest in the banker's daughter. Was his previous interest in Patrice so insubstantial it was easily replaced by a pretty, fresh face? Tara began to question her attraction to Lord Gavin, or more correctly, his attraction to her. Had she allowed herself to believe he felt more than he actually did? For a while, it seemed as if he had encouraged her attentions, deliberately seeking out her company, but after his curt dismissal of her at the sculpture garden, she doubted his feelings. What if his earlier interest was only an instinctual male response to a new encounter, as her mother had suggested, and nothing more?

Still dwelling on her thoughts, she glanced over at Lord Gavin. He was watching her, as if hoping to catch her eye. For one brief moment, he intensely held her gaze, before he looked away, returning his attention to the conversation taking place around him. The experience sent her butterflies back into motion. She wondered what he saw in her, or if he even really saw her at all. Did his gaze go beyond her pretty face?

Based on his repeated glances her way, it appeared his questionable behavior at the sculpture garden was not indicative of complete disinterest, as she had feared. Perhaps all was not lost. It was encouraging enough to suggest his interest was still engaged; however, it wasn't enough to know for certain how he really felt. As such, Tara decided it was best to keep her feelings in check and not allow them to rule her actions as they usually did.

At dinner, Tara found she was seated next to Lord Gavin on his left. Usually, this place of honor would be reserved for the woman of highest rank, but since they were in his home, the duke was free to set the seating arrangement anyway he pleased. However, since her father and mother were seated right across from her and Lord Gavin, any conversation they might share was easily overheard and completely public. The arrangement did have its advantages as it allowed her to observe Lord Gavin as he interacted with her family. Tara could tell her parents were reasonably charmed by the grand duke and his gracious, though somewhat guarded, conversation. They had eventually suspended their mildly probing questions and moved on to talk of the weather, governments, and other socially acceptable topics of conversation.

Tara smiled inwardly as she watched him interact with her uncle. She could tell he was growing quite fond of the old military man by the way he listened to him and drew upon his opinion. Even with the hindrance of her parents across from them, she was pleased to note that on several occasions throughout the dinner they shared private and rather telling glances. As the night wore on, she felt his desire rising.

After dinner, when they returned to the grand salon, Tara moved to once again take up her position next to Marina on the rose colored settee. With subtle, but unmistakable intent, she noticed Lord Gavin sat in the armchair next to her. His attentions seemed an unmistakable show of interest, if not possession. Ushered in on the arm of her husband, Lady Chandra took a seat across from Tara and Lord Gavin, leaving Tara to believe her mother would be watching their every move. Loclyn managed to secure a settee at the outer edge of the social circle which he shared with the finance minister's daughter, their heads drawn together in quiet conversation.

"Mrs. Metwick, your mother tells me you are quite accomplished at the piano," Lord Gavin stated. It was one of the few times he had addressed Tara's cousin directly and Marina reacted with enthusiastic delight.

"I do like to play, but I hope Mama has not overstated my abilities." Marina exchanged an excited glance with Tara, her eagerness to play for the duke clearly showing.

"Perhaps you would consider giving us the pleasure of sharing your talent," Lord Gavin graciously suggested.

"Certainly, Your Grace. It would be my pleasure." Marina nearly leapt from her place beside Tara and immediately took a seat at the piano. "Do you have any preferences?" she asked.

Lord Gavin indicated a stack of sheet music neatly piled atop a nearby table. "I have a fair variety of music to choose from. I'm sure you can find something to your liking."

Shuffling quickly through the reams of sheet music, Marina pulled a few selections from the stack. "Should I start with a ballad or would you prefer something classical?"

"Choose as you wish. I'm sure anything you pick will be quite pleasing," the duke replied.

Marina beamed and launched into a favored ballad.

Lord Gavin appeared suitably impressed. He kept his focus turned toward the musical instrument and player, but when he shifted in his chair Tara felt him lean toward her, leaving only inches of space between them. Acutely aware of his presence, Tara forced herself to hold her position, moving neither away nor closer to Lord Gavin.

Marina was an accomplished pianist and earnest applause greeted the ending of her piece. Aunt Jeanine encouraged her daughter to play another. After Marina's third piece, Lady Chandra turned to Tara with a discrete smile. "Tara, my dear, wouldn't you like to take a turn at the piano?"

"Mother, you know my talents cannot compare to Marina's," she rebuked the suggestion. Her mother's ever-present polite smile didn't fool Tara for a moment. She knew she was no match for Marina's talent and was loath to display her limited abilities against those of her cousin.

"You needn't be so modest. You're among friends and family, and it's been too long since I've heard you play," Lady Chandra persisted.

Lord Gavin spoke up, leaning toward her and all but eliminating the space between them. "Would you mind if I joined you? Perhaps we could play a duet together, if that would please you. It will make it harder for them to know if one of us plays badly, although I'm sure it will be me far more than you."

Tara blinked. "You play?" she asked.

"Yes," he admitted. "One of my few indulgences is to sit for long hours lost to the muse of music. As much as I enjoy hearing music played well, and Mrs. Metwick does play well, I enjoy being the one to play it even more. It has taken many years of practice, but I believe I have developed my abilities fairly well." Dropping his voice to a husky whisper, he added, "It would be my honor if you would allow me to impose my limited talents upon you."

Stark anticipation glowed in his dark, coffee-colored eyes, shining in the candle light. Thick waves of rich, chocolate-brown hair haloed his face, softening the hard lines of his jaw. He looked delicious. Tara breathed deeply and released a long, low sigh.

Was he teasing or taunting her? The amusement she saw dancing across his eyes, and the slight curve of his lips, made her wonder if he believed she would decline his challenge. Yes, that's what it was, a challenge to force her hand, testing her will. To refuse would be petty and rude, but to accept would expose her to failure. Neither rudeness nor failure was an option.

"How can I refuse?" she answered with renewed determination. "Daunting as it may be to expose my talent next to yours, I would be remiss to pass up an opportunity to share the keyboard with you. It isn't often a grand duke offers his musical skills for the benefit of his guests. I am quite intrigued." She also welcomed the opportunity to sit next to him on the piano bench.

Marina graciously made way for the duke and her cousin, showing her interest along with everyone else in the room as they encouraged the duke to play.

Lord Gavin and Tara riffled through half a dozen pages of sheet music until she found one to her liking. The duke nodded his agreement.

Tara took a seat at the piano bench, smoothing her skirts beneath her. She took a moment to breathe it all in, to settle her nerves, and to absorb the sensation of Lord Gavin sitting next to her, his strong muscular thigh nearly touching hers. No matter how badly she played, the pleasure of this moment made it all worthwhile.

They set their fingers upon the keyboard and with a signal from Lord Gavin she began to play. The piece began slowly as Tara sought their rhythm, but Lord Gavin, being more of a master than he had led her to believe, easily followed her lead. Although hesitant at first, Tara quickly felt their momentum climb as her fingers leaped upon the keys. Back and forth, between melody and harmony, their fingers danced in tune as if they had played together for years. Perhaps for the first time in her life, Tara truly felt the music flowing from her fingers to the keys, while also feeling his music surging through her. It was exhilarating. By the time they reached the crescendo and played the final chords, Tara's chest heaved with breathless excitement. She noted Lord Gavin's breath, though more controlled, came slightly labored as well. It took every ounce of restraint she could command not to throw her arms around him with a feeling of elation. She imagined him pulling her into his arms and engulfing her with a passionate kiss. Instead, closing her eyes, she forced her fingers to rest a second longer upon the keys before she slowly brought her hands down to her lap and released a wistful sigh.

The room erupted into applause.

Lord Gavin turned his head to whisper into her ear, his breath warm on her heated skin. "It appears you undersold your abilities."

"I believe that was the best I have ever played," she said, her voice whisper soft for his ears only.

"Should we play another?" His question felt not so much as a request but as an open invitation to test her reaction.

"Another, another," Lord Tyrus stood, applauding loudly in a display of fatherly pride.

Tara looked to her mother, who appeared to understand the effect the episode had on her. "Perhaps you should leave them wanting more," Lady Chandra spoke pointedly to her daughter.

"Yes, perhaps we should," Tara agreed with her mother. Their first time together had been special, perhaps a bit of beginner's luck, but Tara doubted she could repeat such a spectacular performance.

~~

Becoming aware of his need to break their connection to avoid risking a public display of affection, Lord Gavin looked up and spoke to the room in general. "Can I offer anyone a drink? Wine, port, brandy, you only need to name your preference."

"Have you no Scottish whisky in this fine manor home?" General Gregerson asked.

Gavin smiled, pleased by the older man's request. "Of course sir, and for you, only the finest."

While drinks were being served, and before Tara could slip from his side, he turned to her and placed his hand upon her bare forearm, his fingers seductively enfolding her slender wrist. He took note of the warmth still emanating from her skin. Her ardent gaze was a mixture of passion and pain, giving Lord Gavin cause to reconsider his initial assessment. Upon meeting her, he had believed she was an innocent young beauty, now he was once again reminded her youthful appearance was deceiving. Closer inspection revealed something akin to weary wisdom swimming in the deepest depths of her liquid blue eyes. Maybe her exposure to travel had placed it there, but he suspected something more personal than exotic sights had contributed to her fragile pain.

Speaking privately to Lady Tara, he said, "I must apologize for my abrupt departure the other day. My mind was focused on my building project and I was anxious to oversee the progress being made on the gazebo. It should be finished soon." He hoped the appeal of the gazebo would lure her back to the garden, and perhaps another meeting, if she so desired.

"So you are building a gazebo. I suspected as much." Her smile brightened with delight.

"Yes. Apparently the master gardener felt your suggestion had merit."

"And you, sir, did you not feel it had merit?" Her expression turned serious.

"If I did not, I would not have recommended it to the gardener," he assured her.

Lady Tara's delightful smile returned in full force.

"I'm hoping you will find the design to your liking. I was allowed to make a few creative suggestions for the carpenter. The unveiling will be next week, if you are interested." Actually, he had nearly total control of the design process, but that could go without saying.

"I will look forward to receiving your notice." Lady Tara accepted his unspoken invitation with a charming smile lingering upon her lips.

"As will I." He planned to return to the building site tomorrow to check on its progress. He had to admit, he rather enjoyed the feeling of anticipation created by the thought of seeing her again. All he needed to do was release his never-ending need for control of a situation and let fate take over. Besides, he mused, fate was usually the one who held the winning hand.

When his guests began to take their leave, Lord Gavin called for his butler to issue a private request. "I want Lady Tara to be the last one departing the manor. I trust that you'll do what is needed to make that happen."

"Certainly, my lord. Leave it to me," Millinsworth replied.

The butler's style was to be admired. When it came time to usher his guests out the front door to their waiting carriages, Millinsworth instructed the footmen as to which order the carriages should be presented. Under his guidance, the Millard family was the first to say their good-byes and file into their carriage. Degraw followed them out the door to bid Miss Brandie Millard a fond farewell. The finance minister and his family were followed by the occupants of General Gregerson's carriage with Jeanine Gregerson leading the way. Finally, Lord Zanders' carriage began to load. Lady Tara however, was delayed for a few moments when it was discovered her shawl had been misplaced. The impeccable timing of the announcement by Millinsworth was enough to give Lord Gavin a moment alone with her, as he had requested, while the missing garment was located.

"Thank you, Lady Tara, for a most pleasant evening. I'm so glad you were able to attend."

"The pleasure was mine, Lord Gavin. Thank you for extending such a gracious invitation to my family."

"My door is always open to you and your family."

When the wayward shawl was finally found, Lord Gavin took the liberty of personally assisting Lady Tara with her wrap. More than a mere gesture of good manners, he used it as an opportunity to take his pleasure. As he draped the garment over her shoulders, he boldly touched the delicate skin of her neck and was rewarded by a noticeable shiver.

"I will send word when the gazebo is finished," he reminded her in a hushed voice.

"I'll be waiting," she replied. There was no mistaking the sly smile that graced her lips.

Gavin dipped his head closer, placing his lips upon the tender skin of her long white neck. She gasped, her breath catching in her chest. With a sigh she turned her head ever so slightly to better accept his attentions. Her acceptance of his actions brought a surge of heated relief to his body. Placing his fingers below her chin, he turned her face to his. "May I?" he whispered.

She met his gaze, her eyes bright and shining. Her lips parted ever so slightly. A hushed "Yes," escaped with her breath.

He brought his mouth full upon her lips. She shuddered at his touch, clutching handfuls of her cloak in her fists. Her passion, though restrained, was profound.

With a gasping breath, she broke away. "Lord Gavin, I must go. My parents are waiting."

Beguiled by the heated look in her eyes, it took an amazing amount of effort for him to heed her request. "Certainly, as you wish." Gavin stepped away and bowed, once again the picture of propriety. "Good night, my lady," he said.

Her eyes searched his face, intense, full of meaning. She gathered her composure, turned from him, and slipped out the door to her parent's waiting carriage.

Watching the footman assist her into the carriage from the candlelit foyer, Gavin had a comforting feeling that all-in-all it had been an evening well worth his efforts.

~~

Lord Tyrus and Lady Chandra waited and watched as Tara settled into her seat beside Loclyn. "I trust all went well?" her mother asked.

"As you can see, they were able to locate my shawl," Tara replied, not wishing to discuss what had transpired between her and Lord Gavin.

"A splendid evening, don't you think?" Lord Tyrus remarked.

"Were you able to question the duke to your satisfaction?" Tara asked, turning to face her father. She believed her mother was much better at reading her expressions and wanted to avoid meeting her gaze.

"I think we have learned enough for now," Lady Chandra offered, keeping her eyes on her daughter.

Tara settled back into her seat and closed her eyes before responding. "Well then, I would agree, it was a splendid evening."

CHAPTER 10

As soon as Tara's head settled upon the pillow, she began dreaming of her charming prince, the handsome grand duke, Lord Gavin. In peaceful slumber she imagined herself standing in the gazebo, moonbeams lighting the night with its soft pale glow. Standing at the railing, she looked up to see a full moon shining high above in the night sky. Her long, sheer nightgown swirled gently around her ankles, blown by the night breeze. The scent of sawdust mingled with night blooming flowers offering up their heady fragrance from the nearby garden. Turning her face to the moon, she stepped and twirled, dancing to music floating on the wind. Feeling his presence, she stopped and turned. There he was.

Lord Gavin slowly climbed the steps to the gazebo. "It seems you are destined to invade my dreams," he said as he reached the top step.

"It is you, sir, who fills my dreams." She smiled, grateful for his presence.

"Is it not you who have summoned me here?" he asked, taking a step toward her.

"It appears we are in this dream together." She took a hesitant step forward, waiting, yearning for him to close the distance.

"So it does," Gavin murmured. Closing the gap, he swept her into his arms. "Shall we dance, or may I just hold you?"

She gazed into his eyes, dark and intense, and full of emotions only dreams could release. "Hold me, Gavin. Please, hold me close, as if you will never let me go."

Answering her plea, he kissed her. It was a kiss full of passion and desire and unspoken wishes that could never be granted. In the quiet of the night, lit only by moonbeams and twinkling stars, he held her, running his fingers through her long golden hair as she wrapped her arms around him, clinging to his body with heated desire. He gathered her into his arms as if to never let her go, and as he held her, she wished with all her heart this dream could come true.

Gavin rode out early the next morning to check on the progress of the gazebo. Upon arriving at the site, he was somewhat surprised to see it looked exactly as he expected. Lumber and building materials sat stacked nearby, waiting to be put to use. The scent of sawdust filled the air. It was exactly as he had dreamed. Glancing down, he spied two sets of footprints impressed in the fine layer of sawdust covering the gazebo floor. One set of prints looked like men's shoes, nothing unusual there, but the other was that of bare feet. Crouching low to examine the prints, he wondered if magic was at work here.

~*~

As the family drifted into the front salon after dinner, Lady Chandra drew her husband aside for quiet conversation. "Have you noticed how happy our daughter has been for the past few days? Not at all like the upset school girl who greeted us upon our arrival."

"It hasn't escaped my notice. What do you make of it?"

"I'm not at all surprised," Lady Chandra replied, glancing over to her daughter. "She believes herself to be in love." She watched as Tara participated in a game of backgammon against Marina, distracted and losing badly.

"Is that what she told you?" Lord Tyrus asked with a raised brow, following the gaze of his wife.

"She doesn't have to. I can see it plainly on her face." A sad and knowing smile played across Lady Chandra's lips. "I'm worried she's unprepared to confront such powerful emotions. Her freedom to travel has been her focus for far too long."

"Do you think Lord Gavin knows?" Lord Tyrus turned his gaze back to his wife.

"Perhaps not yet, but surely he will in time. As you've noticed, our daughter has a charming inability to hide her emotions." Lady Chandra leaned closer to her husband, enjoying the warmth of his body next to hers. "She would never make it in our line of work," she whispered.

"Thank heavens for that," Lord Tyrus replied. "It's enough I have my wife running about in disguise, beguiling every man she sees to garnish information from him. I don't need to think of my daughter following in your footsteps."

"But darling, you must agree, I'm very good at what I do." Lady Chandra graced her husband with a coy look.

"My darling, I learned long ago you are very good at *everything* you do, which is one of the reasons I love you so much."

"You, my dear sir, are very good at flattery, which is one of the reasons why I love you."

Running his hand along his wife's bare arm Lord Tyrus whispered into her ear, "I believe you're looking a little tired, my love. Perhaps it's time to put you to bed." The gleam in his eye easily revealed his true intentions.

"Don't you think it's a bit early to slip away?" she teased, delighting in the touch of his hands.

"To slip away is exactly what I had in mind," he said for her ears only. Speaking louder, he continued, "I'm only thinking of your well-being. It's off to bed with you or I will drag you there myself." To the room in general he added, "My wife grows weary and must retire for the night. Please excuse our early departure."

Iain looked up from the military journal he was reading and exchanged a knowing glance with his wife. "You seem to make a habit of retiring early," Iain teased his sister and her husband.

"Early to bed, early to rise, keeps a man healthy, or some such rot," Lord Tyrus quipped, pulling Lady Chandra toward the doorway. She offered no resistance.

"Quite right. Early to rise, my arse," Iain shot back with a wolfish grin. "You best be off. We don't want you snoring in the salon." He took a sip of Scottish whisky from the half-full glass he was holding.

"Or arriving late to breakfast," Jeanine said, joining the jest.

"I can assure you, there's little risk of that. He'd hate to miss his tea, toast, and jam," Lady Chandra stated, referring to her husband.

Lord Tyrus bowed to the occupants of the room before shepherding Lady Chandra out the door. She did her best to disguise her bemused smile behind her hand, feigning a polite little yawn.

~~~

Too distracted to focus on her game of backgammon with Marian, Tara paused to observe her parents. Her mother didn't look unduly tired and she was quite sure her father's concern for her mother's well-being was just an excuse for them to retire early. A smile spread across her face. It warmed her heart to see her parents still so very much in love. As role models, they set the bar for a loving relationship very high indeed.

When she returned her attention back to the board game, Marina had rolled the dice and was moving her final stones from the playing field.

Tara's cousin clapped her hands in delight. "Look at this Darren! I've won my first game against Tara."

"So I see." Darren moved to take a seat next to his wife.

"You played very well," Tara complimented Marina. She knew her head wasn't in the game but she had no desire to diminish her cousin's enjoyment. As promised, Tara had received a message from Lord Gavin that the gazebo was finished and ready for viewing. The brief note asked her to meet him at Wiltzer Park early the next morning. Throughout the day and into the night she had floated on clouds, feeling distracted by thoughts of happiness, and unanswered questions.

Following Tara's lead, Loclyn adding his support to Marina. "Well done. I believe you're the first to defeat a Zanders."

Marina beamed, lit by their praise. "So I am. I believe I'll stop while I'm ahead and take some time to savor my victory. Darren, I'm ready to retire. Will you join me?"

Darren stood and offered his hand to Marina as she rose from her chair. "Of course, my love. You need your rest." His eyes briefly surveyed his wife's slightly swelling abdomen. Linking his wife's hand over his arm, he rested his hand atop hers. "If you will excuse us?" He gave a nod to his in-laws.

The room rang with a round of good night wishes as Darren escorted his wife from the room.

"I don't suppose you're interested in playing another game?" Loclyn addressed Tara.

"No, I'm done for the night. I think I'll go to my room to read." Her mind was too distracted to read or sleep but she welcomed the opportunity to cuddle up with her dreams.

"Allow me to walk with you," Loclyn offered.

Tara nodded. "Good night, Aunt Jeanine. Good night, Uncle Iain," she offered her parting salute.

"Don't burn the midnight oil," Loclyn advised Uncle Iain.

"Don't sass your elders," Uncle Iain retorted, taking another sip of his whisky.

They had hardly passed beyond the doorway of the salon when Loclyn questioned Tara. "I heard you received a message from the duke today. Anything you want to share?"

She rested a hand on his coat sleeve as they crossed through the connecting foyer toward the central staircase. "He sent word that the gazebo is finished, and has invited me to see it." She attempted an air of nonchalance, hoping to conceal the full extent of her excitement.

Loclyn didn't appear fooled. "Do you think that's a good idea? I'm worried he'll upset you again, as he did the last time," he said. He had seen first-hand her gloomy reaction to her experience in the sculpture garden.

"I do not expect a repeat of that . . . that day. Besides, you're a fine one to talk. One day you're fawning over Miss Patrice, the banker's daughter, and the next you're flirting with Miss Brandie. Who is to believe your attentions?" She wasn't exactly playing fair by turning the topic against him like this, but it was a subject she had long wanted to discuss.

"I have not claimed a match with either of them, but if you must know, my interests are with Miss Patrice."

"Then what was that business with Miss Brandie Millard? You latched onto her at the duke's dinner party like a moth to a flame." She stopped at the bottom of the staircase, awaiting his response.

Loclyn shrugged. "The opportunity presented itself. She's a beautiful woman. But I can assure you, it was no more than a momentary distraction."

"A momentary distraction? What if she took your attentions seriously?" Tara persisted, hoping Loclyn would reveal his true intentions. She needed to understand.

"She didn't. It wasn't like that." Loclyn began climbing the stairs, trying to shake off her concerns.

"How can you be sure? How would she know?" Tara was right at his heels.

"Believe me, she knows. Miss Brandie was well aware of my true intentions. What about you and the duke? Are you sure of his intentions?"

Tara hesitated, pausing in the middle of the stairs. "I'd like to think so, but how can I be sure? What if his interest is only a momentary distraction, as you say?" They had tapped into the core of her uncertainty.

Loclyn also stopped and turned to look at her. His voice softened. "What does your heart tell you?"

She swallowed hard. "I don't know. This is all so new. I want to believe." She gazed up at him from a lower stair.

He stepped back down and looked into her eyes. "Then believe. Tara, you have to follow your heart. Which is worse, to know or not know?"

"And if I'm wrong?" she questioned in earnest.

Loclyn guided her to resume climbing the stairs. "Then it's best to hope for a safe place to land."

CHAPTER 11

Standing in front of the full-length windows of her bed chamber, Tara looked out upon the landscape of the Maynard villa. To her eyes everything looked greener, more brilliant. The sun shone in a bright blue sky with scattered wisps of white fluffy clouds. It couldn't be a more perfect day. Tara pushed aside her concerns from the night before, determined to meet her challenge head on.

Dressing for her meeting with Lord Gavin, she chose a simple white empire-waist dress with lavender flowers sprinkled throughout the fabric and trimmed with lavender ribbon along the neck and sleeves. To accompany it she chose her plum colored cloak and shawl, the same one she had worn to the dinner party.

Holding the shawl to her cheek, she recalled the way she felt when Lord Gavin danced his fingers across her skin. Closing her eyes, she returned to that evening, savoring every detail, from the moment their eyes met in the grand salon, to their moment alone in the foyer for a parting kiss.

The whole evening had sparked with tension, like a summer thunderstorm threatening on the horizon, but their parting kiss had been nothing less than tempestuous, brazen in its passion. If she had been an innocent, unfamiliar with the customs of courtship, she might have been shocked by the boldness of his actions. Instead, she had welcomed his passionate attentions, taking full responsibility for her choices.

Perhaps it would be easier if her parents had raised a prig, a feeble-thinking woman afraid of her own emotions. But no, they had raised a free-thinking, sensual woman who all too often acted before thinking. Tara was well aware of her carnal desires and her need for passion. Both a blessing and a curse, her untamed sensual desires had driven her to accept a marriage proposal from Captain James Millhouse, a man she hardly knew, and he had abandoned her.

In a moment of self-doubt, she wondered if part of Lord Gavin's appeal was his inability to leave his kingdom. If anyone was at risk of being abandoned, it was him. She was free to come and go as she pleased, although lately, it seemed her familiar desire for travel had deserted her. For now, the intriguing secrets of Lord Gavin held greater sway. Upon further consideration, she dismissed her concerns as insignificant. As she had already seen, a man didn't need miles of earth to make a woman feel rejected.

With Lord Gavin, she was beginning to feel special again, even desired. God—and her mother—knew she desired him. She wanted to believe he truly was her prince charming and not just playing with her affections. He was intelligent, strong, and deeply handsome. It was obvious he was well educated and a man of many talents. At times he displayed a rather witty sense of humor that could easily pass unnoticed if one was not paying attention.

Still, she wondered if he saw her as his heart's desire or merely a momentary diversion, much as Loclyn had with Miss Brandie. How was she to know?

His attentions at Sunday's dinner seemed genuine and sincere, but he hadn't actually declared he wanted more than to see her again. For all she knew he could be playing with her emotions, taking advantage of her passionate nature, much like Loclyn had with Brandie Millard.

Except for her failed engagement, she had very little experience when it came to matters of the heart. After Captain Millhouse, she had shut herself off from men, in effect creating her own invisible wall. It had taken months for her to recover, not from his death, but from his desertion. Disappointed that she had subjected herself to such rejection, she was determined to avoid a repeat performance. She had been a fool in love, and he had abandoned her.

Growing up with only brothers, and surrounded by a multitude of male cousins, she had always viewed herself as one of the gang. In return, they had doted on her, and usually tried to protect her from their rough and tumble games. Most of all, she felt loved and accepted. She had learned how to ride and could sit a horse well, both sidesaddle and astride. She could shoot a gun, and her aim was sharp at close range. She was known to speak her mind, and had heard more cuss words than a lady of her rank should ever know.

In spite of all that, or maybe because of it, she had neglected to learn the fine art of seduction. Disappointing as it was to admit, when it came to Lord Gavin Richard Montague, she often felt like an outsider looking in, and the view into Lord Gavin's heart was far from clear. That bothered her. It was something she couldn't ignore. There were times when he was charming and charismatic, but others when he was solemn and distant, as if he had seen too much of the world and was no longer engaged.

She wanted to believe he was interested in her. She wanted to believe his attentions went beyond momentary flirtation. She wanted to believe, but she couldn't be sure. She hoped their meeting at the gazebo would give her reason to believe her feelings were returned.

Moments after breakfast had finished, Tara grabbed her cloak and headed out the back door towards the carriage house. She had already asked her parents for the use of their carriage and her father had informed the groomsmen to have it ready. Loclyn, Marina, and Darren caught up with her as she made her way across the graveled courtyard.

"We've come to escort you into town," Marina greeted her cheerfully, clutching her husband's arm as she trotted slightly to keep up with the two long-legged men. Her grey cloak fluttered in the breeze, revealing a pale blue day dress. Matching ribbons adorned her straw bonnet.

"We can't very well let you make the trip on your own," Loclyn offered, looking perfectly serious if not for his sardonic grin. He looked fine in his tan britches with black polished boots, and hunter green coat.

"There's really no need," Tara tried to dissuade them. She maintained her brisk stride towards the carriage house. "I'm perfectly fine on my own."

"I was planning a trip into the village anyway," Marina insisted. "And Darren has kindly agreed to come with me."

"It's not as though I had a choice," Darren spoke. "I couldn't very well leave my wife to wander on her own." His attire, pale grey trousers and a dark grey greatcoat, was far more subdued than Loclyn's.

"I'm of a mind to visit the dear Miss Patrice. It only makes sense we should all take the same carriage," Loclyn put in. "And who knows, you may welcome the company on the return trip. You may need someone to talk to."

"If that is a reference to my previous meeting with Lord Gavin in the park, I can assure you I expect a very different outcome," Tara replied.

"Exactly, you'll want someone to share your good news," Marina said, her face sparkled with anticipation.

"Who better than your loving cousins?" Loclyn added. While his smile was distinctly mischievous, his eyes showed loving support.

Standing at the open doors of the carriage house, Tara surveyed their faces. Loclyn and Marina gave her the impression of lap dogs, following along behind their master, in grand anticipation of a run in the park, while Darren looked slightly amused.

"All right," she conceded, "But I expect you to behave yourselves. Lord Gavin is not on display."

"Oh, of course not," Marina said, her eyes open wide.

"We'll be quite discreet," Loclyn said, still smiling.

"That's to be seen," Darren snickered under his breath.

"Come now, climb aboard," Loclyn chimed, opening the carriage door for them. He bowed low and ushered them in with a broad sweeping wave of his arm. "We don't want to keep the grand duke waiting."

As the carriage made its way from the villa and down the hill towards the village of Larinda, Tara was beset with comments from Marina and Loclyn.

"It must be nice to have a gazebo erected in your honor," Loclyn teased her.

"The duke did not have the gazebo erected in my honor," Tara bristled, attempting to correct him. "He was only responding to a suggestion I made."

"You must have great influence with the duke for him to act on your suggestion," Marina speculated.

"I'm sure it's only because he agreed with its merit." Tara once again attempted to deflect their comments. Privately she hoped her cousins were right.

In a rare show of affability, Darren spoke up, placing his hand atop Tara's as they lay clasped in her lap. "Pay them no mind," he said kindly. "They mean you no harm. Actually, I believe it's their way of showing their support."

Tara was taken aback by his show of kindness, but saw immediately the rightness of his words. This is why Marina loves him, she thought. He understands and accepts her just as she is. What a precious commodity to have in a husband.

Tara couldn't send her cousins away fast enough when they reached the entrance to Wiltzer Park. From the roadway, she could see Lord Gavin standing beside the gazebo, waiting for her. Just seeing him made her chest swell with joy and her beating heart broke into a gallop. Every time she saw him, he took her breath away. She paused for a moment to take in the sight. He stood tall, his hands clasped behind his back, a serene smile indicating his pride and pleasure. She couldn't overlook the tight fit of his dark tan breeches, and the highly polished shine on his black leather boots. Wearing a dark blue greatcoat that fit him to perfection, he presented an awe-inspiring figure of a man, a true leader.

Tearing her eyes away from him, she turned her gaze to the gazebo. It was magnificent, everything she had dreamed it would be and more. The curved arches mimicked the lines of temples from India and its brightly painted colors spoke of exotic bazaars.

Meeting her half-way—as far as the limitations of his border would allow—he greeted her with a chaste kiss upon her cheek. "It's a pleasure to see you again, Lady Tara."

"The pleasure is mine, your Grace," she said, pleased by the mere touch of his lips upon her skin.

"Come, let me show you the gazebo," he said, turning towards the structure. "I hope you will find it to your liking." He offered her his arm. She placed her hand neatly in the bend of his elbow. It felt warm and right.

The gazebo was fairly large, rising to a height of twenty feet or more, including the raised platform. The graceful lines of the eight-sided structure gave it the illusion of being round. Onion-shaped arches and filigree trellises connected the large supporting columns, allowing the early morning sunlight to dance upon the polished hardwood floor. Wrought iron hand railings graced the four short stairways providing access to the gazebo. Atop it all was a domed roof with a crescent-moon weather vane.

"Lord Gavin, it's perfect, just as I pictured it. It's as if you slipped into my mind and knew my dreams," she marveled.

His eyes lit with delight, pleased by her response. "I believe it is you who have slipped into my dreams," he said.

She wondered if he really knew. Surely not.

Clasping his hand over hers, he led her up the short set of stairs and into the gazebo's interior. Jewel colored cushions adorned the benches lining the interior walls. Sheer gauze curtains of royal blue trimmed with gold hung from rods above the arches and were secured against each of the columns with heavy braded ropes adorned with long flowing tassels. It gave the gazebo the feeling of an exotic, middle-eastern temple. The dark blond wood was freshly polished, and shined in the morning sun.

Tara walked to the middle of the gazebo and did a slow twirl before she turned to Lord Gavin in awe. She spoke in a whisper. "It's beautiful. Even grander than I imagined."

Lord Gavin gave a short nod, watching her.

"It's rather large. Are you planning to hold another ball?" Her teasing jest was her best attempt at flirtation.

He joined her in the center of the gazebo, bowed, and held out his hand. "May I have this dance?"

Delighted her flirtation had worked, she placed her hand in his. He drew her into his arms and together they stepped to a silent waltz, gliding across the floor. They took one turn about the gazebo then stopped. He continued to hold her, not dropping his arms. A thin smile curved his lips, but his eyes were serious. "Do you approve?"

"How could I not?" Standing so close like this, she was certain he could feel her beating heart, her chest swelling with each pounding pulse.

"I'm glad. I had hoped to please you."

"Did you really do this for me?" Tara looked up at him, searching his eyes.

"In a manner, yes," he replied. "Certainly your suggestion had merit. But more than that, I wanted to please you."

"But why?" Tara asked, waiting, hoping. He had yet to say if he cared for her.

Lord Gavin hesitated a moment before answering. "Because this makes me happy. You make me happy." He placed a hand on each of her cheeks, cradling her face. "You bring light into my darkness."

His answer thrilled her. Her pounding heart increased its tempo. Still uncertain, she searched the depth of his eyes, looking for evidence his words were true. Was he truly pleased by her presence, or was he just sprouting the type of empty flattery that came easily from too many years of aristocratic practice? It was hard to tell what emotions hid behind those deep, shadowed eyes, he masked his feelings too well. Eyes should be a window to one's soul, but his were dark and unyielding. She wanted to believe she saw a spark of honest affection, but it seemed subdued by a prevailing presence of weary sadness. She told herself to be cautious, but it was a difficult warning to heed. She had so little practice, and her emotions were already racing far ahead of her thoughts.

Drawing a breath, she forced herself to boldly venture further. "May I ask you a question?" It was one she needed to ask, the one that had been niggling at her brain.

"Certainly," he said.

"The other day, in the sculpture garden, was it just my imagination, or did I do something to offend you? Did you intentionally send me away?" Her breathing stilled as she waited for his answer. There was so much she needed to understand before she could go on.

He cringed, dropping his hands to his sides. "That was not my intent." Stepping back, he walked away, taking a seat on one of the cushioned benches. He was doing it again, blocking her out.

She shook her head, trying to understand. "That's how it felt, as though you had dismissed me." Hesitantly, she followed him to the bench, taking a seat beside him.

"It was not you I sent away from me. It was me I sent away from you. A slight difference perhaps, but significant." Lord Gavin faced the center of the gazebo with his eyes turned away from her and hunched over to brace his arms atop his knees.

Tara blinked, wondering at his meaning. "But why? Why would you do that?"

"You must understand. I've spent a number of years alone. I've grown more accustomed to solitude than to the company of strangers."

"Do you think me a stranger?" A sinking feeling settled in the pit of her stomach.

"No. I think you're a threat to my solitude." He turned to look at her.

"Is that so bad?" she asked.

"It was unexpected. It took me by surprise."

"It was so abrupt. You seemed so cold and distant." Even now, as she tried to read his expression, it was like a mask, void of emotion.

He looked away again. "One needs to be cold and distant when one rules a kingdom. People's lives are at stake. I have not allowed myself the luxury of true companionship since the passing of my wife and son."

"How long ago was that?"

"Years ago, too many to count, but a day can last forever when you're grieving the loss of a loved one. I have not, cannot, allow myself to become unduly attached." Sadness swept through his eyes.

Tara's heart sank. "Do you feel that way now?" She was still so confused. He had been attentive to her at the dinner party, and had kissed her. He had built this beautiful gazebo, and had invited her for a special showing. And yet, it seemed as if he had no desire to pursue a relationship with her. What on earth was wrong with this man?

"I am the grand duke of Maninberg, the ruler of my duchy. I have duties here. My life is here, in this kingdom, in my castle. But you, you have the desire and freedom to travel wherever you wish. It is simply an irreconcilable difference."

She understood the merit of his argument, but she would not give up so easily. She also noted he had not truly answered her question, refusing to reveal how he felt about her. "It is not so irreconcilable, as you say. If you wished, I could stay." The quick jerk of his head in her direction unnerved her, as if she had spoken too boldly. She hastily added, "My uncle said I am welcome to stay as long as I want." And she would stay, if only he would ask. If only he wanted her. But she would not beg, she would not plead. She would accept only what he freely gave.

"I cannot ask you to stay. You are free to wander the world and I am not. I am tied to my kingdom. I am their ruler."

"Is that the only reason?" she asked, thinking of the invisible wall blocking his departure.

"It is reason enough," he answered, clenching his jaw.

She nibbled at her bottom lip and then lifted her chin as determination set in. "What if I want to stay? Would you still seek to send me away?"

~~~

Gavin struggled with his answer. He wanted to tell her to leave for her own sake. He wanted her to stay for his. But most of all, he wanted her to choose freely. This was his dilemma, his irreconcilable conflict.

Here, in his kingdom, he had total authority and it took all of his control not to take what she offered, to take her here and now and never let her go. It would not be a kind or gentle act. No, it would be a purely possessive taking, an act that would claim her as his, chaining her to him forever. Such a lover's embrace would soon become an imprisonment, breeding resentment. Even if she could not openly declare her frustrations, they would be there nonetheless, growing beneath the surface, choking her soul like an insidious vine that would eventually overtake its host.

As much as he wanted her, he respected her too much to take away her spirit.

"Tara, the facts are plain. This is my kingdom, where I belong. I must stay, and you are free to go, to pursue that which you love most in the world."

"Yes, and I'm also free to stay," she stated.

"But if you stay, eventually you'll resent being here. You'll want to leave and you'll resent your ties to me. I couldn't allow that." Silently, he added, *eventually you'll realize I will not age and you will. Eventually you'll realize you must give me anything and everything I ask for. Eventually you'll realize you have no control in our relationship, no free will, and that will be the greatest pain of all.*

"You do not know that to be true. Do you really have so little faith in me?" Tears glistened in her eyes, threatening to leak onto her cheeks. Swallowing hard, she blinked, holding them at bay. "If I tell you I wish to stay, will you not believe me?"

He wanted to comfort her, to dispel her tears, tears he had caused, but what comfort he could possibly provide? Governed by the restraints of his curse, he was a man at war with himself.

Finally, he spoke. "I will admit, I want you to stay." Damn, how it pained him to say that. "Nevertheless, can you honestly tell me when you feel the need to travel again, you will honor that need? You will follow that quest?" His heart weighed heavy in his chest. He tried to reason the feeling away, but it remained. He told himself this was unavoidable. It had been his intention to make no requests of her and yet how quickly he had broken his vow.

Her face brightened and she smiled, breathing deeply once again. "Of course, I would have it no other way."

"You . . ." Gavin was shocked.

"Of course, my lord, we are in complete agreement." She looked extremely pleased with herself.

He looked at her for a moment, cockeyed. *You* would have it no other way. Typically the response was "yes, my lord, as you wish" or some such thing, never "I would have it no other way." He brushed it aside. It didn't matter what words she spoke, she had agreed because she had no other choice. He had given them some time, a delay was all it was, but for now, it would be enough.

Gavin was still recovering from her unexpected response when he heard the sound of an approaching rider. A man was calling his name. Drawing Tara to her feet he led her out of the gazebo.

The rider pulled up on the access road and dismounted. "Lord Gavin, I have a message from Prime Minister Ballistare," he said.

"Can it not wait?" Gavin barked, annoyed to hear his prime minister had sent a messenger looking for him. Such an action was highly unusual.

"As you wish, my lord. I only came because the prime minister was most insistent." The messenger looked confused, as if not sure of how to handle the situation.

Gavin knew he shouldn't simply dismiss the issue, not with Tara watching. "What is the message?" he asked abruptly.

"He asked for you to return to the castle. He has urgent news that needs your attention," the messenger replied. "This is all I know," he added.

While Gavin was talking with the messenger, he noticed the Zanders' carriage approaching from the village road. When it reached the park, Lieutenant Degraw jumped out and hurried towards them.

"Tara, we must return to the villa. General Gregerson has sent word," he called out to them, foregoing any formal greeting.

"What is this about?" Lady Tara asked.

"I don't know, but the general sent word we're to return to the villa, and that's good enough for me," Degraw replied.

Gavin and Lady Tara exchanged glances.

Gavin spoke. "I trust General Gregerson's judgment. If he feels the need to order you back to the villa, I'm sure he has good reasons."

Lady Tara looked up at Gavin. "I know I must go. Will I see you again?"

"I don't know. First I must find out what has the general and my prime minister in such a fit." Addressing the messenger, he added, "Ride ahead to the castle. Inform them of my return."

"Aye, my lord, as you wish." The messenger rushed back to his horse.

Degraw stepped forward, motioning to Tara, "Come, we must go."

"Stop. One moment," Gavin barked at the first lieutenant. The man stopped and stood his ground.

Gavin reached for Tara and drew her into his arms. Fearful instincts set his senses on fire. "I'll send word when I know what this is about," he promised.

She nodded, her innocent wide eyes gazing up at him, showing her reluctance to leave. He flicked a glance over her shoulder to Degraw and the waiting carriage. The first lieutenant stood frozen in his tracks. No one stirred in the carriage. For a moment time stood still and all Gavin could think of was how much he wanted her with him. He didn't want her to leave. Not now, not ever. But now was not the right time. Holding her in his arms, he gave in to his desires and kissed her full upon her mouth, not caring if all the world could see. Wrapping her arms around him, she returned his passion in full measure, willingly giving herself to him.

Reminding himself of his duties, he pulled back. With a final brief embrace, he sent her on her way. He was the ruler of his kingdom. He had obligations and responsibilities to fulfill.

~*~

Loclyn hurried Tara into the coach and closed the door behind them before rapping on the wall to alert the driver to be off. Turning his attention to her, he glared. "That was quite a display back there," he remarked, his eyes focused small and precise upon her. His irritation was quite evident.

"Loclyn, don't," Tara replied.

"If we were in England . . ." he began.

"But we're not in England. You've traveled enough to know the rest of the world doesn't live and breathe by England's standards." She knew she was being haughty, but she was too upset to be polite.

"I've traveled enough, little sister, to know my place in the world." Anger infused his term of endearment, making it sound offensive. "I am well aware of what is proper and what is not."

"Do you imply I am not?" Sinking against the cushions, Tara felt his anger slam against her. She was appalled.

"Nothing of the sort. It's the duke who abuses his rank." Loclyn thumped his fist against the carriage wall.

Marina and Darren exchanged glances but remained silent.

It wasn't like Loclyn to react so harshly toward her. This was serious. "Why are you so peevish? You know something, don't you?" Tara tried to control the pounding in her chest but her anxiety was too great.

"I know we've been ordered to return to the villa. General Gregerson wouldn't make such a request unless it was justified."

"Yes, and the duke received a similar request from his prime minister. You must have a guess what this is all about."

Loclyn crossed his arms over his chest and looked out of the coach window toward the far horizon. Tara realized he wasn't ignoring her. He was carefully choosing his words. When he looked back at her, the anger lines on his face had softened but the worry still remained. "I'm sure you'll know soon enough. There have been rumors of raiders coming out of France."

"But we're not in France," Marina squeaked as she reached for Darren's hand.

"Raiders do not respect borders. They won't confine their actions to the countryside of France." Loclyn slowly turned to look at Tara sitting next to him. "It's quite possible they're setting their sights on Maninberg."

"But why? Why would they attack Maninberg? The duke has done nothing to provoke a war." Tara was at a loss, nothing seemed to make sense.

"Greed, my good little sister, greed. Maninberg is a rich country. Small but rich. The raiders are counting on being able to overrun the place and make off with the spoils. Land pirates," Loclyn informed her.

"Surely they'll be stopped. They cannot hope to succeed," Darren put in, sounding hopeful if not confident.

"They've experienced enough success to believe they will," Loclyn countered.

"How do you know all this?" Tara asked.

"General Gregerson has been receiving reports about these raiders for some time now. He had hoped they wouldn't bring their troubles to his doorstep, but he knows he can't ignore the threat any longer." As he spoke, Loclyn's voice softened. His anger seemed to be fading, losing its hard edge, but only slightly.

Tara dropped her eyes to her lap, too frightened to hold Loclyn's gaze. He reached out to clasp her hands. "The general has gone to see the duke, to ask him to rally his forces. He's hoping Montague has enough resources to hold off an attack, at least until additional support can be found."

"Why have they gone to the castle? Wouldn't it be quicker to meet at Wessington?" Darren asked.

"Because that's where Montague keeps his army," Loclyn replied.

"Do you think he'll be successful?" Tara looked to her cousin, grasping for hope.

"General Gregerson? He's never failed yet," Loclyn assured her.

~*~

Gavin rode fast and hard back to Maninberg castle, using the exertion of the ride to clear his mind. It angered him to think he had broken his vow to make no requests of Lady Tara. This was how it always started. One request would lead to another, and another, and before long, he wouldn't know where his demands ended and her desires began. They would be buried beneath the burden of his ultimate control. Soon she would be acquiescing to everything he wanted and the true essence of Tara would be lost, submerged within the curse of his existence.

As he rode, he forced himself to focus only on the task at hand, barring any thoughts of Tara from entering his mind. Such a futile endeavor only produced frustration. There were no easy answers to his dilemma and searching for them only caused him pain.

Gavin entered the large majestic castle and hurried past his staff toward his office. Along the way he barked out a command for a cold glass of ale to quench his thirst. The ride had tapped his energies and he needed a moment to relax or he risked facing his prime minster with unchecked anger.

When the ale was delivered, he drank it down in one long swallow before taking a seat behind his oversized desk. The soft leather gave a welcoming groan as he lowered his body into the well-worn chair.

He had once been a warrior prince. Years of experience and well-honed instincts told him something major was afoot. While he was confident there was no real threat to his kingdom, he was concerned for the surrounding lands and General Gregerson's alarm. One thing was certain. He would do whatever it took to protect Lady Tara and her family.

His thoughts were interrupted when the royal secretary came knocking on the door.

"The Prime Minister Ballistare and General Gregerson are here to see you," Rollins informed him. "They report they have an urgent matter to discuss."

"Ballistare and Gregerson?" he asked. He hadn't expected the general.

"Yes, my lord."

"Very well. Show them in," Lord Gavin instructed. He remained seated behind the large desk, his unofficial throne.

Prime Minister Ballistare and General Gregerson entered, bowed, and stood waiting for the grand duke to address them. Lord Gavin noticed with amused acceptance that General Gregerson's bow was noticeably less deep than the prime minister's. He took no offense, knowing the general had a rather relaxed view of protocol.

"Prime Minister Ballistarc, I was surprised by your summons. This is so unlike you. Could it not wait until our meeting scheduled for tomorrow?" Lord Gavin regularly met with his cabinet of ministers to discuss the affairs of his kingdom. Usually there was very little news to report, the kingdom had settled into a well-run organization. Still, he felt it was important to keep his ministers actively engaged in the day-to-day business of running the duchy. He had learned it was easier than doing it all alone, and it increased their sense of value to him and his people.

"Pardon our interruption, but we have information that needs to be discussed with you outside of our regularly scheduled meeting," Ballistare replied.

Gavin gestured to the chairs across from his desk. "Please, be seated."

"Thank you, Your Grace. I'll get right to the point," the prime minister began. "As you know, the French have endured a number of years of unrest and revolution. Now it seems there are some who would use the guise of revolution to spread further destruction. There are reports that a band of rebels under the leadership of a man named Ghilslain is raiding and looting along the border lands."

"None of that affects this kingdom. We are too far removed from such things." Lord Gavin shrugged off the disturbing news.

"Not only Maninberg is at risk, it's also the surrounding villages," General Gregerson broke in. "These distant villages are of little or no concern to the monarchs ensconced behind their castle walls. We are being left to fend for ourselves." General Gregerson's pointed comment led Gavin to believe he could easily be included in the general's list of uncooperative monarchs.

"Shouldn't the French be addressing this matter?" Lord Gavin countered.

"The French have too much on their hands to concern themselves with rebel revolutionaries. As long as the destruction is not aimed at Paris they're content to turn a blind eye to the problem. At best they send out meager bands of soldiers ill equipped and poorly trained to fend off the raiders. These inadequate attempts have failed to halt these marauders. If the raiders are allowed to go undefeated they will eventually reach the border of Maninberg. Then the problem will be deposited neatly at your doorstep. Is that what you want?" General Gregerson leaned forward slightly in his chair with a look of hardened determination as he presented his argument.

"My little kingdom is well equipped to deal with such a threat. You need only to look at our history to see we have not been successfully invaded for over one hundred years." Gavin felt no threat. Since the beginning of his reign he had insisted on maintaining a well-equipped and well trained army for the benefit of his kingdom. Every able-bodied man, upon reaching his maturity, served at least two years in training and service to his kingdom. It made his people feel safe and presented a show of force to the outside world. Regardless of all that, an invading army need only to step foot across his border and he could command them to lay down their arms. The few minor attempts made since he came into power had been completely unsuccessful.

"That is certainly an enviable record, but how can you be sure this new threat will not be the one that breaches your defenses?"

Lord Gavin eyed General Gregerson. He had to admire the man. It seemed the general didn't give up easily.

"Let me assure you, there will be no fighting within my borders," Gavin said with a confident grin. It was tempting to tell General Gregerson he had no time or patience for rumors of war. The outside world could not harm him or his people. His borders were safe and secure.

"Even if you're not concerned for your kingdom, are you not concerned for your neighbors? I have reports the raiders are only days from reaching our lands. They have shown no mercy to the farms and villages they have already raided. The farms are laid to waste, often torched and burnt to the ground. The women are raped and abused, the families are left without resources. Can you honestly tell me you have no sense of obligation to provide help to those who do not reside within your borders?" General Gregerson met Gavin's gaze unflinchingly, with hardened determination. It was obvious he was willing to push his cause as far as necessary to provoke the grand duke into action.

Gavin didn't like to be pushed, and his first instinct was to push back. He thought about ordering General Gregerson to leave Maninberg, but just as quickly dismissed the idea. That would only reinforce his isolation, and the wizard's enforced confinement of him from the rest of the world. Besides, the general's argument was too convincing. It couldn't go unaddressed. He couldn't allow the rebels to threaten the safety of Lady Tara and her family. He wouldn't turn his back on them.

"What do you suggest I do?" he asked, sounding more irritated than he had intended.

"You need not fear for your own safety. No one is asking you to put your life or limb on the battle front. I only ask for the necessary men and resources to soundly defeat these marauding rebels."

Obviously General Gregerson had misunderstood him. He held back his cynicism, refusing to feel insulted by the man's unknowing comment. It wasn't a matter of fear that kept him from personally engaging this threat. Yes, he could feel pain and experience injuries, the last ninety-nine years had demonstrated that time and time again, but his body always healed quickly, completely rejuvenated. He believed he would die if the injuries were truly severe, a separation of his head from his body would certainly do the trick, but it would take more than a bullet, or a sword, or even being struck by lightning, which he had already experienced twice, to cause his death. If nothing else, he was fairly certain severing his head from his body would make it a done deed, not that he wanted to test that theory. He had heard of the gruesome consequences of the guillotine, a device recently being used to bring death to the aristocracy of France. The mere thought of executing someone by slicing off their head brought shivers to his spine. Thankfully, by his own command, decapitations were not allowed in his kingdom. As such, he believed he had a very strong chance of continued survival.

"You're obviously a military man of considerable experience. I'll trust your knowledge. How many men, and what resources do you need to take down these rebels?" Gavin asked.

"Thank God," General Gregerson breathed, voicing a prayer of gratitude. "Our sources tell us Ghilslain has an army of about two hundred men at most, perhaps less. There have been some deserters from his cause. I'll need a force equal to that or greater to ensure victory."

"His cause?" Lord Gavin wondered aloud.

"Greed, my lord. As I said earlier, it appears his only quest is to bring death and destruction to the farms and villages in his path. I believe he sees them as easy prey, and until now, he has not been successfully challenged. Your kingdom may very well be at risk if he isn't stopped. With your help I plan to put an end to his destructive campaign."

The general's words suddenly held great appeal to Gavin. He could still recall how his kingdom had been left to its own resources at that last decisive battle nearly one hundred years ago. The battle where he had gained control of his kingdom, but lost his freedom. He had often wondered if the assistance of a willing ally could have turned the tide and saved him from making his outlandish demand for total control. It was a question that could never be answered. Now he was being presented with an opportunity to set right a wrong, to extend the assistance he had once so sorely lacked.

Lord Gavin looked pointedly at General Gregerson. "There is only one stipulation I will impose. The men who accompany you must be volunteers, and you must be the one to ask them to risk their lives. This is your battle." It was a fair enough request. He believed any man who wanted another to put his life on the line should personally make that request.

"I understand completely. It shall be as you wish, my lord," General Gregerson agreed.

"I also suggest you send any women and children who are at risk to come to my castle. You'll need every available man to assist you. Refuge within my castle walls is the only way we can ensure their safety until this skirmish. . ."

"Battle," General Gregerson broke in.

"Until this battle is over." Gavin eyed the general with a touch of disdain. He wasn't accustomed to being interrupted. Tamping down his irritation, Gavin called for Rollins and began issuing orders to his staff. "Ballistare, take General Gregerson over to the armory to meet Commander Walker. Rollins, take stock of our foodstuffs and provisions. Make sure we have all that we need. We'll be taking on visitors. General, I'll be returning to Wessington Manor near the border. It will provide easier access for me to be kept abreast of the fighting. I'll set up a war room there. We'll use it to coordinate all correspondence."

The duke's demands were met with a chorus of, "As you wish," from the men as each of them received their orders. It was as he expected. Now that he had agreed to lend his support to his neighbors, he was fully committed to ensuring their success. Even though he couldn't physically join them on the battlefield, he would be there in spirit. A feeling of well-being settled over Lord Gavin that he hadn't experienced in years, perhaps decades. This, he told himself, was the right thing to do.

CHAPTER 12

The setting sun threatened to steal the last fleeting rays of light from the sky, and still there was no word from her uncle or Maninberg castle. Tara looked up from the book she held in her lap and watched as her mother and aunt entered the front salon, lighting candles to combat the dark. She hadn't been reading, only staring at the words on the page, as if they could distract her from her wandering mind. She tried to keep her thoughts and worries in check, but her efforts had not been successful. She knew too little and feared too much.

"Any news?" Tara asked, forcing her voice to remain calm.

"Not yet," Aunt Jeanine shook her head. She took a seat next to her daughter. Marina had quietly and diligently spent the last hour embroidering an intricate rose pattern onto a square of linen. Her ability to focus on her task amazed Tara. She envied her cousin. No doubt the complex weaving of needle and thread through the fabric had served to occupy Marina's mind while it kept her fingers busy, diverting her thoughts away from the tedious task of waiting.

"What about Father?" Tara asked her mother.

179

"He's out doing what he does best, gathering any information from the neighbors that can be useful. I expect he'll return soon. It's nearly dark." Lady Chandra took a seat near her daughter, close to the front windows.

"Loclyn and Darren are busy searching the villa, gathering anything that can serve as weapons. They want to be prepared if there is a battle," Jeanine said.

Marina secured her needle in the fabric, set her work aside, and collapsed into her mother's arms. "I cannot believe this is happening. I don't know what to do." A strangled sob accompanied her plea.

"I know, Marina. I know. The waiting is never easy." Jeanine stroked her daughter's hair, trying to offer comfort. Jeanine's eyes looked weary with worry. Perhaps she had learned to endure, but even her years of experience as a general's wife could only do so much to ease the pain of waiting, and it was doubtful she had experienced the threat of an enemy so close to home.

Finally they were alerted by the sound of a rider coming into the courtyard. Lady Chandra pulled back the drapes and peered out the window. "Iain has returned," she announced.

Led by Aunt Jeanine, the women rushed to the kitchen at the back of the villa, ready to greet him. A moment later, General Gregerson strode through the back door accompanied by Loclyn and Darren. Marina rushed to her husband's side, burying her face in his chest. He wrapped a protective arm around her.

Jeanine calmly greeted her husband. "I expect you're hungry." The ride to Maninberg castle and back again had taken most of the day.

"And thirsty," Uncle Iain added.

"Let me serve you." She motioned for him to take a seat at the kitchen table and immediately began gathering leftover roast beef, some cheese, and a hunk of crusty bread from the sideboard. Iain pulled back one of the chairs from the large plank table and sat, stretching out his legs. A low burning fire in the compact brick oven occupying the far corner dispersed warmth into the room.

Loclyn darted down to the storage cellar and retrieved a jug of ale before taking a seat next to General Gregerson. Lady Chandra pulled dishes and glasses from one of the cupboards and set them on the table.

Tara watched them as they went about their tasks. They all seemed so calm, as if their only concern was preparing a late evening snack for her uncle. She could wait no longer. "Aren't you going to tell us what happened? What did Lord Gavin say?" She'd been standing near the doorway of the large kitchen and now moved to take a seat at the far end of the table.

Her uncle looked about the room, a cock-sure look on his face. "The duke has agreed to lend his support. I'll have all the men and arms I need to put down the raiders." He poured ale into three of the glasses set down by Tara's mother and passed two of them to Loclyn and Darren before taking one for himself. He raised his glass in a silent salute to the men. "I wouldn't have guessed, but Montague maintains a very impressive army. They're outfitted with the latest weaponry. We'll have no problems with Ghilslain." More than pleased, he looked confident.

"How soon do you plan to leave? At dawn?" Aunt Jeanine asked. She had obviously been through this before.

"At first light," Uncle Iain confirmed after downing his first glass of ale. He immediately poured another. "The duke has offered refuge to anyone at risk. Jeanine, I want you to take the ladies of this house up to the Maninberg castle. You know the drill. Take only what you need and leave the rest. Make sure none of the female staff are left behind. From what I've heard, these marauders do not treat the women folk kindly."

Jeanine set a plate full of food in front of her husband and he nodded, gratefully accepting the meal she'd set before him. Before she could withdraw her hand, he grabbed it and brought it to his lips. For a moment their eyes met, his smiling, hers fearful.

Jeanine seemed to welcome the gesture. "Did you have any trouble getting the duke to help you?" she asked. She stepped away to lean against the kitchen counter, folding her arms in front of her.

Tara was aware of her aunt's reservations about Lord Gavin. Life seemed to come too easily to him, and Aunt Jeanine didn't believe the duke truly appreciated all the blessings his position afforded him. Tara didn't necessarily agree with her aunt.

"It wasn't until I provoked him with the guilt of helping his neighbors that he agreed to provide the assistance we need. I had expected the duke to be far more concerned with defending his borders. Why else would he maintain such an impressive army?" Iain took a large bite of the roast beef and washed it down with ale.

"It was the threat to his neighbors, not to his own kingdom, that swayed his view?" Aunt Jeanine asked, her mouth agape. Tara suppressed a grin. Maybe her aunt had been too harsh in her assessment after all.

"Well, yes. When you put it that way," Iain answered between bites of his dinner. "He seemed confident his borders are safe. He said there hadn't been a successful invasion of his kingdom for nearly one hundred years, and insisted I be the one to ask for volunteers. Can you believe that? Volunteers! Said he wouldn't order his men to fight. But no one refused, not a one. They're ready and able to assist their neighbors. I think they're eager for a fight, they've been without one for too long."

"More likely they're eager to defend their kingdom before the battle hits home. Only fools go looking for a fight," Loclyn put in.

"I've never seen a more dedicated group of soldiers," General Gregerson continued. "It's no wonder the duke showed no concern. He has unlimited faith in their abilities."

"What an impressive record." Aunt Jeanine raised her dark brown brows.

"Aye, an impressive record indeed. Let's hope his luck holds true." Iain sat back, wiping the back of his hand across his mouth, satisfied and finished with his meal.

Tara took a moment to look around the kitchen. Her uncle was obviously enjoying the experience of having his family gathered around him and being the center of attention. He was rallying his troops, preparing to march off to war. He was a man in his element. Even if it was only a minor battle with a marauding rebel, he would give it his all.

As she glanced around, she noticed her mother suddenly cock her head towards the door. A few seconds later her father entered. He looked about the kitchen filled with family, and closed the door behind him. Leaning against the door-jam, he smiled broadly. Even though he was dressed as a common horse groomer, in rough woolen breeches and a coarse linen shirt, he looked confident and charming. His large-weave wool jacket hung loose on his frame, giving him the appearance of being swallowed up by the cast-off garment. It was a fair disguise for a man wishing to blend in with his neighbors.

Lady Chandra rose to greet her husband. "My dear, it's good to see you." She stepped into his arms. Her nose crinkled a bit as she took in the scent of his clothing, a mixture of hay, horse sweat, and manure. Apparently it was worse than she had expected.

"The pleasure is mine," Lord Tyrus said, pulling her deeper into his embrace. She endured for a moment longer before she pushed him away, his odor getting the better of her. She waved her hand in front of her nose.

Lord Tyrus eyed the jug and drinking glasses set around the table. "I'll have one of those," he said, indicating a half-full glass of ale. Lady Chandra rushed to respond, taking a fresh glass and filling it with ale.

"What have you learned?" Iain asked.

Tara's father took a seat at the table across from his brother-in-law. "I've had a rather interesting afternoon," he said, catching everyone's interest. "It's as you suspected," Tyrus said, speaking to Loclyn. "They're making their way through the valley."

"That puts us at risk," Iain said. His face hardened with a scowl.

"They've set their sights on Maninberg," Tyrus finished.

"Maninberg!" Tara squeaked. "Why Maninberg?" It was just as she had feared. She had hoped against hope that Loclyn had been wrong, but her father was leaving no doubt.

"It's a rich, little country, hasn't been bothered for a good long while. They think it's ripe for the picking," her father answered before taking a long swallow of ale.

"Ha! They're in for a surprise. The duke has an army England would envy, with all the latest weaponry," Uncle Iain informed her father, looking rather pleased.

"The marauders don't know that. They see a small kingdom that's been idle for too long. The common folk of France have become quite disenchanted with kings, rulers, and monarchies. They're using any excuse they can find to grab the wealth from the rich. Spreading it around, they say." Tara saw the disappointment imprinted in her father's eyes as his demeanor turned serious. It fueled her fears.

"Lord Gavin has worked hard to bring prosperity to his kingdom, they're not idle. And he's offered to help us quell this rebellion," Tara argued.

"Were you able to speak with the duke?" Lord Tyrus turned his attention back to Iain.

"Aye. It took a little persuasion, but he has agreed to supply all the men and arms we need. Rather fitting, now that we know his kingdom is the target. How did you come across this bit of information?" Iain cast a sideways glance at this brother-in-law. It was always questionable how much Tyrus would reveal with it came to his information gathering techniques.

"Scouted out a few of the roadside taverns along the main roads. It isn't hard to pick out the outsiders from the locals. I claimed I was looking for any work that would pay. Latched on to a couple of forward scouts for Ghilslain and plied them with some of the finest Scottish whisky this side of the English Channel. Thanks for the flask, old boy," Tyrus said, nodding at Iain. "Worked quite well, I must say."

Tara took stock of the family positioned around the kitchen. Marina was still standing, locked in Darren's arms. Her father, Uncle Iain, and Loclyn sat around the table discussing battles and strategies while her mother and Aunt Jeanine hovered over them, ready to attend to their needs. Tara felt displaced. Her family was preparing for war and there was no turning back.

~*~

Fearful visions occupied Tara's sleep that night as she tossed fitfully in her bed. Rather than being in control of her dreams, she felt confused, swept along by her churning emotions.

One moment she was running, lost in the hedgerow maze, then suddenly she was in the shadowy halls of Maninberg castle. She felt lost and afraid, alone in the dark, unable to see what lie ahead. She seemed to be wandering in circles, running down one long corridor after another.

Finally, as she turned yet another corner, she saw a light up ahead, and ran toward the light. Gavin was there, waiting for her. She ran to his arms, seeking comfort.

"It's alright, my dear. I'm here for you," he said.

"Gavin, I'm scared." She burrowed into his embrace.

"I know, Tara. I can feel it. It's as though we're connected." He held her close, wrapping his arms around her.

Tara relaxed into his arms, her fears subsiding. "How did you find me?"

"I thought you found me." Pulling back, he searched her upturned face. "What is this strange magic?"

"It's the grandest magic of all. The magic of dreams, and love, and life." A radiant, glowing light surrounded them.

"I've not been able to dream for so long. Not until I found you." Gavin stroked his hand down her back.

Tara rested her head upon his chest. "If you never let me go it can always be this way."

"I cannot have what is not mine. You must be free." His voice became distant but his arms remained encircled around her.

"Why do you say such things?" Tara stammered.

"You have no idea the darkness my kingdom holds." Gavin's face receded into the shadows.

Tara's fears returned. "Gavin, I don't understand. Talk to me." Shadows crept upon them, dimming the light.

"Hush. We're here now. That's all that matters." Gavin continued to stroke her hair.

"But soon we will awake," Tara sighed.

"It matters not. It's only a dream." His voice became strange and distant.

"No. Stay. Please stay."

The last of the light faded away and Tara awoke, alone in her bed.

CHAPTER 13

The gray morning sun cast deep shadows across the courtyard as Tara stepped onto the large front veranda of the villa. Her traveling bag was packed and ready to be loaded onto her father's coach. Dark circles shadowed her eyes, a reminder of her restless night. She had not slept well, and now the family was up with the sun, preparing to depart for Maninberg Castle. Everyone was in a hurry to leave for the castle, except her aunt.

"If you're so sure about this, I don't see why we can't stay here in the villa." Aunt Jeanine stood defiantly, arguing with Uncle Iain. From the look on his face it was evident they'd been over this before, and he was resigned to going over it again.

"Jeanine, my darling, you don't want me out on the battlefield worrying about you. I need to be focused on the battle." Uncle Iain spoke to his wife as he continued to pack his saddlebags.

"You keep telling me there will be no problems, that it will all be over in a few days," Aunt Jeanine persisted.

Tara cringed upon hearing the whine in her aunt's voice. She had never seen her looking so conflicted. Typically her aunt was the practical one, keeping everything and everyone under control.

Tara wondered what made this situation so different. Aunt Jeanine must have seen her husband go off to battle several times before, and according to her uncle, all of those had been greater threats than the one they now faced.

Her uncle stopped his packing and turned his attentions to his wife. "You need to believe me. I'll be commanding Montague's army along with Commander Walker. My job will be easy."

"Then why must we go to the castle? Why must I leave my home?" Jeanine continued to argue with her husband.

Uncle Iain sighed. "Because there will be no one here to defend you. Fighting is not always contained to the battlefield, you know that. If raiders were to stray from the battlefield and come looking for trouble – I don't want you here unprotected."

"I can take care of myself," she insisted.

"Of that I have no doubt, but there are others. . ."

"I thought we left England to get away from war," Jeanine broke in.

The look on the General's face softened, as if he finally understood her distress. He cupped his wife's face in his large rough-skinned hands. "Jeanine, it's one thing to fight for your country. It's so much different when you're fighting for your home. This makes it personal. But trust me, it's a minor skirmish, nothing we can't handle."

"You better be right. You promised to grow old with me." Though dry-eyed, her aunt looked to be on the verge of tears.

"Aha, now there's my girl, already planning for the future."

Lady Chandra stepped out on to the veranda next to her daughter. "I have no doubt Iain will be here for the birth of his grandbaby," she said. Unlike Tara, it seemed her mother had chosen to do her listening from the shadows of the doorway.

Suddenly becoming aware of her audience, Jeanine resumed her usual business-like demeanor. "Come now, let's get these carriages loaded. The quicker these men take care of the raiders, the quicker we'll all be home, where we belong." Jeanine cast a meaningful glance at her husband.

"That's my Jeanine," General Gregerson said with pride. He brushed her lips with a kiss before returning to the task of packing his bags.

Tara traveled with her mother, aunt, and cousin in her father's carriage. Her uncle's coach, filled with women from the villa, followed close behind. As they passed through the large, fortified gates of Maninberg, she surveyed the structure. The walls of the fortress were easily six feet wide. Built to be strong and formidable, they looked as though they could hold back the world.

She had expected to be happy upon her return to Lord Gavin's castle. Instead, an uneasy feeling gnawed at her nerves. Men she loved and held dear to her heart, including her father and cousin, were preparing to go to war. While the women's carriages had traveled to Maninberg, they had set off to engage in a battle with rebels, men who apparently had no sense of morals or consideration for the rights of others. Their only aim was to take all they could, regardless of who was hurt along the way. Such thoughts and actions were beyond her ability to comprehend.

When they pulled into the courtyard of the castle there was very little evidence of the turmoil developing only miles away. Footmen stood ready to assist them the moment their carriages rolled to a stop. Lord Gavin, followed by his royal secretary, Bruno Rollins, was there to greet them.

"I trust your ride into Maninberg was uneventful," Lord Gavin addressed Lady Chandra and Aunt Jeanine as they stepped down from the coach.

"Thankfully, we have arrived unscathed. We welcome your hospitality and are grateful for the invitation," Lady Chandra replied. She turned to nod at Jeanine, as if prompting her to speak.

"Yes, we appreciate your hospitality," Jeanine said. "Although it seems a little over-protective if you ask me. Heaven only knows what we'll do to occupy our time."

Tara wanted to poke her aunt in the ribs for being impolite. It pleased her when she saw her mother take on the task herself.

"I've arranged for Rollins to be available to you. Ask, and he'll do his best to provide. You'll have the whole castle and citadel to explore. I do hope you will find something within our walls to ease the burden of waiting. You may find our infirmary to be of particular interest. It possesses the latest in medical equipment, and our doctors adhere to the most modern practices. Our birthing facilities are particularly well outfitted. I cannot abide having women suffer needlessly."

Marina and Aunt Jeanine exchanged startled glances. Lord Gavin's words had successfully captured their interest.

Jeanine's brows raised in a furrow. "An infirmary with birthing facilities? I've never heard of such a thing. Women give birth at home," she stated flatly.

"That is usually true. However, if the need arises, I believe there is comfort in knowing such services are available," Lord Gavin said. From his demeanor one would think he was talking about the weather, not intimate medical conditions. Tara found it hard to believe her aunt and Lord Gavin were having this discussion.

"An infirmary – with birthing facilities?" Marina reached for her mother with an excited little bounce. "Mother, we really should take a tour. Just to have a look, don't you think?"

"I suppose it may be of interest," Aunt Jeanine conceded. She folded her arms tightly across her chest, looking less than pleased.

Rollins stepped forward, greeting the women with a bow. "Ladies, if you will follow me, I will show you to your rooms." With Lady Chandra's assistance he ushered Aunt Jeanine and

Marina into the castle. The master chamberlain had also arrived and was directing the village women to their quarters.

"When can I see the infirmary?" Marina asked Rollins as she followed him into the castle.

Lord Gavin turned to Tara, silently motioning for her to stay behind. Nodding her agreement, she watched as her family followed Rollins, leaving her alone with the duke. She wasn't exactly sure how it happened so quickly, but she was pleased with the results.

"It's a pleasure to see you again, my lord," Tara said when the others had dispersed. "Although I am a bit surprised. I heard you were returning to Wessington."

"I couldn't leave until I knew you were safe. Perhaps I'm being overly cautious, but I was worried about you." He hesitated a moment before asking, "Did you sleep well last night?"

"No, not so well. I suppose I look weary." She rubbed lightly at her eyes.

"Bad dreams?"

Tara sighed. "I'm sure this talk of war is enough to give us all bad dreams. I doubt I will sleep well until this danger has passed."

Although she understood the reason for his questions, she needed to feign innocence. She had been wondering if he would address their nocturnal meetings, but she wasn't ready or able to discuss the merits of her talents, not just yet. And she was still too distraught over their recent nightmarish encounter. Unlike her usual dream weaving, last night's dream had been out of her control. She shivered as she recalled the unpleasant experience.

Most importantly, her loyalty to Tazire demanded her continued secrecy. She realized she was reaching a point where it would be best if she fully understood her Grand Papa's connection to Lord Gavin, but until such information was revealed to her, her first loyalty was to her family. She wondered how much her Grand Papa would reveal and when.

"Commander Walker and your uncle both assure me it will only be a minor battle, little more than a skirmish at most, but I want to do everything I can to ensure your safety. Rest assured you and your family are completely safe here at my castle." He stepped forward and ran a hand up along her arm, a casual yet intimate gesture. "I won't allow any harm to come to you. Not while you're in my kingdom." His eyes bore into her. He seemed so confident, as if he could single-handedly hold back an invading army.

"Your assurance is comforting. I hope you weren't offended by my Aunt Jeanine. I believe she's feeling distraught about Uncle Iain being so close to the fighting. Back home in Scotland his military career was carried out at a distance."

"I took no offense," Gavin assured her. "Her reaction is understandable. We can only hope the need for her to take refuge here at Maninberg will not be unduly long."

A footman approached Lord Gavin from inside the castle and stood a few feet away, awaiting instructions. Lord Gavin acknowledged him. "Have my horse made ready for travel and brought here."

The footman bowed. "As you wish, my lord," he said and hurried on his way.

Lord Gavin turned back to Tara. She noticed he was dressed for travel in finely polished black boots, thigh hugging breeches, and a dark hunter green wool coat stylishly tailored to fit across his broad shoulders.

"I've instructed Rollins to do his utmost to ensure your comfort. We have some lovely gardens here at the castle."

"If they are anything like the gardens at Wiltzer Park, I'm sure they will be quite pleasant," Tara said.

"As nice or better, I would say. There's also a well-stocked library, if you are interested. I hope you will take advantage of all the castle has to offer." Though their conversation was casual,

Lord Gavin appeared slightly on edge, as if there was something more he wanted to say.

"I'm sure we'll be comfortable, but there is very little that can be done to alleviate the burden of waiting. A day can last forever when you're concerned for a loved one, as I'm sure you understand," she said.

"Yes, only too well. It's a sentiment I believe we can all agree upon. Under better circumstances, I would welcome the opportunity to personally oversee your stay here at Maninberg, but I've made a commitment to be at Wessington. It's my duty to oversee the management of my duchy's resources in order to support Commander Walker and General Gregerson."

Now she understood. He was torn between sovereign duty and personal preference. She wanted to make the choice easier for him and lessen some of his concerns. "Of course, you must go where you are needed, where you can do the most good. You needn't worry about a bunch of women taking refuge in your castle. As you've said, we'll have everything we need."

A groomsman brought the duke's horse into the courtyard, saddled and ready for travel. Tara glanced from the saddled horse to Lord Gavin. "You're traveling by horseback?" she asked. This wasn't what she had expected.

"Whenever possible. It's quicker and more efficient," Lord Gavin replied.

"Shouldn't you travel by carriage with guards, or at least footmen?" She reached for him, placing a shaking hand upon his forearm. It unnerved her to realize how strongly she feared for his safety. Maybe she was more like her aunt than she wanted to admit.

Lord Gavin's face softened, as if he understood her concerns. "I can assure you, I am safe within the borders of my kingdom. No harm will come to me."

"But there are rebels about, my Uncle said so, and my father encountered rebel scouts in a village not far from your border.

Aren't you. . ." Pulling back her hand, she stopped her nervous ramblings before she said too much.

"Afraid? No Tara, I'm safe. But if it makes you feel any better, I'm riding with two of my most trusted guards." He pointed to the far end of the courtyard, indicating the riders waiting there.

Tara hadn't noticed them before. Either they had suddenly appeared, or she'd been too focused on Lord Gavin to see anything else around her. She tried to make light of her fears. "Please forgive me. I must sound like an old nag."

"No, not at all. I appreciate your concern. It isn't often I have someone worrying over me." His smile spread to his eyes.

"That can't be right, Lord Gavin. You have a whole kingdom to worry over you." His lighthearted comment helped to boost her confidence.

"If they do, their concern is for their sovereign, a figurehead, not the man behind the title. I would hope your concerns are of a more personal nature."

"They are, my lord. I can assure you, they are." Tara's hand rose again, as if to reach out and touch him, but she stayed the movement.

This wasn't like Wiltzer Park. There, they had created their own little world. Here, they were surrounded by his subjects, and she was an outsider taking refuge in his realm. She looked about. A groomsman stood patiently nearby with the duke's mount as his guards waited in the distance.

Lord Gavin appeared to hesitate for a moment longer, as if reluctant to leave her. She had observed her Aunt's reluctance to be parted from her Uncle Iain and she had no desire to place such a burden upon the duke. She didn't want him to see her as any more fearful or needy than she already appeared. She forced a brave smile. "You must go and do your duty. I'm sure we'll be fine."

"I'll send messengers to the castle daily to keep you informed on our progress." He was leaning closer to her, his voice dropped low. "I would not wish you to worry."

"That's very kind of you. I'm sure we will all appreciate your efforts." She could feel herself shaking. Her discomfort was growing. Saying good-bye was proving harder than she had expected. Drawing it out, as they were, only made it worse. "You must go now, my lord. Please, I cannot say good-bye."

A broad smile swept across his face, lighting his eyes. He looked pleased. He pulled her into his arms, slowly, as if seeking her permission as well as her acceptance. She leaned into his embrace, giving her unspoken approval. His head bent to hers and he kissed her long, slowly, and tenderly. Unlike the hurried kiss they had exchanged back at Wiltzer Park, this time he lingered, his lips tantalizingly soft against her mouth. She breathed in the scent of his skin, musk and leather laced with fresh pine soap. She filled her senses with his touch. Her heart beat rapidly, not from fear as it had earlier, but from the passion he provoked. For one brief moment, time stood still, and she wished, as lovers often do, the moment could last forever.

Stepping back, he smiled. "This is not good-bye, Tara." He gave her a short bow before he turned and stepped away to mount his horse.

She stood there watching as he rode away. Her fingers rose to softly touch her lips, savoring the heat still lingering there. She sent up a silent prayer of protection for all the men marching off to war, but for him she said a special, heartfelt prayer that they would be together soon.

~*~

Tara was greeted by Rollins as soon as she stepped into the castle. He escorted her to the suite of rooms she would be sharing with Marina. Lord Gavin had provided them with splendid, spacious accommodations. Adjoining the large bed chamber was a sitting room and a separate dressing room with its own bathing tub. The rooms were painted ivory with pale blue trim. Wallpaper delicately depicting exotic birds and plants graced the paneled cutouts. The quilt covering the bed was pale blue silk and excessively puffy, providing an image of comfort and warmth.

She had hardly settled into the chamber when Marina excitedly burst in. "Isn't it grand, Tara? We're back at the castle and have the whole grounds to explore."

Tara was too concerned for her loved ones marching off to war to fully appreciate her luxurious surroundings. "How can you be excited about this? Your husband's life is at stake."

"I doubt my father will allow Darren to be put at risk. I'm sure he'll protect him. He's my husband."

"Marina, every man who goes to war is at risk. Whether he's a general, a first lieutenant, or the general's son-in-law, they're all at risk. Someone always dies." Even the duke, who would not be leaving his kingdom, was at risk, if the rebels managed to cross into Maninberg. For all she knew, those rebels could be anywhere, and the way Lord Gavin rode about on horseback alarmed her. She was amazed, and somewhat envious of his overwhelming confidence. Gavin acted as if nothing in the world could harm him or anyone else in his kingdom.

Marina's eyes fell to the floor, her expression turning childlike with anguish. She reached for Tara's hands. "Tara, I pray, do not be mad at me. I'm not as strong as you. If I were to believe for one moment that Darren's life was at stake I'm sure I would melt into a puddle of mush right here on the carpet."

Tara reached out to comfort her cousin. She knew the waiting would be hard on them all.

"I'm sorry, Marina, I did not mean to be harsh. All this talk of war and battles has me undone. I'm more afraid than I'd like to admit. My father, your father, and other men we love are putting their lives at risk to fight against a ruthless rebel. I cannot make sense of it."

"But we have to believe they'll be alright. We have to believe," Marina whispered.

"You're right, we have to believe," Tara responded. "I could use some of your faith right now."

"I've always thought you were the strong one. The way you've traveled and seen the world, I thought nothing frightened you."

"Yes, I've traveled much, and seen a lot. I've seen that the world isn't always a welcoming place. It's not like home, Marina." She slumped into the cushions of a nearby sofa. This was one time when Tara was grateful the duke could not leave his kingdom. She was grateful he would not be putting his life at risk and join the battle. She was grateful his position afforded him such luxury. It was selfish, she knew, but she couldn't help but feel better knowing he was safely ensconced within the borders of his kingdom.

CHAPTER 14

After one hundred years of unchallenged reign, Lord Gavin Richard Montague had come to expect flawless efficiency, and he was rarely disappointed. Upon his arrival at Wessington, he hoped to receive regular and complete reports from General Gregerson and Commander Walker, but fighting, as he dimly remembered, had a timetable all its own. It infuriated him that he wasn't able to lend his physical support to General Gregerson, even though Gavin knew he was not expected to ride out with his countrymen to the battlefield.

On the first day he received only a brief note informing him the troops were advancing on Ghilslain's position, along with a short list of supplies the troops needed. It wasn't much, barrels of gun powder and some additional foodstuffs. He immediately ordered the provisions be transported to the troops. The courier accompanying the transport was instructed to return immediately with news of the battle, but even that communication encountered delays. Messengers and progress reports were an extravagance not always afforded while a battle was being waged. For the first time in nearly one hundred years, he was once again forced to face the chaos of war, even if only from a distance.

Within days after arriving at Wessington, Lord Gavin finally received word General Gregerson and his men had encountered the rebels in full force near the southern rim of the valley. They had the marauders contained, but for the moment they were at a standoff, neither side making significant progress. The battle was lasting longer than General Gregerson had expected. Ghilslain was proving to be a more formable foe than any of them had anticipated. The rebels had reaped the benefits of a series of victories and his followers had grown bolder, filled with the type of confidence and arrogance that came with repeated success.

General Gregerson had expected the battle to be over within a few days, but it was two weeks before they were able to put an end to Ghilslain's threat. Finally, Gavin received news the rebels were seen fleeing the battlefield. Apparently, even the spoils of war weren't sufficient to hold their interest, as their supplies ran low during the prolonged battle, and their chances for winning ran even lower.

Shortly after being informed that the battle was nearing a successful end, Gavin also received a visit from his old nemesis, Tazire. The wizard strolled into the duke's office and sat in the largest armchair, nearest to the fireplace, making himself comfortably at home.

"I'm pleased to see how well things are progressing," Tazire said, stretching his legs out before him. He settled in, setting his shiny black boots, one atop the other, upon a conveniently placed foot stool.

Lord Gavin set aside his paperwork and glared at the wizard. Tazire had not asked for entrance, but then again, he never did. He just showed up. "I suppose you're referring to the battle," Gavin said, taking pains to sound more courteous than he felt.

"Among other things," Tazire smirked. "I'm quite impressed to learn how you've provided assistance to your neighbors in need, rather than do nothing and wait for the threat to reach your borders. So unlike you. I understand you've supplied ample resources, including men and supplies, to General Gregerson. Everything he needs to ensure his success. I've heard you've even given refuge to many of the villagers who live near the fields of battle, taking them out of harm's way. Yes, quite impressive indeed."

"I can't believe you've come here to congratulate me on a job well done." Lord Gavin sat back in his chair and tried to relax. Tazire was being uncommonly kind, but that didn't mean he could lower his guard.

"Not yet." Tazire sent him a pointed look. "I've heard General Gregerson's family is among the individuals benefiting from your hospitality."

"That's correct. The General is fighting to defeat the rebels. He should not have to worry about his family."

"Isn't his niece the young lady you danced with at the Summer Solstice Ball?"

Gavin didn't like the wizard's line of questioning. "What's your point?"

"I'm wondering how things are going. Have you made any progress with her?" Tazire's grin was suspiciously wicked.

"I cannot believe you're asking me such things." Gavin's eyes raked over the old man with disdain.

Tazire narrowed his eyes, focusing his stare at Gavin. "I have a personal interest in you, lad. I'll ask anything I want." He flicked his wrist and the fire in the hearth blazed brighter.

Gavin huffed, but he remained silent. It would do no good to get into an argument with the wizard. Tazire would only endeavor to make his life more miserable, if that were even possible.

"So the niece, what was her name?" Tazire asked, returning to his subject of inquiry.

"Lady Tara Zanders. Her parents are Lord Tyrus and Lady Chandra of Cullenwood, as I'm sure you already know."

"Of course I know. I make it my business to know these things. You still have not answered my question. How is your relationship with Lady Tara progressing?"

Gavin crossed his arms over his chest. There was no avoiding Tazire's inquisitiveness. "I cannot say there is a relationship. I am fond of Lady Tara and am relieved to know she is well protected within my borders, but . . ." Gavin hesitated, reluctant to discuss his feelings for Lady Tara with Tazire.

"But what?" Tazire flared.

"But more I cannot say. I'm letting Lady Tara dictate how the relationship progresses. I've made no requests of her and I don't intend to. I've been careful to ensure she's acting of her own free will. She was invited, along with the rest of the General's family, to take refuge at the castle, but she's free to do as she pleases."

Tazire looked impressed, his eyes widened with surprise. "You want me to believe you've made no requests of her? Even though she can't deny you?"

"It is precisely because she can't deny me that I refuse to make any requests. I prefer to leave it up to her." Gavin felt good about his revelation. He rather liked shocking Tazire with something new and unexpected.

"This must be a new experience for you, to allow for circumstances beyond your control. How does it feel?"

"You mock me, I know. Take your pleasure, but I've found a great deal of satisfaction in letting her lead the way and know her actions are based on her desires, not mine."

Tazire's smile turned triumphant. "There's hope for you yet, lad."

"When are you going to stop calling me lad?"

"When you grow up and mature, so maybe never. But there is hope. You are learning. You're learning you can't control the world around you, you can only control yourself. I would say that's progress." Tazire stood and strolled about the room. He picked up an ornately carved wooden box, examined it, and then set it back down.

"That's nonsense. You know better than anyone that I have complete control over everyone within my kingdom. They do whatever I tell them."

"You also have complete control over what you request of them, or not request, as the case may be." Tazire next examined a reflecting globe, holding it up to the light, turning it this way and that.

"Correct. I've learned to be mindful of what I ask for. I no longer make unreasonable requests of my subjects."

"Then it's only fitting they should want to please you. After all, you are their sovereign."

"No one ever refuses me, no matter how absurd the request." *Because they can't.*

Tazire began tossing the reflecting globe back and forth, from hand to hand. "And in return your subjects live happy and productive lives. You brought them out of darkness when all seemed lost. Together you've built a prosperous duchy. For that, do you think they should rebel?"

Gavin watched the ball flick back and forth in the wizard's hands. "I would expect someone to disagree with me once in a while. Believe it or not, I know I am not always right."

Tazire stopped tossing the globe and laughed. "That's what I'm here for."

Gavin shot Tazire a look of disgust before he continued. "Too easily I recall the string of mistresses I pursued, like a strand of pearls, each beautiful and yet each so like the other. I had hoped one of them would refuse my attentions, but of course, none ever did. They were unable to refuse." Gavin shook with the memory of his deviant behavior. Like a drunkard obsessed with the mind-numbing escape found in a bottle, he had taken his desire for physical pleasure too far.

"Yes, that was quite a nasty mess. The way I saw it, you surrounded yourself with people who demonstrated a willingness to give into debauchery, which doesn't surprise me, given the circumstances. They were a wretched group of courtiers only seeking to gain your favor. You finally realized everyone didn't share your misguided idea of pleasure."

"Your censure is well deserved. I've come to realize that affection, or should I say compliance to duty, without true love is not worth having."

"I did not judge you. It was simply a statement of fact. However, your words are reassuring. What is life, if not for learning?" Tazire tossed the reflecting ball one last time before setting it down on the table.

Gavin looked at Tazire with fresh eyes, and for the first time in his long life, saw him as a friend. He had known the wizard for nearly a hundred years. To Tazire, his life was an open book. He had no secrets from this man, and it suddenly struck him what a luxury this was. It was a blessing to have someone to talk to, even someone who could argue with him, disagree with him, tell him he was wrong, or even offer a dissenting opinion. As much as he had resented the wizard's intrusion, he also realized the benefit of having him as a confidant.

He wondered what it would be like to have such an honest and open relationship with Tara. How would she react if she knew his deepest, darkest secrets? Hell, forget about his affairs, they were in the past. What would she do if she knew he couldn't leave his kingdom, that he was immortal, and had complete control over his subjects? Surely it would be enough to send her packing. Once again, he found his desires at odds with the reality of his situation. No matter how strongly she might be attracted to him there was too much deception between them. If she were to learn his secrets, he was certain she would flee from his kingdom in an instant, never to return.

Tazire broke into his thoughts. "Why so gloomy? You look as though you've just lost your best friend."

"I was thinking about Lady Tara. She knows nothing about my condition. If she did, I expect she would abandon me."

"You think she doesn't suspect?" Tazire raised his brow with a quizzical look.

"How could she? I've been careful to hide my truth. It's disheartening to think you are the only one who knows me as I truly am. I realize I haven't always appreciated your counsel or the companionship you provide, and yet, you are the one person I can count on to always be honest with me. That is the mark of a true friend. Can you forgive me?"

"Forgive you? Now you're asking me for forgiveness. You are full of surprises." For a moment Tazire looked touched by Gavin's admission, but his expression soon turned lighthearted. "Do not trouble yourself. There is nothing to forgive. I know you're only doing the best you can, given who you are. Too bad about that." At Gavin's expense Tazire released a mirthful laugh, delighting in his own joke.

"I don't know why I even bother to try." Gavin intended to sound offended, but Tazire's laughter was too contagious, too delightful. The wizard was right and he knew it. Gavin's lips curved in a tentative grin.

"You really need to take it easy. You take yourself entirely too seriously. You should laugh more. Enjoy yourself more." Tazire picked up a small carving of a bird with spread wings, ready to take flight.

"We are in the middle of a battle, if you haven't noticed."

"I understand it's nearly over, but still, it won't hurt the troops in the field one bit if you break down and enjoy a laugh or two. In fact, I think this calls for a celebration. Where's that butler of yours?" Tazire had barely spoken the words when Millinsworth appeared at the door.

"You called, my lord?" Millinsworth bowed low to Tazire and the duke.

"Bring us some of the duke's finest brandy, and serve it in crystal glasses. Only the best in times of troubles, don't you agree?" Tazire said.

Millinsworth looked to Lord Gavin for confirmation.

"Do as he asks. It looks like I'm taking a break, although I have no idea what we're celebrating," Gavin said.

"Enlightenment, Lord Gavin Richard Montague. We're celebrating enlightenment."

~*~

True to his word, Lord Gavin was considerate of the women who were separated from their loved ones. He sent communications to the castle nearly every day to keep them informed about the battle being waged so close to his kingdom. Usually the reports were encouraging, and Tara could tell Lord Gavin was doing his best to present positive communications, but nothing could prevent the women from thinking the worst. Waiting was hard. Nothing would change that.

While it was reassuring to be kept informed of the ongoing battle, Tara was much more interested in the personal notes Lord Gavin sent addressed to her, folded and sealed in their own envelope. The notes were always short, little more than a line or two wishing her well in his crisp, bold script, but it was enough to let her know he was thinking of her. In a time of war, this was more than she should expect, and it was more than enough to let her know that he cared.

The women had been at the castle for several days, days that dragged on with the waiting, when Darren finally arrived with one of the duke's messengers. News of their arrival spread swiftly through the castle, and the women rushed to gather in the grand salon where the men were waiting. Tara and Marina were among the first to arrive, having recently returned to the castle from a stroll in the gardens.

Upon seeing her husband, Marina was overcome with emotion, and flew to him, weeping with joy. Darren welcomed his wife with open arms.

Tara was happy for them. As carefree as her cousin had tried to appear, she knew Marina's fears and insecurities had heavily weighed on her. Within days of moving into the castle Marina had become quiet, losing her natural tendency to be excited over every new adventure they encountered. Even the duke's peacocks failed to rouse her delight by the end of the first week.

"The battle is over. Ghilslain has been defeated. The men are returning to their homes." The news was repeated several times over as each new group of women made their way into the salon.

Darren waited until both Lady Chandra and Tara were in the salon before he pulled them aside. He looked tired. His usually impeccable clothing was filthy with the dust of travel and the grime of battle. "The news is not all good," he began. "Loclyn has been wounded and Lord Tyrus is missing."

Tara and Lady Chandra both gasped. Lady Chandra sank onto the nearest settee. Tara took a seat beside her mother.

"It's not all bad," Darren continued. "Lord Tyrus has not been found among the dead or wounded. We just don't know where he is."

Lady Chandra breathed a sigh, appearing somewhat relieved, but her color was still pale.

"But what of Loclyn? You said he was wounded," Tara asked. A wave of fear grew in her stomach, taking root.

"He took a bullet and was thrown from his horse. He's been taken to the General's villa. It was the closest location with the proper facilities," Darren said.

Tara was beside herself with fear for her cousin's life. "I must reach Loclyn, I must see him." Unable to remain still, she stood and began pacing the room.

"I've come to escort all of you back to the villa. We'll travel together," Darren said, holding Marina close.

"We'll all go. Have our carriage brought about," Lady Chandra instructed Rollins.

The royal secretary bowed. "As you wish, my lady." He turned to walk away.

"No, Rollins. Wait," Tara spoke loudly.

Rollins stopped in mid-stride.

"Mother, that's too slow. I need a horse. I'll ride on ahead. I can get there faster by myself." Tara's mind was whirling. She needed to act quickly.

"Are you sure you know what you're doing?" Lady Chandra asked.

"Mother, it's Loclyn. I must go to him. You know how close we are."

Lady Chandra hesitated, her face filled with worry.

"I'll climb the walls if I have to travel by carriage," Tara pleaded.

"You're right. You should go. He needs you," her mother acquiesced.

Tara was grateful. She didn't want to argue with her mother. There was no time for such delays and she was determined to go. She needed to be at Loclyn's side.

She turned to Rollins. "Prepare a horse for me, please. With a proper saddle."

Rollins bowed. "As you wish, my lady." He hurried off toward the stables.

By the time Tara had changed into her squire's breeches, a horse, along with an escort, stood ready and waiting for her in the courtyard.

~*~

While Tara was riding away from Maninberg, Lord Gavin was occupied with the battle's aftermath. He'd been delayed by the flow of incoming soldiers. Each new wave of men brought news from the battle and more of the wounded. He couldn't leave Wessington until he was sure his men were safe and well cared for. It was hours before he returned to Maninberg castle. The moment he walked through the front door of his castle he was greeted by Rollins.

"How is everything here? Have the women been informed of the outcome?"

"Yes, my lord. Most of the women have already made their departure."

"What about the General's family? Have they left?" Gavin knew Darren Metwick had ridden on ahead to personally see to his wife and family. He had heard about Lord Tyrus' disappearance from the battlefield and he was concerned for both Tara and her mother. He had sent extra men in search of Lord Tyrus.

"General Gregerson's family was among the first to leave. Mr. Metwick was here to escort them."

"And Lady Tara, did she leave with her mother?" He had little reason to believe she had stayed behind, not with her father missing, but he held enough hope to ask.

"She left before them, my lord. She was informed by Mr. Metwick that First Lieutenant Degraw was among the wounded and insisted on riding ahead by horseback. She said it was faster and that she needed to reach the first lieutenant as quickly as possible."

"On horseback? You allowed her leave on horseback? Did she ride out alone?" Gavin was livid. His concern for Tara vied with anger over her hasty departure.

Rollins' face fell, dread plain in his eyes. "I sent a guard with her. He has already returned and reports she arrived safely at the villa. You told me to do whatever they asked, my lord."

The knowledge that Gavin had inadvertently contributed to her departure only added to his anger. It was another example of unanticipated consequences created by total submission to his demands. He also knew it made no difference, not in the end. He had vowed she would be allowed to leave, if that was what she wanted to do, and that was exactly what she did.

"Did she say anything else? Did she leave me a message?"

"No, my lord, no message for you. Do you want me to send word that you've returned?" Rollins' brow furrowed with worry.

"No. That's not necessary. I'll be contacting General Gregerson with closing reports. It can wait until then." Lord Gavin dismissed Rollins with a wave of his hand. He wanted to be alone.

His initial fear for her safety slowly dissipated into dismal regret. Apparently, Lady Tara's first obligation was to Loclyn Degraw, the General's blasted first lieutenant. Without a word, she had left in haste as soon as she heard Degraw was wounded. It was a stinging blow.

Her departure disappointed him more than he wanted to admit, but Gavin refused to do anything to sway her decision. The choice was hers to make. He had been hoping against logic that she would be there to meet him, but somewhere in the back of his mind he had known this was inevitable. He had always known that sooner or later she was destined to leave him.

Perhaps it was best it happened now. If she had stayed, she would have become just another compliant mistress unable to utter a word of disagreement, unable to voice her own opinion. He couldn't do that to her. He admired her wit and intelligence too much to threaten their existence.

As much as it pained him, the right thing to do—the only thing he could do—was to let her go.

CHAPTER 15

General Gregerson's butler met Tara as she stormed through the gates of the villa. "Loclyn, where's Loclyn?" she shouted at him.

"He's over at the workhouse. They've turned it into an infirmary. All the wounded soldiers have been taken there," Parker informed her. Frowning, he cast a judgmental look at her unusual attire. She didn't care. A proper riding habit would have been too much of a hindrance at a time like this.

Though she was weary from her long ride, she rushed across the graveled courtyard to the distant workhouse, grateful for the freedom of breeches. She needed reassurance that her cousin was alive and well.

Several wounded soldiers were laid out on two rows of cots lining the walls of the workhouse. She spied an older man who appeared to be a doctor. Silver streaks painted his jet black hair. His shirt sleeves were rolled up to his elbows and he wore a blood spattered apron as he tended to the wounded, assisted by a younger man.

"Loclyn, First Lieutenant Degraw, do you know where he is?" she asked.

"He's near the end, you'll find him down there," the younger man answered. He pointed to the far side of the building.

She rushed down the row of wounded, checking their faces. Over and over again she saw pain, exhaustion, and despair. They were haggard looking men in ragged clothing, stained by dirt and grime from the battlefield, and blood from their injuries. This was what war brought. There was little glory to this.

She found Loclyn near the end of the row as the doctor's assistant had indicated. He was asleep, but even in slumber his face was distorted with pain. The blood-soaked bandage on his right shoulder signaled the depth of his injuries. A layer of filth clung to his clothes. His unshaved chin contrasted with the pallor of his skin, and dark circles framed his lidded eyes. Sweat and blood matted his hair, masking his blond curls.

Her hand reached out to touch him. His skin felt cold and clammy. "Loclyn," she whispered, breaking into a sob. It pained her to see her cousin's wrecked body. She dropped to her knees beside the cot, crying.

"I think he'll live." A man's voice startled her. She turned to see the doctor. His assistant stood nearby holding a foot stool.

"Here Miss, this may help." The younger man held the stool out to her, unable to meet her eyes. He was obviously uncomfortable with her display of emotion.

She rose from her knees and wiped her eyes. Gratefully accepting the stool, she set it down beside Loclyn's cot. "How bad is he?" she asked, hoping the doctor would tell her the truth, even though she was afraid to know.

"We've removed the bullet from his shoulder and hope to avoid infection. The wound was clean, but his left hip was seriously injured when he was thrown from his horse. It doesn't look broken, but it's too soon to tell. It'll be a long time before he can walk again, but hopefully he will."

"What do you mean, hopefully?" Tara asked.

"Like I said, it's too soon to tell, but the swelling doesn't look good." The doctor squarely met her gaze. "Are you family?"

Tara didn't hesitate. "I'm his cousin, Lady Tara Zanders."

For the first time since their meeting the doctor took stock of her manly breeches. His eyes raked over her body from head to toe. Whatever judgment he made, he kept it to himself. "We need all the help we can get. Are you able to lend a hand?"

"I'll do whatever I can. I'm staying at the villa. I'm General Gregerson's niece."

"That's fine. You can start now. At least you're dressed for work. We need to keep this place clean. You can start by giving your cousin a bath."

Her eyes widened and her jaw dropped. Shocking images of the doctor's suggestion poured over her.

"A sponge bath, I dare say, nothing more. Davy will show you the way." The doctor gestured over his shoulder to his assistant. "Start with Degraw and keep on working. They all need to be cleaned and tended. War does its best to kill them. I can only do my best to keep them alive." The doctor turned and walked away with a sad shake of his head.

Tara turned to look at Davy. She wasn't sure if his fearful expression was due to her presence or the daunting task they'd been assigned. Either way, she figured the best course of action was to get to work. "We'll need water, fresh rags, and buckets. Do you know where we can find these things?" she asked him.

"Yes, Miss. Follow me." The call to action put the young man at ease. She followed him to a storage locker where he helped her gather fresh linens. Davy took the empty buckets out to the well, filled them, and hauled them back inside the work house. It was an exercise he would repeat several times before the day was done.

As the doctor suggested, they started with Loclyn, wiping the dirt, grime, and blood from his face, hands, and body as best they could without causing him unnecessary pain. They kept going until they reached the end of the row. She had taken extra care with her cousin and went on to apply the same loving care to all of the men. They were all someone's brother, son, or husband. They all deserved to be treated with kindness.

By the end of the day she was bone-weary, filthy dirty, and smelled like a stink-hole. She was too tired to join her family for dinner. Instead she took a hot bath and asked to have a tray of food sent to her room.

As Tara was preparing for bed, Lady Chandra entered her room. Shadows darkened her smoke-grey eyes, betraying her weary sadness. Her shoulders slumped with fatigue. Though well-schooled in the art of deception, her mother couldn't hide her concern for her husband. "We've still no word on your father," she said.

"He must be found. We cannot lose him." The exhaustion of the day got the better of Tara and tears spilled from her eyes.

"Now Tara, there's no need to worry so. Keep in mind, your father is a sly one. I have every hope he will be found. Iain has men looking for him." Lady Chandra sat next to Tara and pulled her into her arms, comforting her. "How is Loclyn doing?"

"He's badly wounded, but the doctor says he'll recover. There's some question about him being able to walk again. His leg was badly injured. He may have to leave Uncle Iain's service."

"Your uncle would never send Loclyn away. He'll always have a home here."

"I can't imagine Loclyn being anything less than whole. I can't imagine Father being gone."

"Then don't. Imagine the best. Believe in the best, and keep believing until you're proven right." Lady Chandra rubbed her hands up and down Tara's back, massaging her aching muscles.

"I don't know how you do it, Mother. How do you keep believing, even when everything seems lost?"

Lady Chandra gave her daughter a weak smile. "It's the only way to keep going. It would be too much to bear if I didn't."

Tara sat snuggled in her mother's arms, grateful for her comforting presence. It wasn't long before a loud commotion from downstairs drew their attention. They could hear Darren shouting in the entrance hall. "It's Lord Tyrus. He's returned."

Jumping up, hand-in-hand, Tara and her mother rushed to the hallway. Lord Tyrus came bounding up the staircase, taking the steps two at a time. Lady Chandra flew into his arms. He picked her up and spun her around. As they came to a stop, Tara threw her arms around them both, crying with happiness. Her father was dirty and smelly, but the sight of him was better than presents at Christmas.

"Is this any way to greet a man returning from battle?" Lord Tyrus teased, smiling broadly at his wife and daughter.

"I'm sure it's highly improper," Lady Chandra laughed through her tears.

"You're all right." Tara hugged him tightly. "Where have you been?"

"Fact-finding, my dear. Fact-finding, of course." He pulled away from Lady Chandra and Tara so he could see their faces. "We need to return to England. I need to report to the King."

"We can't leave now. Loclyn's been hurt," Tara said.

"I know, I saw him in the infirmary, but in a few days, after everything's settled. I need to report to King George. There's a new military leader making waves in France, General Napoleon Bonaparte."

CHAPTER 16

Tara busied herself by helping the doctor, doing all she could to comfort the men in his care. Each day she rose with the sun and went to bed by candle light, falling into an exhausted slumber. She checked on Loclyn several times each day. He was showing signs of improvement but his wounds were serious and he was unable to rise from his bed. A slight fever had come and gone, but the doctor expected it would be days, perhaps weeks, before his leg fully recovered. Tara asked to have Loclyn moved into the villa, but he insisted on staying in the make-shift infirmary with the rest of the wounded soldiers.

On the fourth day, he surprised her beyond all expectations when she found him miraculously standing beside his cot, tucking his shirt into his trousers. "What are you doing? You shouldn't be up!" She rushed to his side.

He reached for his jacket and Tara instinctively held it out for him to slip over his arms. "Believe it or not, I feel quite well," he said, doing up the buttons on his military jacket.

"How can that be? Yesterday you could barely move."

"I can only guess. I don't know if I was delusional or dreaming, but last night, I believe I saw Tazire."

"Grand Papa? He was here? Why haven't I seen him?"

"Perhaps I was dreaming, but I'm fairly certain Tazire paid me a visit, and now I feel fine. I can't explain it, but as you can see, I am up and walking." He linked her arm over his and headed for the villa.

She stamped her foot. "Darn! I wish I had known he was here. I need to talk with him." Tara had questions only her Grand Papa could answer. She also knew he would only provide answers of his choosing when the time was right.

Loclyn chuckled. "You know Tazire. He comes and goes as he pleases. He's a mysterious one."

Tara nodded. She understood perfectly well. "I suppose this means we'll be returning to London soon. Father wants to get back to report to King George. Will you be staying here?"

"General Gregerson has invited me to stay at the villa as long as I want. I suspect his generous offer was prompted more by my inability to leave than a true need for my services. But he assures me my assistance during the battle was quiet valuable. For the time being, I expect I will stay." He walked steady at her side without a trace of a limp.

"I noticed Patrice visited you yesterday. Does she have anything to do with your decision to stay?"

Loclyn grinned, looking pleased. "She has everything to do with my decision. Can you blame me?"

"Oh, Loclyn, I'm happy for you." She squeezed his arm with affection, but worried she may have caused him pain, immediately soften her grip, pulling away.

"It's all right. I assure you, I'm in no pain." Loclyn retrieved her hand and replaced it in the crook of his arm.

For the first time in days, Tara allowed herself to think about Lord Gavin. She wondered why she had not heard from him since she returned to the villa. While she was attending to the wounded, she had pushed thoughts of him aside, preferring to focus on the soldier's needs rather than her own. Now that Loclyn was fully recovered, and fewer men needed her care, her mind was able to indulge in speculation.

When she had last seen Lord Gavin at the castle, she felt certain he cared for her. Everything about their parting kiss confirmed her belief. Throughout her stay at the castle, every communiqué from the duke had included a personal message to her. Usually it was no more than a line or two, but she had grown accustomed to receiving his letters.

Now, even though the battle was over, she had received no word from him. He had not asked to see her or even asked if she was well. In fact, since she had returned to the villa, he had not sent her any message at all. She knew Lord Gavin was back at the castle in Maninberg, and that he was still communicating with Uncle Iain. She also knew her uncle had informed the duke of their status. So if he knew she had returned to the villa, why hadn't he sent her a message? It was as if he suddenly just abandoned her, and she didn't know why.

~*~

Tara sat at the window in her room, her head resting against the glass as she looked out over the vineyards and the valley below. Cold air from outside seeped in through the window, chilling her skin. The warmth of the fading sunlight was quickly being replaced by the deep, dark, chill of night. In the far distance, she could faintly see the silhouette of Wessington manor. If Lord Gavin was there, she could no longer feel him.

A soft knock on the door drew her attention as her mother quietly entered the room. "Here you are. I've not seen you all day. I've come to tell you that your father and I will be leaving in the morning. Will you be coming with us?"

Tara sighed heavily. "No, I think not. I'm not ready to leave. Marina has asked me to stay while she is carrying. Loclyn is also staying." Her voice sounded foreign to her ears, as if someone else was talking.

"Yes, Iain told me. His recovery is quite amazing, one could even say miraculous." Her mother picked up a brush from the dresser and began stroking Tara's long blond hair.

"Did he tell you he thinks Grand Papa had something to do with it?" Tara felt comforted by her mother's gentle gesture of affection.

"Tazire? It doesn't surprise me. He has his ways, you know." Lady Chandra pulled the brush slowly through Tara's hair to remove any lingering tangles.

"Yes, I know." Tara returned her gaze to the view outside her window. Darkness had settled in and she could no longer see the distant hillside.

Her mother stopped her brushing and looked at Tara. "Are you feeling alright?"

Tara could muster no more than a sad smile. "I haven't been sleeping well."

"Tell me what's wrong. Maybe I can help."

Tara cast her eyes downward. "I was weaving dreams, hoping to see Lord Gavin. He hasn't appeared."

Her mother breathed deeply, noticeably stiffening her spine. "I see. Have you been doing this for long?"

"Only since Locyln's recovery. Before that I was too tired and focused on Locyln and the other wounded."

"Was this your only attempt to weave Lord Gavin into your dreams?"

Tara understood her mother's question and heard the concern in her voice. "No. There were several times before when I was able to see him in my dreams. It was grand. But ever since the battle, I feel I've lost our connection."

"I understand you've not heard from him, that there have been no messages."

"None for me. I know he's been communicating with Uncle Iain, but I've heard nothing. Perhaps I should go to him." Tara watched for her mother's reaction reflected in the darken window panes.

"No. You cannot. He has not sent for you." Lady Chandra's voice was firm, leaving little room for argument.

Tara turned to face her mother. "But I need to see him. I don't care if it's proper or not. I need to see him."

"Tara, this is not about what's proper. This is about what's best for you and your heart."

"What if I don't agree?"

"If the duke wanted to see you, he would have sent for you. He knows where you are. He has been informed. Think about it. His silence speaks loudly."

Tara stood and stepped away. "No, I can't believe that. The last time I saw him, at the castle, he told me he wanted me safe. He . . . he let me know he cared, that I was important to him.

"And yet you've not heard from him since. Not since you've come back to tend to Loclyn."

Tara looked at her mother, searching her face. Love shone in her mother's eyes, along with something else. There was a sense of sadness Tara had not seen before.

Her mother spoke. "You're beautiful Tara, amazingly beautiful. To my eyes, perfect. Your beauty radiates from within. It's part of your sweet, gentle nature, even if it is spiced with strong opinions. But my darling, you're the queen of wishful thinking. That's why this rejection is so hard for you."

Tara shook her head, not wanting to hear. "How can he abandon me like this, without even a word? I don't believe it. I can't." Tears gathered in Tara's eyes. She sniffed, trying to hold them inside.

"He's the ruler of his kingdom, the grand duke of Maninberg. He can do as he pleases."

"How can you say such a thing? How could he be so cruel?" A tear slid down her cheek.

Lady Chandra stood and gathered Tara into her arms, embracing her fully grown daughter as if she were still a small child. "I know this hurts, Tara. Really I do. I wish I had some magical words I could say to take it all away, but I don't. Life brings joy and pain, and both bring blessings in their own way. Trust me, the gift hidden in your disappointment may take longer to unwrap, longer to be revealed, but pain does have its blessings."

"That's not how it feels, Mother. Right now, that's not how it feels at all." Tara swiped her hands across her face, attempting to dry the tears streaming down her checks.

"I know, darling, I know. Right now all you feel is pain. Go ahead, darling, let yourself cry. The blessings will come later."

Lady Chandra held Tara, stroking her hair and patting her back, while Tara sobbed in her arms until she felt exhausted and drained. If nothing else, Tara knew she was loved and supported by her mother, and for that, she was deeply grateful.

~*~

Lord Tyrus and Lady Chandra were preparing to leave the villa. Their bags were packed and loaded on their carriage. All that was left were good-byes.

"Are you sure you don't want to come with us? We've plenty of room," Lady Chandra asked Tara once again. Her lips were pressed into a thin, unsure smile, and her eyes were darkened with sadness.

Tara understood. Her mother didn't want to leave her like this, but Tara knew she needed to stay. She had unfinished business. "I assure you Mother, I'm fine. I'm surrounded by family."

"When will you return to London?"

"Marina has asked me to stay until the baby is born and I told her I would. Loclyn has offered to escort me back to London whenever I want to go. I'll be fine."

Even though it was the truth, she knew it was also a convenient excuse. She was staying because she hoped to see Lord Gavin, hoping that sooner or later he would contact her. She was grateful her mother had given her a shoulder to cry on, but now she needed to carry on. She gathered her wits and put on a brave face.

"Only if you're sure." Lady Chandra stood near the open door of the carriage, her hands clasped before her. She seemed hesitant to leave her daughter behind.

Tara forced a bright smile, as bright as she could manage, trying to give her mother reassurance. "I've been to Egypt and back, Mother. I've crossed the Atlantic Ocean. I'll be fine here with Uncle Iain. He is your brother."

"Yes, all right then, we must be off." Lady Chandra resumed her usual brave expression, clear eyed with a serene smile. She gave Tara a parting embrace and kissed her cheek before stepping into the carriage. Fighting back her own tears, Tara admired her mother's self-control.

Tara's father pulled her to his side, giving her a kiss upon her cheek. "I have perfect faith in you, my darling. You may be impetuous, but you're still my daughter, strong willed and determined. I trust you to have a level head when needed. I know you'll do the right thing, whatever that may be."

"Oh, thank you, Father. I so appreciate your support." She gave him one last hug before he joined his wife in the carriage.

With a brave smile, Tara waved as her parents rode away. As she lingered to watch her parents' coach disappear down the drive of the villa, Loclyn stepped across the graveled lane to stand by her side.

"How did that go?" he asked as they turned to head back inside the villa.

"Well enough. For a moment I thought Mother was going to insist I leave with them. She's worried I'll do something foolish, like contacting Lord Gavin." Tara shrugged her shoulders followed by a shake of her head.

"Do you really think that's foolish?" He followed her into the front salon where they could speak in private.

"Honestly, I'm not sure. I don't know what to think. I haven't heard from him since I left Maninberg." Smoothing her skirts, she took a seat on a rose-colored settee. Loclyn sat down beside her.

"Do you have any idea why?" Loclyn reached for her hand, stroking the backside.

"Maybe because I left in such haste, without leaving a message. When I heard you were injured, I left as fast as I could. I couldn't think of anything else."

"What does your heart tell you?"

Tara cocked her head, giving him a puzzled look. "I don't know if it's my heart or my head, but I feel as though I need to contact Lord Gavin. I tell myself it's only because I can't walk away without knowing what happened. I'm hoping he'll tell me."

Tara had never been one to walk away from a project or endeavor once begun. Whether it was learning how to dig for artifacts in Egypt or scouting for ancient texts in Rome, she had always given her assignments her full attention, at least until the next project caught her eye, but she never left a job undone. She had no desire to be with a man who didn't want to be with her, but her innate standards of human decency demanded he give her the benefit of an explanation, or at least a final farewell.

"Then you should contact him. You should know what happened. At least give him a chance to tell his side of the story."

"That isn't what you said last time." She recalled Locyln's previous harsh judgment of Lord Gavin. "Last time you wanted me to stay away, afraid he wouldn't do right by me."

"Things can change."

"Really?" Tara gave him a half-hearted smile.

Loclyn's expression turned serious. "After the battle, after I had been shot and thrown from my horse, there was a time when I thought I might die. It's true what they say about a dying man. I saw life differently. My first regret was that I hadn't told Patrice how I feel about her. I feared I might die and never have an opportunity. That she was lost to me forever."

Tara reached for his arm. "Oh, Loclyn. I had no idea."

"That was the problem, neither did she. I was encouraged when she came to see me. I made sure she knew. I told her plain that I wanted to see her again."

"Did you ask her to marry you?" Tara's eyes opened wide.

"No, I didn't want her to take pity on an injured man. I wanted to wait until I was healthy and whole to court her. She's the reason I'm staying."

"I'm so happy for you." Tara smiled, hugging her cousin.

"I will admit, I haven't always thought highly of the duke. I judged him to be royally pompous, at times arrogant, and usually self-important. I have found I was wrong. We couldn't have won that battle without his support. It's true, he refused to join us on the battlefield, and at first I judged him harshly for that. I thought he was choosing to remain safely ensconced within his kingdom."

"Oh no, Loclyn, you mustn't. I'm sure he had his reasons." Tara interrupted, knowing perfectly well what his reasons were.

Loclyn held up his hand, waving off her concern as he continued. "I soon realized he was doing everything he could to ensure our success. He set up a command post at Wessington and sent us supplies, everything the general requested and more. He kept the lines of communication open between General Gregerson and his family, and he sent men to look for your father when he was missing. Never throughout the battle did his support fail us. He could have waited until the rebels were at his borders. He had more than enough men and armaments to defeat them. He didn't need our help, we needed his. His only gain was to see his neighbors protected against an invading force."

Tara had watched Loclyn intently as he told his tale. Now her eyes sought the floor, looking for a hole she could crawl into. "The thanks I gave him was my hasty departure, without even a word. It must have looked as though I was the one abandoning him."

"Don't be so hard on yourself. I'm sure he knows of our kinship."

"How could he? I've said nothing about you. I didn't feel the need."

Loclyn frowned, his previously pleasant expression turning dismal. "If that's true, he could easily believe you left to be with me, not because I'm your cousin and think of you as my little sister, but because I'm your lover."

Tara drew back, appalled. "Oh, no, he couldn't."

"Oh, yes, he could. Men love to believe the worst with it comes to the women we care about. We'd rather be silent and wrong, than risk speaking out and appearing foolish."

"That's awful." *And stupid.*

"It's true," Loclyn stated. "I've often thought that's what happened to your Captain Millhouse."

"I don't understand."

"Millhouse obviously wanted to travel, but I don't think he ever believed you'd be willing to leave your family or your home in Scotland. Rather than risk your rejection, he simply choose to take assignments that took him out of the country."

"That's ridiculous," Tara huffed. "I love to travel."

"How was he to know? Did you ever offer to join him in India?"

"No, of course not, we weren't married. But I traveled to Spain while we were still engaged."

"Yes, with your parents. But visiting the court in Spain is far different than being the wife of an army captain stationed in India.

Besides, by then, he had already accepted the assignment in Russia."

Loclyn was right. Men were a pig-headed lot. It was time she took control.

Tara stood abruptly. "I must send Lord Gavin a message. I need to set things right." She started to walk away, heading for her room.

Loclyn stood also. "What are you going to say?" he called after her.

She paused at the doorway. "I don't know. I'm sure I'll think of something."

Tara had wasted enough time, she could wait no longer. She immediately requested a messenger be sent to Maninberg with her letter for the duke. Her note was short and simple, and she hoped effective.

Lord Gavin,

I will be at the gazebo in Wiltzer Park tomorrow at noon. Please meet me there.

Lady Tara Zanders

She had no way of knowing for certain if he would be there. She had not asked for a reply, or even an acknowledgement, only his presence.

CHAPTER 17

G avin read over the message again and again, hoping to find some hidden meaning. He could detect nothing. She had given no clue as to why she wanted to see him. She made no mention of wanting to return to Maninberg, nor did she give any excuse for her hasty departure. The letter had been delivered without even a request for a reply. It appeared she was the one making the demands.

For weeks he had been hoping she would return, knowing all the while she was with that damned Degraw, and now this was the message she sent.

He crumpled the letter in his hand, ready to discard her request, when he thought differently. It was time he put an end to their charade and stop longing for a relationship that held no future. He owed her the honor and respect of explaining his actions, or inactions, as was the case. It was only fitting he should meet her at the park, at the gazebo he had erected in her honor.

Somehow, he had always known the gazebo was where they would say their good-byes.

~*~

The next morning Tara dressed in her finest day dress, a pale yellow gown with rich velvet trim. She had one of the maids arrange her hair in an attractive style, with golden curls cascading down her back. And once again she chose her plum colored cloak, the one she had worn to his dinner party when he had first kissed her. She knew much of her preparation was sentimental and frivolous, but she hoped to present the appearance of a desirable woman.

Loclyn had offered to ride to Larinda with her, and she was grateful for his moral support, but respectfully declined his offer. This was something she needed to face alone. She was challenging herself to step off a ledge, to take a leap of faith, and to trust in her feelings. She would risk taking the fall. All of her worldly travels were nothing compared to exposing her heart to rejection once again.

She arrived early, wondering if he would be there waiting for her. He wasn't. She could see the gazebo was empty as the carriage pulled to stop at the entrance to the park.

After stepping down from the carriage, she turned to the driver. "You may return to the village to wait for me there. I will send for you when I'm ready to leave," she informed him. She didn't want him waiting within sight. She wanted a private moment alone with Lord Gavin without the encumbrance of a waiting carriage.

"As you wish, my lady." He gave a hee-haw to the team and left her standing alone.

She pulled out her locket watch and checked the time. It was still ten minutes before the hour. She did her best to control her nervous quivering, and slowly mounted the steps of the gazebo. Taking a seat on one of the plush cushions, she told herself to be brave. Still, she couldn't shake the feeling of dread that they would be saying their last good-byes here at the gazebo. That wasn't how she wanted it to end, but feared the outcome was out of her hands.

At the appointed hour he arrived and her trembling increased. He rode up on a dark black stallion at a leisurely gait, sitting tall in the saddle. He appeared so confident, so fully in control of his emotions, as if he hadn't a care in the world. He certainly didn't appear to be as nervous as she felt. He mounted the steps of the gazebo but did not approach her.

"Lord Gavin, I'm honored you accepted my request for a meeting." She stood to greet him, her hands clasped together in front of her trying to hold them steady. When that didn't work, she clutched them to her sides.

"You left me with little choice. It was the only polite thing to do." His voice was flat, as if drained of emotion. This wasn't at all like the man she had last seen at the Maninberg castle, the man who had kissed her with such deep desire. This felt more like the man who had dismissed her so abruptly from the sculpture garden.

Tara lifted her chin. "I had hoped to hear from you, after I returned to the villa, but you didn't contact me. Why have I not heard from you?"

"It was your choice to leave the castle." Steely eyed, he did not attempt to hide his anger.

Or was it disappointment? Looking deeper, below his hardened mask, she believed she saw pain. At least that's what she wanted to believe. She could only hope she wasn't being misled once again by her foolish desires.

"Have I been deceived? Do you not care?" She held her breathe in anticipation of his answer.

His eyes held hers, but his shoulders sagged ever so slightly. He spoke low, barely above a whisper. "You know I do."

A candle-like flame flickered in her chest. It gave her hope. "Then why did you not contact me?"

"I left it up to you."

"I don't understand." Her hands flashed with irritation. "Why do you act like this? One moment you show me you care and the next you're as cold as a fish in winter. Have I been a fool to believe you ever cared?" She couldn't understand how he could stand there, appearing nearly lifeless, devoid of emotion, while her feelings surged through her with such heart-wrenching force.

He stood motionless for a long moment. She feared the worst.

Finally he spoke, speaking slowly, as if carefully choosing his words. "I will agree to answer your questions and tell you everything you want to know, if you will agree to stand over there on the road to Larinda." Lord Gavin turned and pointed at the village path.

"You mean outside of your kingdom? You want me to stand outside your kingdom before you will answer me?" Tara furrowed her brow, wondering why that would make any difference. Did he have the ability to lock her out?

Lord Gavin looked stunned. "You know where my border lies?"

It was time for some truth-telling. "If you mean the magical wall surrounding your kingdom, then yes, I do."

His dazed expression told her she had scored a direct hit.

She left the gazebo and marched toward the invisible wall. As always, when she crossed over his kingdom's border, she saw the sparks of light dance around her. She took another full step, and then turned to face him.

He followed her down the steps of the gazebo and then stopped, still well inside his kingdom. "How – when?" Emotion had returned to his voice. His face lit with amazement, visibly stunned by her revelation.

"Nearly from the beginning. I suspected there was something unusual about Maninberg when I visited your castle for the ball. I confirmed it that first day here at the park. I can't see the wall unless I touch it. Then lights are released, like tiny sparks or embers from a flame. It only happens when I touch it or cross your border." She held her hand up to the unseen wall and watched the sparks of light dance about her fingers.

"I cannot see the lights you describe. I see nothing, but I know exactly where my border lies. Does it hurt?"

"No, I feel nothing. Though I'll admit, it's rather strange." *No stranger than being a dream weaver, or the great-granddaughter of a wizard.*

"You knew, and yet you didn't say anything?" Frustration seeped into his voice, or maybe it was anger. His eyes became small and focused.

"No, and neither did you," Tara defended herself. "From what I could see, I reasoned you are imprisoned behind this wall, unable to pass through it, unable to leave. Am I right?"

Lord Gavin gave a curt nod. "Correct. I can never leave."

Tara gasped. Though she had expected as much, his confirmation stunned her. "Why? What have you done to deserve this punishment?"

Lord Gavin's lips became a pale, thin line as his face hardened with pride.

"You said you would answer my questions," she reminded him.

"I did not always consider this to be a punishment, or imprisonment, as you so aptly called it. When the spell was cast I believed it to be an answer to my prayers. My kingdom was at war. We were engaged in a battle we could not win. I prayed – no, I demanded, to claim my birth-right, seeking control of my kingdom and all the people who lived here. A great wizard appeared and granted my request." He paused.

"Was it Tazire?" she asked.

"Yes. Do you know of him?"

She bit back her smile. "I am familiar with his reputation. Please, do go on."

He breathed deeply before speaking. "There were certain conditions that accompanied the spell. I was granted complete and total control over my kingdom in exchange for accepting immortality. I thought it was the most magnificent blessing possible, the ultimate fulfillment of my grand desires, to live forever with complete control. However, there were consequences to my demands, consequences which I hadn't considered. It wasn't until later that I discovered I am absolutely, positively, and completely limited to inhabiting this domain, and only this domain, always and forever, for as long as I shall live. As you have seen, I cannot leave."

Tara forcefully held herself from taking a step back.

"You said you were given immortality. How do you know?" She was tempted to judge him for his past mistakes, but a part of her ached for him. He was paying dearly for his youthful arrogance.

"The battle I speak of happened when I was thirty years old, nearly one hundred years ago."

She stared at him, her eyes frozen. "You're telling me you're one hundred and thirty years old?" She could scarcely believe it.

"That is correct."

"And all this time, you've been unable to leave Maninberg?"

"Correct. I have tried many times, in many ways. All have failed."

Her heart sank, like a stone tossed away into a murky pond. She didn't know what to feel. It was too much to take in. Although her suspicions were correct, this was not what she had expected. There was pain for him, but also outrage, anger, and betrayal at his deception. It was too much too fast. She needed time to digest what he had told her, to see if she could make sense of it all. Already her mind was working to sort through his story, trying to understand what could have prompted him to act so rashly and what he had gone through. She needed time to think through this, and apparently time was the one thing Lord Gavin had an abundance of.

"You've been imprisoned for one hundred years? And you do not grow old? I'm sorry, but this isn't what I expected. I need time to think this all through." She began pacing back and forth outside the wall, looking from the ground, to Lord Gavin, and back to the ground again. "Right now, I don't know what to think, but I think I need time." Tara shook her head, annoyed with herself, knowing she sounded like a babbling idiot.

"Understandable," he offered calmly. "I've had years to deal with my condition. This can't be easy for you."

Tara stopped her pacing. "Your condition! Is that what you call it? Your condition?"

"I am sure you could come up with any number of ways to label my life."

"Oh, I'm sure I could." Spitting mad, and totally confused, Tara turned to walk away, determined to return to the village to seek out her driver. She took a few steps then paused and looked back. "I think I should go now."

"Yes, of course." Lord Gavin stoically stood his ground, unmoving. Of course. Where could he go?

She stepped away, and then paused again to look back at him. Even his pride could not mask the sadness in his eyes. "Is there anything else I should know? Why did you ask me to stand outside your kingdom before you told me about this?" A thought suddenly occurred to her. "Have you locked me out?"

"Not quite. As I said, I have complete and total control of my kingdom and all the people who reside here. If you are within my borders you cannot refuse any request I make. It is beyond your control."

"I don't believe you." She was incredulous. She thought back over all their times together, recalling all their conversations. Not once had she felt as if her actions were out of her control. Never had she acted in a manner which was not her own, nor had she ever felt compelled to do so.

"If you were standing here and I asked you to believe me, you would," he responded with complete confidence. "And if I asked you to stay, you could not leave."

She considered his predicament. It was truly a chilling thought. To think he could ask for anything, anything at all, and it would be granted was daunting. To know all the people around him had no choice but to obey his will was intimidating and somewhat frightening. It also explained why he had so adamantly refused to ask her to stay. Why he had never asked her to return to Maninberg. Why he had never asked her for anything.

"For now, I will take your word on the matter," she said.

"As well you should," he agreed.

She started to walk away, but again she stopped. She turned to face him. "I'd like to see it for myself."

"What do you mean?" He drew back in surprise.

"I want to see if you can truly make me do anything you ask."

"You want to feel the effects of the spell?"

"Yes," she nodded. "But first, I must ask you to promise, as a man of honor, that you will not ask me to stay against my will or do anything improper." She felt it was a reasonable and even sensible request.

He solemnly raised his right hand. "I, Lord Gavin Richard Montague, as a man of honor, give you my word I will not ask you to stay against your will or do anything improper. I will not ask you to do anything that you should not do." He finished by placing his hand over his heart.

Satisfied with his declaration, she watched the sparks dance about her as she walked back across his boundary. She took three more steps into his kingdom, and stood before him. "Make a request of me," she stated boldly.

"Slap me," he ordered.

"Excuse me?" She couldn't believe she had heard him correctly, or that he would say such a thing.

He repeated the demand, loud and clear. "Slap me. Slap my face."

She was about to refuse when she was suddenly overcome by a new thought, a new emotion. An impulse surged through her body so strong she could not deny it. The desire took control, replacing her initial reaction of denial with something new, powerful, and exciting. She felt its power, and the impulse could not be denied. She quickly raised her hand above his face and brought it down in a swift cutting motion.

It ended with the lightest touch as her fingers danced across his cheek in a playful caress.

A sly and rather mischievous smile crept into the corners of her lips. "Is this what you had in mind, my lord?" she asked, her smile growing wider.

His expression jolted from bland detachment to stunned surprise. "I cannot believe . . ." His voice trailed off.

"Did you not ask for my hand to grace your face, my lord?" She thoroughly enjoyed the moment as her fingers continued their playful assault upon his skin.

His eyes were wide. "Do not touch me," he spoke, his voice firm and clear.

She understood him well this time, understood what he was attempting to prove. Suddenly everything fell into place and she knew exactly what she should do. She stepped closer and kissed him full upon his mouth.

~~

His resolve broke, shattered by her simple acts of defiance. He had no rule over her, no control over her actions. She was free to act as she chose. He wrapped his arms around her, holding her tight, deepening the kiss. She melted into his embrace, showing him the full power of her passion.

"You can deny me?" He was still reeling in shock. After a hundred years of unquestionable authority over everyone he encountered it was still too much to believe, too much to hope for. Had she broken the spell?

"I can do whatever I want." She kissed him again. Laughter bubbled up from inside her.

Gavin buried himself in her embrace, lost in his joy and desire. Had she broken the spell? Could she free him from his cage? It didn't matter. She had acted of her own free will, and she had kissed him.

Suddenly, a bird screeched, pulling him back from his bliss as he detected a disturbance in the upper reaches of the gazebo. A large grey owl sat nestled in the eves. It ruffled its feathers and spread its wings, swooping out of the building to gain his full attention. The owl flew over to the lawn, setting down near the garden path.

"I've seen that owl before," Gavin said, pointing out the bird to Tara.

"I have too," she replied.

With a puff of smoke, the owl transformed and Tazire appeared. "It is done," he said to them.

Tara giggled. "A rather grand entrance, don't you think, Grand Papa?"

"Lovely to see you also, my jewel," Tazire greeted Lady Tara.

Lord Gavin turned to Tara with eyes wide and mouth agape. "Grand Papa? You know this man?"

"Yes, I do," she said, with an unapologetic look of guilt.

"Tazire is your Grand Papa? You're the granddaughter of a wizard?" Lord Gavin asked, unbelieving.

"Actually, he's my great-grandfather." She shrugged. "I expect that's why I can see the magical wall surrounding your kingdom."

"Can you see it now?" Tazire asked her.

"Not right now, Grand Papa. Only if I walk up and touch it," she said.

"I'd like you to show me," Tazire requested.

From the devilish look in the old man's eyes, Gavin suspected the wizard was up to no good. He held on to Tara. "Wait! Is she also now imprisoned?"

"Seriously, lad."

Tara shook off his grasp and walked toward the border. *If Tazire truly is her great-grandfather, surly he will not harm her,* Gavin assured himself. Hesitantly, she stepped up to the magical wall, and then breeched it without stopping. *Thank God, she's still free.* She took several more steps, zigzagging along the path. Finally, she stopped and shrugged.

"I can't find it," she said.

"Lord Gavin, can you find it for her?" Tazire asked.

"I am very much aware of my boundaries," Lord Gavin replied with a heavy sigh.

"Really? Show me," Tazire demanded.

"I have no desire to demonstrate my limitations," Lord Gavin replied. He believed the wizard was playing him for a fool, trying to embarrass him in front of Tara, knowing he would walk smack into the invisible barrier and be repelled.

"Do it for me. Humor an old man." Arms crossed before him, his smile turned serious.

Lord Gavin walked slowly toward his border. His steps faltered as he approached the same section of pathway where Tara was standing. In a slow, steady measure he continued walking, taking one hesitant step, and then another. When he was certain he had stepped beyond the border of his kingdom he turned and looked about, then took several more quick steps further into freedom.

His eyes flash from Tara to Tazire. "What just happened?"

"Obviously, you are no longer confined to your kingdom," Tazire said.

"But why? What prompted you to break the spell?" A mixture of joy and disbelief washed over him as one hundred years of confinement came to an end. He didn't know if he should laugh or cry for joy. His emotions felt suspended in overwhelming confusion, it seemed too good to be true.

"I did not break the spell. You did," Tazire stated plainly.

"How? How did that happen? And why now?" Why, after nearly one hundred years, was he suddenly being set free? Gavin looked at Tara, but she merely shrugged.

"You had some tasks to perform. Hurdles to overcome. Lessons to learn."

"What lessons, what hurdles? I had no idea."

"That was precisely the point. You had to complete the tasks without ever knowing what the requirements were, of your own free will."

"Now that they're done, can you tell me what they were?" Lord Gavin asked.

"Certainly. First, you needed to aid someone outside of your kingdom for no other reason than because they needed your help. It had to be of little or no benefit to you. You did that when you aided General Gregerson and gave refuge to the people of Larinda. You could have waited until the rebels reached your borders, knowing your kingdom was completely safe, but instead you reached out to help your neighbors, protecting them as best you could."

Gavin scowled, feeling chagrin over the wizard's truthful assessment. "It's not as though I've never helped anyone before. I've often been generous and considerate with my subjects. I've always been fair to the merchants of Larinda."

Tazire nodded in agreement. "True, you've been kind to your own subjects, or when it served you. This was the first time you reached beyond your borders to provide assistance to others in need."

Gavin was about to argue that it was the impenetrable wall that had kept his efforts confined to his own kingdom, but as quick as the thought emerged, he knew it was false. The wall hadn't prevented him from reaching out to his neighbors, it had been his pride, and his belief that he was above and beyond those outside his kingdom.

"Second," Tazire continued, "you needed to love someone enough to let them do as they pleased. To let them be in control and accept unconditionally their choices. I needed to see you relinquish your power over them. You had to love someone enough to let them go." Tazire gazed fondly at Lady Tara standing next to him. "You demonstrated this with Tara. You placed her happiness above your own, and accepted her choices at a great cost to your own desires, believing her happiness was more important than yours. You have completed your tasks. The spell is broken. You did it yourself."

"All of it?" Gavin asked.

"All of it. The only one you have any control over is yourself. You are free to leave your kingdom and go wherever you please. And you will age. You will live a natural life and grow old, if you don't kill yourself first. Of course, I expect your subjects will still do as you request for some time. They've grown too accustomed to accepting your authority to change right away. But over time they will begin to question you. They will voice their opinions and perhaps even rebel, if you do not rule them well."

Tara leaned in, clutching her great grandfather's arm as she whispered in his ear. Gavin strained to hear her words. "Grand Papa, he has not yet said he loves me."

Gavin coughed, clearing his throat.

Tazire laughed. "My dear, I know him well. His actions have spoken louder than any words."

Tara blushed and by God, if it wasn't one of the most beautiful sights Gavin had ever seen. He cocked his finger, beckoning her to him. When she reached his side he cupped her face in his hands. "My darling, let it be known throughout my kingdom and beyond, I love you. Now and forever, I love you." And then he kissed her. Wrapping her in his arms, he pressed her to him and held on tight, no longer afraid she couldn't refuse.

Gavin broke their embrace and turned to Tazire. "I have learned my lessons. I assure you I have learned my lessons."

"I believe you have," Tazire said. "But still, I think it's only fair to warn you, I shall be watching.

Gavin chuckled with amusement. "I have no doubts."

Tazire spoke to Tara. "I trust you can handle it from here."

"Yes, Grand Papa. I'll be fine."

The wizard kissed his great-granddaughter sweetly on her forehead and then stepped away. A moment later, he became an owl once again and flew to the skies.

Gavin wanted to cry, to laugh and sing, and dance about. He wanted to fall upon his knees and offer up his gratitude. But he did none of that. He still had enough pride and common sense to behave properly. Certainly, his ego was much smaller than it was before, but it was still enough to keep him standing. Instead, he reached for the one thing he wanted above anything else. He reached for Tara.

Still holding her in his arms, he said, "Now that I know you can deny me . . ."

"And that I have always been acting with my own free will."

"Yes, of your own free will," Gavin agreed.

"Yes," Tara said with sly expectation.

"I'm wondering if you'd like to accompany me back to my castle."

Tara's expression turned thoughtful and she shook her head. "No, I think not."

Gavin's heart skipped a beat as he registered her denial. "No? Do you wish to return to your uncle's villa?" As much as her answer disappointed him, it thrilled him to know she could refuse him.

"Your castle sounds quite nice, but isn't Wessington manor much closer? After all, I think I've waited long enough for you to declare your feelings, do you really want me to wait any longer than needed?"

His smile felt as though it would split his face in two. It was his turn to bow down to her wishes, and he did so gladly. "Wessington manor it is."

~*~

Gavin was consumed by a feeling of youthful expectations. After one hundred years of unconditional control, how did one go about courting an independent woman, much less the great-granddaughter of a wizard? Surely he couldn't just whisk her off to his bed chamber. She would want to be wooed and courted and assured his feelings were true, especially considering how he had doubted her.

Within minutes after their arrival at Wessington, he found his concerns were rather insignificant. He offered her tea and refreshments, which she politely declined, asking instead if he would give her a tour of his home. Her request was completely understandable. If she were to become his wife, an idea that nearly sent him to the moon, it made perfect sense she would want to see her new home.

He had finished showing her all of the public entertaining rooms on the first and second floors, and was about to suggest a walk through the gardens, when she presented him with an astonishingly bold request.

"I think this is all very wonderful and really quite lovely, but I wonder if you wouldn't mind showing me your bed chamber."

"My bed chamber? You want to see my bed chamber?" Had she been reading his mind?

"Yes, if that's not too much to ask. I've often dreamed of how it looks."

"You may ask for anything you want. I am sure I could not deny you." He too had dreamed of her in his bedchamber, visiting him in his dreams.

"I hope that's not true. While mutual agreement is often sought and usually preferred, unconditional control holds no interest for me."

"Yes, so I have learned." He smiled happily.

"Then you don't mind showing me your bed chamber?" she asked again.

He'd be a fool to refuse. "I would be delighted."

He took her hand and led her up the grand staircase to his master bedroom. He paused with his hand on the door handle to give her a chance to change her mind. She stood there with wide-eyed anticipation, waiting. Accepting her silent appeal, he opened the door and let her in.

She stepped inside the room and headed straight for the windows overlooking the terrace, they stretched from floor to ceiling. "It must have a lovely view of the moon at night."

"Why yes, it does. When the moon is full, as it will be tonight, these windows are bathed in the glow of moonbeams."

"Surely bright enough to dance by the light of the moon."

"Correct again."

Her sigh carried lustful longing. "Ahh, it is just as I have dreamed. As *we* have dreamed."

Stark realization settled in. "Then it *was* you."

"Yes, Gavin, I visited you in your dreams. Another one of my talents." She stepped away from the window and into his arms. "Will you dance with me now?"

"It would be my pleasure."

He took her in his arms and suddenly he was surrounded by music. Birds chirped in the trees as the breeze rustled their branches. Curtains fluttered softly at the open windows and off in the distance he heard the mellow sounds of sheep baying in the fields. As she swayed in his arms, he pulled the pins from her hair and let them fall upon the floor with tinkling notes.

Soon he was lost in her flowing blonde hair and pale alabaster skin. He ran his hands through her hair and along her bare shoulders, pushing the sleeves of her gown lower down her arms. Her skin warmed to his touch.

Before he could proceed much further, she halted his progress by placing her hands solidly on his shoulders and bid him to look at her. Her simple gesture reminded him he had not asked for her permission, nor had it been granted. Being with a woman who could accept or deny his affections of her own free will was still new to him and he bristled to think he may have offended her. He was about to ask for her forgiveness when she brought her hands to his cravat.

"Do you mind?" she asked as she began to untie the knot.

"No, not at all," he replied, amused by her daring.

After releasing him from his neckwear, she reached for the top button of his coat. "Do you not find this garment confining?" she asked coyly.

"Yes, quite confining," he agreed. He watched in fascination as she undid the buttons of his coat, one by one, and then removed it from his shoulders, casting it aside. Could it be that the little minx was seducing him?

She ran her hands over the fine silk fabric of his waistcoat. "And this waistcoat, it is most handsome, but would you not be more comfortable without it?"

"Yes, much more comfortable, I'm sure." Though he had seen how shamelessly she had touched the Poseidon statue, he now realized how greatly he had underestimated her abilities, and her boldness.

Following her lead, he rained kisses along the smooth contours of her shoulders, pushing the bodice of her dress even lower so he could caress her breasts. She tilted her head, arching against his touch. Her beautiful firm breasts filled his hands to overflowing.

"You may have believed I am innocent and unschooled in the ways of the world," she said, her voice hushed and breathless.

"Yes, that image has crossed my mind." Although it wasn't the image he was now contemplating.

"While I have never actually been with a man, I can assure you, I know what transpires between a man and a woman."

"Really? How have you come about this information?" He continued to explore her slender neck and shoulders with his lips slipping closer and closer to the erect nipple of her breast.

"In my travels I have heard tales and seen sights typically withheld from the delicate eyes of fragile young women."

"Extraordinary. How fortunate for you."

"Yes. And, I believe, for you."

Oh yes, he could easily see how he was about to reap the benefits of her worldly travels.

"Would you be alarmed if I asked you to help me disrobe?" she asked shamelessly.

He stopped for a moment to smile against her skin. Plain spoken as always. "I'd be more alarmed if you didn't." He reached for the lacings of her gown, loosening them until he was able to slip the garment from her body and let it fall in a puddle upon the floor.

Piece by piece, they undressed each other. She stepped out of her gown, and then removed his shirt. He undid her corset and tossed it aside. Wearing little more than her chemise and stockings, she directed him to sit in an overstuffed armchair and bent before him to pull his boots from his feet. He'd never had a more enticing valet. When she helped him removed his breeches, he could swear she sighed with delight.

He scooped her up in his arms and carried her to his bed. Finally, he would fulfill the longing her dreams had sparked within him. Fueled by the passion she ignited, he wanted to devour her, to wrap himself around her and never let her go. For the first time in years, no, decades, he felt the full force of his passion rushing through his veins, feeding every cell of his being. Savoring the sweet taste of her lips, he claimed her mouth in a fiercely possessive kiss. She was his and only for him.

"You may have traveled the world and seen sights I can only imagine, but today I will be the one to show you the fine art of making love," he whispered as he brushed his lips across her taut nipple.

"Oh my goodness," she gasped, "I certainly hope so."

"My sweet Tara, you are goodness, and light, and love, my darling." He kissed her again, softly teasing her senses into heightened awareness. His hands moved slowly and methodically to explore every curve of her shapely body.

She was everything he had ever wanted in a woman, everything he had ever wanted in his life. He held her close, feeling her need, bursting with a need of his own. When he could wait no longer, when he felt her body crying out for him, he moved to join with her, sinking deep into the soft folds of her welcoming flesh. He felt her body clench and quiver in response to their union and felt the oneness of the bodies united together in sacred passion.

When he awoke, later in the night, he saw the moon shining its light through his open windows, casting its glorious glow upon the polished wood floor. He recalled how he had once compared Tara to a moonbeam, and how, much like a moonlit dream, she had come to shed light on his dark world of shadows and despair.

He turned and brushed a pale strand of hair from Tara's cheek as she slept. Such a beauty. What a thrill it was to wake and find her by his side, not because he had asked and she could not refuse, but because she had chosen—demanded—and who was he to argue with the great-granddaughter of a powerful wizard.

A happy smile curved his lips. It thrilled him to think that, God willing, he would grow old with this woman. The idea was far more appealing than the possibility of living forever, alone.

~*~

Tara gazed around the room at her family and friends, all of them people she loved. She would be leaving soon on another grand adventure, and they had come to see her off. Her parents had come to visit before heading out to France on another fact-finding mission for the Crown. Even her great-grandfather, Tazire, had come to wish her well.

Loclyn sat with Patrice by his side, beaming with joy. Earlier they had announced their plans to marry. Her Uncle Iain and Aunt Jeanine were insisting the wedding be held at the villa instead of the castle, as Lord Gavin had offered. Though the castle was an impressive site, Loclyn and Patrice had respectfully declined in favor of the villa. It was only fitting. It had become Loclyn's home.

Tara gazed down at the babe in her arms. "She's beautiful, don't you agree?" She pulled her eyes away from the sleeping child and looked up at Lord Gavin standing next to her.

His eyes were locked on hers. "So like her mother," he said, not lifting his gaze.

"I believe I'll have to second that," Darren agreed, taking the baby from Tara, "since her mother happens to be my wife." He rubbed a gentle hand over the fine dark hair gracing his daughter's head.

"I'm so glad you stayed until the baby was born. I thought for sure you'd go off on some grand new adventure right after the wedding," Marina said. She sat propped up on a sofa, surrounded by pillows and quilts and looking supremely happy. Marina and Darren had moved into the castle nearly a month ago as they awaited the birth of their child. It allowed them to be close to Tara and the thoroughly modern birthing facility Lord Gavin had installed in the infirmary. Thankfully, Marina had not needed to avail herself of its facilities. With the assistance of her mother, Aunt Jeanine, her delivery had been loud, but relatively easy. It was full of drama, as was the way with Marina, but no unnecessary trauma.

Tara looked at her husband, Lord Gavin Richard Montague, and smiled. "We'll have plenty of time for travel. I was in no hurry to leave Maninberg. Besides, I promised to stay for the birth of your daughter."

Gavin took a seat next to Tara. "You would have thought my lovely wife was tied to Maninberg, the way she refused to leave. Now that Celeste has been properly christened, I believe we can begin our travels."

"I'm sure everything will be fine when you return, although thirty days seems like a long time to be away from your kingdom," Uncle Iain remarked to Lord Gavin.

"Not when I have fine men like you guarding the place. I trust Prime Minster Ballistare, as long as he continues to avail himself of your counsel. You've never steered us wrong. I don't expect you to start just because I'm leaving Maninberg for a few weeks."

Leaving Maninberg. The words sounded sweet to Tara's ears. Not long ago, Lord Gavin had been a prisoner in his own kingdom. Now he was her husband and free to roam the world.

She thought back to the first night she spent at Wessington manor, when she had been brazenly bold in her actions with Lord Gavin. She had practically insisted he take her to bed before he even had a chance to properly court her. She had looked ahead down the road and had known exactly where they were headed. If she had not taken matters into her own hands, it might have taken days, if not weeks, to get where they were going. Such a continued waste of time was simply unacceptable to her.

She considered how Gavin had waited years, perhaps decades, to meet the woman of his dreams. After learning she had been the one he had chosen, she knew precisely what she wanted to do and had immediately set about pursuing her pleasant task. Why should she torture them both by making them wade through weeks of a proper courtship? She had seen no benefit in taking the slow scenic route when a direct shortcut was so much more appealing. At six and twenty, she felt she had waited long enough to share a man's bed, and could think of no good reason, other than for the sake of someone else's sense of proper decorum, to delay the inevitable.

Lord Gavin must have agreed. Within days he had made her his wife. What a grand celebration that had been.

She had been surprised when he insisted on staying in his kingdom until Marina's baby was born, honoring her previous agreement with her cousin. She had expected him to flee to the nearest mountain or ocean, anywhere outside of his kingdom. But he had stayed and maintained his rule. In the preceding months he had used his time well. He had prepared his cabinet of ministers to take charge in his absence, ensuring they were quite capable of leading his subjects without his oversight, and without his control. Gavin had asked Uncle Iain to act as royal privy counselor to his prime minster, trusting the general could handle whatever crisis he encountered. And he had made detailed arrangements to visit every country in central Europe, starting with a trip to the Alps. He wanted to see the view from the top of the mountains. It had been a long time coming, but now with grand anticipation, she looked forward to accompanying her husband as they traveled the world, leaving Maninberg behind, if only for a while.

The End

I hope you have enjoyed reading this stand-alone novel,
Dreaming In Moonlight.
For a sneak peek at the first of my
Jules Vanderzeit novels, please keep reading.
Enjoy Always.

Until We Meet Again

Chapter 1

We may not have chosen the time so much as the time has chosen us.

Present Day

Victoria couldn't be more than a few minutes late for their appointment, and yet the Maestro made a show of pulling out his pocket watch the moment Victoria Winters stepped into his office. Time—and his precious collection of musical artifacts—were the only things Jules Vanderzeit cared about. People were only useful in their ability to function as couriers to retrieve the latest object of his obsession.

"How nice to see you again, Miss Winters. I was beginning to wonder if you would keep our appointment." The Maestro quickly dispensed with any pretense of pleasant greetings and dove directly into chastising her.

Victoria rolled her eyes with a shake of her head. "Please, Jules, try not to exaggerate. I was only momentarily delayed. I was with my daughter." She took a seat in one of the low, plush-leather chairs across from Jules, as he sat perched behind his oversized cherry wood desk. Regrettably, it created the perturbing effect that he was looking down on her.

"If you truly valued time, Miss Winters, you wouldn't be so prone to wasting yours or mine. Someday you may find that a moment of time is all that separates you from that which you desire most." As if to press his point, unnecessary as it was, he continued, "If you will recall, it only took a momentary distraction for you to switch guitars behind that wretchedly disorganized roadie's back, affording you the perfect opportunity to retrieve one of my most prized possessions."

"Yes, I know . . . the Hendrix guitar I swiped at Woodstock on the morning of August 18th, 1969." She spoke with mocking distain at the often-repeated reminder, though privately she agreed it was one of her finest retrievals. It was far superior to the quick, three-day trip she took to retrieve the guitar Ritchie Blackmore tossed into the crowd at the California Jam at the Ontario motor speedway on the evening of April 6th, 1974. At Woodstock, she'd been allowed to spend two weeks as part of the crew that worked behind the scenes to setup the historic festival. It was almost like a vacation until the rains came and swamped the place in mud. What a god-forsaken mess that was, but she had completed her mission through hell and high water.

"Retrieved, not swiped," Jules corrected her. He liked to believe his couriers "retrieved" his cherished collection of artifacts. They didn't swipe, steal, or rob the rightful owners of those items; they simply retrieved, for his careful safekeeping, items that otherwise would have been lost. "And scoff if you must, but that mission stands as the pinnacle of your success. We both know it's the reason I granted you the hiatus you so urgently requested."

"Silly me, I always thought it was because I was pregnant, and needed time to raise my daughter." For the last four years she'd

251

been back home in California with her daughter, Magdalena, living a semi-normal life, but after being summoned back into service by Jules Vanderzeit, any semblance of a normal life had played its final note . . . at least for the foreseeable future.

"Think what you wish, but motherhood does not release you from your contract. Nor does having an affair while on a mission earn you any bonus points; and with a local boy, no less."

How nice of him to remind her of the error of her ways. It seemed Jules actually enjoyed putting her through all manner of tribulation for perverse, eccentric, and mysterious reasons she would surely never understand.

"If it's all the same to you, I'd rather forego this little trip down memory lane and get right to business. Didn't you call me here to discuss my next mission?" Victoria asked impatiently. The sooner she got on with the mission, the sooner she would be reunited with her daughter. At least that's what Jules had promised. To her, it looked as though he was holding her daughter as collateral to ensure her unfailing loyalty. Since her recall into service, neither of them had been allowed to leave his castle. Of course he claimed it was for her own good, and to ensure Maggie's safety while she was away, but Victoria had her doubts. As far as she knew, the Maestro had never lied to her; he might deceive her ten ways to Sunday, but he never outright lied to her. Still, if doing whatever was needed to get whatever he wanted could be considered evil, then yes, Jules Vanderzeit—known to his couriers as "The Maestro"—was indeed an evil little man.

"In a bit of rush now, are we?" Jules mocked her, referring to her earlier tardiness.

"Please, Jules, get on with it. Just tell me where I'm going, and what I need to retrieve."

"You're going back to Manhattan in 1888 to retrieve a Stradivarius violin. This particular violin was from Antonio Stradivari's long period, and at the time of its disappearance belonged to a general in the United States army, if you can believe that. Imagine a military general playing a Stradivarius violin. Totally unexpected. It's reported that the general lent it to a fellow musician and the damn fool left it on a train. Such disrespect for such a valuable instrument deserves to be punished, but fortunately, that's not my area of concern. I'll let karma take care of that. My only concern is retrieving the instrument so it can be preserved for all of time."

For all of *his* time maybe, but he certainly wasn't preserving it for humanity. Once Jules obtained an object of his desire, it was never seen again. He collected rare and priceless musical artifacts, but once they were in his possession, they were as good as gone. The Maestro did not share.

"Sounds easy enough. All I have to do is be on the same train and retrieve the violin when it's left behind. Why the intense study period?" For the last several days Jules had packed her brain with information about the manners of the 1880s and the Gilded Age in America.

"Yes, well, one would think, but it's really not that easy. After being left on the train, it was picked up by another man; and that's where it disappears from history. I've already sent three of my best couriers, and each one tells me the same story. A man was sitting next to the absentminded musician and as soon as the violin was left unattended, this man—this thieving poacher—snatched up the case and took off." Jules ran his hands down the front of his impeccable jacket, as if to sooth himself by pressing out non-existing wrinkles before he continued. "Thankfully, I know the identity of the man. Now I need you to go back and establish yourself in his household and retrieve my prize from him."

Interesting. Three failed attempts, and he was still trying. Obviously, this violin had become an obsession with the Maestro. It gave her some bargaining power.

She knew better than to ask, but she did it anyway. She liked to push his buttons. "Why not send me back to the moment before the musician gets on the train and let me sit with him? I could even flirt with him. That would give me an opportunity to swipe the violin before your poacher can get his hands on it." She smiled inwardly, knowing how much her question peeved Jules' sense of time management.

"You know very well, perhaps not as well as I do, but very well nonetheless, that events of history cannot be changed. We do not change history, we act within it. It has already been recorded that this musician, if he can even be called such, lost this particular violin on a train. It is not our job to change *his* story, and any interaction with him creates that risk. If you flirt with him, as you so woefully suggest, his report of what happened will certainly change how history records this event. Not acceptable." Jules gave a sad shake of his head, and again she had the feeling he was talking down to her.

"Worth a try," she commented with a shrug.

Jules shook his head condescendingly. "I've already determined how this will proceed and how this will end."

"Really, Jules, don't you think that's a bit presumptuous? You said yourself that you've already had three failed attempts."

"I always know how things will proceed, and yet the effort must be made, the experience must be allowed to play out. How else can we achieve what we want? I want the violin and you want to be with your daughter. For each of us to get what we want, we must work together. Wouldn't you agree?"

"Agreed," she said, although she wasn't truly convinced. With Jules, she often had the feeling he knew something she didn't. And her feelings were usually right.

"Now, as for the man who found the violin . . ." Jules continued.

"You mean your poacher?"

Jules glared at her as if his small piercing grey eyes could bring her into submission. "Regarding the man who found the violin, there is nearly nothing recorded about him, nothing to create a noticeable effect on recorded history. History doesn't know who he is, but I do."

"I see." She tried to look suitably impressed. "I expect you have a plan for how I am going to gain access to his household; something that will cause little or no disturbance to his already unremarkable life."

"Of *course*." Jules rolled his eyes dismissively. She had to admit, she enjoyed making him do that; it was as if she had scored a tiny victory against his staid and overly composed demeanor. "After he has snatched the Stradivarius, his wife will die in the Great White Blizzard in March of 1888, and he will become the sole guardian of their adopted daughter. In June of that year, he will contact the Arthur A. Anderson Agency looking for a governess. It's all here in his file. We will arrange for you to register with the agency at the proper time to take the job as governess to the child."

"Hmmm, very good. Not exactly a servant, but with nearly full access to the man's life. By the way, does our poacher have a name?" She glanced at the manila folder lying on the desk in front of Jules.

"Robert Lucius Stevenson. He's an investment banker. He's done quite well for himself, but in a time of excessive wealth, he's still one of the little people. However, I doubt he sees himself as such."

"You mean he's not an Astor or a Vanderbilt?" she asked mockingly. It was amazing how Jules could judge a man he had never even met.

"Hardly," he said with another roll of his eyes. "History won't even miss him when he's gone."

Victoria had scored one more tiny victory, but his harsh assessment made her wonder; would anyone miss her if she were gone? Probably not. Disappointing as it might be, she'd been estranged from her family for too long to expect prolonged grieving from any of them, and at only four years old her daughter's memories would be short-lived at best.

Jules picked up the folder, but didn't immediately hand it to her. "You'll need to be familiar with his file. And while I'm sure you know, it's my legal and moral duty to remind you that you are contractually prohibited from telling anyone who you really are, where you come from, or why you're there. You will maintain your cover at all times. If you share any classified information, for any reason, you will be recalled immediately and sent directly into seclusion. No more missions, no daughter, and no life. I have agents everywhere, and as you know, Victoria, if you discuss your mission, you fail."

She had heard it all before, several times over. It was just one more thing to regret about her life. Victoria resented being forced to do the Maestro's bidding, but as one of his indentured couriers, as long as he held her contract, she really had very little choice. No matter where she went, or when, the Maestro could track her.

Some people had property and mortgages to pay off, or they risked losing their homes. She had to pay off a contractual obligation of *time,* or risk losing everything she held dear, including her life.

When she'd been struck by a drunk driver and on the verge of dying, agreeing to work for Jules Vanderzeit had seemed like a good idea. Ten years of being a well-paid time traveler with an opportunity to see the world—not to mention that part about being alive—had sounded great. And it was, for a while. But good times don't last forever, and after paying down six years of her ten year contract she wanted out. The four remaining years of her contract felt like an eternity.

Jules pulled a single sheet of paper from the file he was holding and handed it to her. "Read this before you go."

She quickly scanned the paper, front and back. "Is this all you have? I expected more."

"It will have to do. It's important that this mission go as planned. I've already tried to get the violin before it leaves the train. That hasn't worked. I need you in Stevenson's house. I need you to learn his secrets. And please, use finesse. Try not to be a bull in a china shop but rather a fly on the wall. If Stevenson finds out what you are up to, who knows what will happen to the violin."

Leave it to Jules to be dramatic. "How long do I have to accomplish my mission?"

"Three weeks. That should be more than sufficient."

"Why so long? If this man has the violin as you believe . . ."

"I'm quite certain."

"Then why do I need three weeks to find it? How big is his place? Surely I can search the house in less than a week. Why do I have to be away from my daughter for so long?"

"Your daughter will be fine. She will be in my safekeeping. You will need at least that much time to gain Stevenson's trust. He's not a man who gives up his secrets to any pretty little face that comes along. While I have no doubt you'll put your feminine guile to good use as you've so successfully done in the past, Stevenson will not be an easy mark."

It was the second time he had referenced her affair with the stagehand at Woodstock, but she pushed aside the hurt. Yes, she had slept with Robbie Stevers, perhaps foolishly, but the affair had provided her with backstage access and the moment she needed to retrieve the guitar that Jules had so adamantly desired; the one on which Jimmy Hendrix had played his infamous hard-rock version of the Star Spangled Banner.

And while he may have assured her that her daughter would be safe and sound, she knew he wasn't about to let her slide out of her mission or turn in less than successful results. The only thing greater than her desire to pay off her accursed contract, was her desire live out her life with her daughter in the twenty-first century. The moment she paid off her last second of time, she would take Magdalena as far away from the Maestro and his god-awful Grand Central Time Chamber as this little blue planet would allow.

"But I am expected to search the house, right?"

"Of course, search every square inch, leave no stone unturned, but my knowledge of Stevenson tells me he's a cautious man, a planner, and a schemer. He's not one to leave his secrets lying about for all to see."

"How can you be so sure he's the right man?"

"Have you ever known me to be wrong?" He glared at her, but there was no eye rolling. No points scored.

She shrugged, "Not that I know of."

He continued to glare. "As I was saying, you have three weeks to complete this assignment. If you can't gain access to the violin by then, you will have failed and will have to return empty handed."

A failed mission meant extra time would be added to her contract; a double whammy. That was unacceptable.

"And if I'm successful, or able to return early? How much time will I earn?"

"Standard pay; two days off your contract for every day out in the field. I'll also give you time off to be with your daughter before your next assignment."

"Come on, Jules, give me a break." She sat forward in her chair, trying to elevate her eye level equal to his. "This is obviously worth more than standard compensation; the chance to retrieve a lost Stradivarius? How often does that happen?"

He eyed her for a long moment before responding. "All right, all things considered, I can agree to a bonus of two weeks; *if* you're successful."

This was amazing. She had never known Jules to negotiate. She quickly did the math; double time plus the bonus would mean two months compensation for three weeks of work. Not a bad deal, but she wanted more.

"Let's think about this . . . You've already sent three couriers and had three failures. It seems to me, if I'm successful, I deserve at least triple time." She knew she was being unreasonable, but figured it was the only way. She had very little to lose and so much more to gain.

Jules gasped. "You must be joking. Triple time is much too generous for less than one month of work."

"Remember, you're taking me away from my daughter. I think the job is easily worth one month for each week away; maybe even two." She put on her best poker face and held his gaze. In for a penny, in for a pound; it was time to play for the jackpot.

"Six months! You dream."

"Really? Do you have someone else who can do the job? You know, I think I might be coming down with a cold." She faked a cough for good measure.

He stared at her for a moment as if considering his options. "Alright, I can give you six months; if you come back with the violin in hand. And if you come back *without* the violin, but can give me substantial information toward its recovery, I will still give you time served."

She nearly jumped out of her chair. This was great news. This was insurance that she wouldn't suffer a penalty for failure. She let the thrill of victory settle in her bones as she sat back and relaxed for the first time since she'd entered his office. "And if I come back early?"

"Victoria, if you're able to retrieve that violin in less than three weeks, I will take a full year off your contract. But if you come back early by even one day without it, all deals are void."

Dang, this was serious. Jules wanted that violin and he wanted it now. She should have held out for more.

While the Maestro's office back at his castle was clean, neat, and well lit, with a formal wood-and-leather atmosphere that rivaled an old law library, the Grand Central Time Chamber felt musty, ancient, and full of secrets. The dimly lit space was consumed by dark shadows interrupted only by shafts of dust-filtered sunlight cutting soundlessly through the vast circular space. The ever changing rays of light falling from windows lodged high in the arched walls of the time chamber provided hopeful evidence of a world beyond these thick stone walls; one ruled by the logic of day and night. A world where she had recently lived and hoped to soon return.

The exact location of the dome holding the time chamber was, of course, a secret known only to the Maestro. It could be anywhere; an overgrown jungle, a wind-swept barren coastal plain, or a frozen mountain top, but one thing she was sure of, it was well protected. Her trips to and from the time chamber were always at night while she was in a drug-induced sleep. It was nearly comical how intensely Jules protected his secrets. She may have traveled for days or only hours to reach this destination, but she had no way of knowing.

Back at his castle, when Jules was giving her last-minute instructions regarding her assignment, he had assured her that her daughter was in good hands and would be being well cared for while she was away. It angered her to no end that she hadn't been allowed to meet the couple who would be caring for her daughter, but Jules had insisted that there wasn't time for a formal introduction. She would have to trust him on this or decline the assignment. The possible payoff for this job was too high to take that chance. Only Jules had been at the castle to see her off, but he assured her that Maggie was already settled in with her new guardians.

"Take care, and please, do your best to complete this assignment on time," Jules had instructed her one last time. "Much is riding on this."

"Yes, of course, Jules, I will do everything I can to protect your secrets while I'm out retrieving your precious violin."

"Believe it or not, I am concerned for your welfare . . . more than you may think."

The sincerity of his statement surprised her. She didn't know what to say.

Her silence seemed to please him. He smiled. "Well then, I believe you have everything you need. I wish you well until we meet again." With those parting words, he had ushered her into the vehicle that brought her to the Grand Central Time Chamber.

Victoria entered the vast circular chamber dressed from head to toe as a proper governess from 1888. She scanned the room, counting the doors. The number of doors in the chamber was different with each mission; sometimes there were only one or two, sometimes there were more. Once she had counted seven doors; another time there had been twelve. Today, the chamber held three. Three doors leading back through time, but only one door was calibrated to work for her. The others would hold fast against any attempt she might make to test their timely destinations. She knew, because like any good, curious, adventure seeker, she had once tried them all. But that was before, when she was young and daring and brazenly bold in her search for the next grand experience to stir her soul. Now she was a mother, bound by love to do right for her daughter, and every bit as determined as her younger, adventure-seeking self to make the most of this particular opportunity.

If she was lucky, and cunning, and fiercely focused, she could complete her mission early and earn her bonus.

She couldn't help but ruminate that she'd be done by now, free and clear, if she hadn't taken off time to raise her daughter. But it was a useless calculation; meaningless against the priceless years she had spent with her child. Only two months ago she had celebrated Maggie's fourth birthday; now, to think that she'd be away from her for three weeks, was sheer torture.

If only Jules would wait until Maggie was older and in school, this wouldn't be such an issue, but he claimed he had waited long enough to draw on her contract and maintained that she should be more than satisfied with her extended maternity leave. Not everyone was so lucky, he reminded her. And she reminded him that none of his other couriers were single mothers with a daughter who would never know her father because he wasn't from her time.

"And whose fault is that?" he had questioned, pointing out once again the error of her ways.

Ah . . . the perks of time travel.

She wondered if she saw Robbie again if she would even recognize him. Probably not; time-travel had a way of scrambling her memories. She compared it to taking a whirl-wind tour through a foreign country; she might remember the highlights, but it was hard to recall all the details of every place she had seen. Besides, Maggie's father would be an old man by now, if he was even still alive. She laughed, thinking what a shock it would be if he knew he had a four year old daughter.

She questioned the benefit of having all these amazing experiences if she couldn't even remember them; it hardly seemed worth the effort. But that wasn't true. She might not be able to recall every detail of every trip, but the experiences stayed with her nonetheless, adding to the richness of her life. They had brought her to where she was, a proud and happy mother to her beautiful Maggie, and for that she had no regrets. She might not have been able to anticipate the effects of time-travel, but she wouldn't regret the decision to become one of Jules' couriers. It had saved her life.

Until We Meet Again

When Jules had pulled her from the car wreck, he had asked her the strangest question. "What would you be willing to lose, to have everything you've ever wanted?"

She hadn't known how to respond, or even what he meant. Later Jules had explained that his question was a paradox; weighing something we think we want, but would have to lose, against what we really want. She supposed that's what had happened to her. She had agreed to ten years of indentured servitude in exchange for her life. Now it was time to pay down her debits.

She set down the satchel holding her journal and traveling wardrobe, limited as it was, and adjusted her undergarments, again. Nothing she did could compensate for the god-awful, ill-fitting corset. Why couldn't Jules have provided something better; something that actually fit? Whoever had designed this particular garment should be hanged, or at the very least, forced to wear the torturous body-shaping device every day of their godforsaken life, and then be buried in it.

Spandex was so much more practical, as well as comfortable, for containing a woman's figure. And who the hell had determined a woman's figure needed to look like an hourglass anyhow? When she had left for Woodstock, she had worn a long, free flowing, tie-dyed summer dress with cotton panties and no bra. That had truly felt liberating.

Only five years ago she'd been reed thin with long, straight, bleached blonde hair and a golden tan from years of living in Southern California. Now she wore drab grey governess tweeds, her hair had returned to its natural reddish-brown shade, and she was as pale as an English maid due to her prolonged time away from the sun. She had also gained the well-rounded figure of a woman who had given birth. Instead of being a shapeless toothpick, she now sported curves, and best of all, full breasts, which were now being crushed by her confining corset. It was obvious the darn thing was laced too tight. She'd be sure to fix that once she got where she was going.

She needed to pull herself out of the twenty-first century and set her thoughts on 1888. If there was one thing she had learned from her years of traveling through time, it was the value of living in the moment, regardless of where or when she was. It wasn't productive to focus on the vastness of the past, or even on the possibilities of the future. It was best to focus only on the immediacy of the moment before her.

She picked up her satchel and headed for door number three; the one assigned to her. She placed her hand on the door knob and took a deep breath. Within a matter of seconds she would travel through time. She opened the door, stepped into the antechamber, and closed the door tight behind her. On the opposite wall of the small chamber was another door, Victoria took another deep breath as she counted; one-thousand-one, one-thousand-two, one-thousand-three. When she opened the second door again, she was standing on the sidewalk in front of a secondhand bookstore. The large clock tower decorating the bank building across the street read six o'clock. She didn't need to ask anyone to know she was standing in downtown Manhattan on Sunday evening, the tenth of June, 1888. All it took was four small steps and one giant leap of faith.

Tricia Linden, author of timeless romance with a touch of magic.

In this lifetime, Tricia has lived in five states, on two islands, and on a farm, and is now living with her soulmate in Northern California. Her travels have taken her to Canada, Mexico, Australia, Hong Kong, Guam, England, Scotland, several countries in Europe, and several states in the US. Besides her love of reading and writing romance, she has a great fondness for Pink Flamingos. Over the years, she's gathered a rather large collection of the fun pink birds.

Website: https://tricia-linden.com/

Facebook: https://www.facebook.com/TriciaLindenAuthor/

Tweeter: @TriciaLinden69

Email: Tricia.Linden@ymail.com

www.ingramcontent.com/pod-product-compliance
Lightning Source LLC
Chambersburg PA
CBHW022154170626
46807CB00005B/2200